CW01020673

To all of those who have had to pick themselves up and start again.

1

Beth tightened her grip on the steering wheel as she tried hard to focus. She couldn't think straight, couldn't keep her mind on the task in front her as she drove along the road that cut across the fens. She had to get back safely. That was *all* she had to do right now. The wipers were going full pelt to clear the relentless drizzle that the blustering wind was driving sideways across the windscreen. The evening was approaching, and dark muddy fields stretched into the distance either side of the road, which was flanked by deep drainage ditches.

She hated this road, this place. It made her nervous every time she drove along it. The land had come from beneath the sea, and she felt like she was drowning just being in it, her lungs screaming for more air than she could get into them as her chest tightened. It made her light-headed, this irrational fear that something would make her swerve and lose control, crashing off the road and into the cold, dark water. It rose in in her every time despite her telling herself to be logical.

Beth blinked hard, just a fraction too long for someone who

needed to pay attention. The car swerved and she pulled the steering wheel sharply to one side to right her course. Slowly pushing her breath out from her pursed mouth, she turned her gaze away briefly from the glistening tarmac to switch off the radio. She had chosen calming classical music that she did not recognise, so it could not steal any of her focus in the way that songs she could sing along to would. But even these smooth tones were fighting for space in her brain, and she needed them silenced.

'For God's sake!' Beth spat as she noticed just how close the car behind her was driving. 'You don't need to drive up my...' She gripped the steering wheel tighter still as she re-focused on the road in front of her. *Don't let it get to you,* she told herself. Despite being a fen road, theoretically as straight as ones that the Romans made centuries before, this one had a section that twisted this way and that for no good reason. It seemed unnecessary, and it irked Beth every time. It was a road, not a river.

The afternoon had been horrific and she needed to escape to somewhere she could let her nerves settle and regroup. She felt like the muscles in her neck were turning to stone, she was so tense. She felt manic. Beth blinked hard again to stop her tears from falling. She just needed to get to where she was going, take a moment to calm down, and then sort stuff out. Everything was a mess, and it made her brain hurt just thinking about how she was going to even start fixing it. If she even *could* fix it. What was she going to do?

'Just get there. Just. Get. Safe,' Beth said to herself, her jaw clenched with stress. She flicked up her eyes to the rear-view mirror. The driver had backed off a bit, thank goodness, and there were not many other vehicles on the road. Beth could feel her heart thumping against her chest. She felt sick as she focused on this small section of the road, concentrating hard on not thinking about how cold the ditch water would be, how full of weeds that would grab hold of you, prevent you from reaching the surface once you were under.

She couldn't stop picturing it. She couldn't do this. She couldn't. It was too much.

Suddenly and without thinking, Beth slammed on the brakes. Hard. She couldn't focus with all the noise in her head. She couldn't safely drive this road. She had to stop.

Her car screeched to a halt.

The car behind her, the driver checking something on their phone, slammed into the back of her at full pelt. Beth was flung forward, her forehead hitting the steering wheel with a loud crack, before the seatbelt pulled her back into sitting position. The sound of metal being crushed under pressure shrieked into Beth's ears. She could feel warmth and wet as blood started to seep down her face. From where? Was her nose broken? The pain hadn't hit yet, so she couldn't tell.

Beth took a deep gulp of air as her mind tried to process what had just happened. What she needed to do now. It was a matter of moments, barely a collection of seconds, before Beth saw another car coming out of an adjoining junction and seemingly speeding up as it came straight for her. Confused, dazed and in shock, Beth screwed up her eyes to shake this phantom car away. It couldn't be real. No one would drive *into* a collision. They must surely be braking, but the rain-slick surface of the road not giving enough purchase to their brakes. The screeching sound of wet tyre against brake-pads ricocheted though the air as Beth watched the second car come right for her, slamming with force into the passenger side door at some speed.

The cars twisted around each other, like two strands of DNA, spinning across the road, pushing Beth's car back towards the edge, towards the ditch. Beth's vision went fuzzy. She felt the car start to tip and then she lost consciousness as she sank into the blackness.

2

There was nothing.

Beth was suddenly aware of the absence of... everything. She was both present and somehow not there at all. The edges of her perception were fuzzy, like when you close your eyes and it's like looking at a blank screen. There's something there and yet also nothing. She was too warm, like she was underneath a heavy blanket that was keeping her down, yet somehow, she also felt like she was floating. It didn't fit together.

She took a breath. Did she? Was she breathing? Her mind was so confused; all the messages coming into her brain were broken, or distorted somehow. Nothing was making any sense at all.

Then suddenly from nowhere, pain. It hurt, something hurt. A lot. She couldn't tell what, or where, just that pain was radiating from somewhere. From *everywhere*. Then, at the edges of her consciousness, she started to hear noises. Voices. Sounds that she couldn't place, and suddenly it was no longer silent but loud, painfully so. She tried to grit her teeth but found that she couldn't. Why? She started to panic. She tried to swallow only to find more pain.

'Beth?' a gentle voice asked.

Beth tried to swallow once again and then prised open her eyes, which felt heavy, stuck shut, like she'd been on the mother of all nights out, like she'd done more shots than was ever sensible and was now paying the price. Her whole head felt as though it was being squeezed by a tight metal band. What on earth had happened?

The light was piercing despite being at a low level, her eyes seemingly unused to the sensation of dilating. She closed them. It was too much. She craved oblivion again. Whatever this was, it was too much. But... she had to know.

'Yes?' she whispered, croaking out the sound, not being able to raise her voice any further.

'Oh good, great, you can hear me,' the voice said.

Feeling the scratch of sheets surrounding her, Beth realised she was in a bed, lying down. She tried to sit up and immediately felt gentle but insistent hands on her.

'Oh, hold up. Not yet. Lie back. Can you open your eyes again for me? There's a good girl.'

Good girl? Where on earth was she? Who was this? She was at least relieved that it was a woman. With some random man in some random bed was not where she wanted to find herself.

She opened her eyes as requested, as far as she could cope with, and looked around. It quickly became clear to her that she was in hospital. Her heart rate gathered pace. She scanned her memory for how she had ended up here but found that nothing came to her. Blank. Trying to pull any picture into her mind resulted in a black void. Panic started to rise in her.

The voice, which Beth could now see belonged to a senior-looking nurse, spoke again.

'I'm Sister Carmichael, and you're in hospital, Beth. You had a little accident but you're in good hands here. Now, you may be disorientated as you've been sleeping for a couple of days and you sustained a head injury... No, don't try to touch it please...' Beth's hands went instinctively to her forehead where her skin felt taut and sorest. The movement also informed Beth that she was hooked up with various tubes and wires. She must look an absolute state.

'What...'

'Happened? The doctor will be around to explain everything and check you over soon, so I won't give you too much information right now, don't want to overwhelm you, but the short version is that you had a car accident.'

'A wh—' Beth coughed. 'A what?' She shook her head in frustration, which caused spikes of pain to radiate down her neck. She stilled herself. 'My throat... it's...'

'Yes, you were on a ventilator for a while, so your throat is going to be a bit sore I'm afraid. Here, let me get you some water.'

Sister Carmichael poured some water from a jug on the bedside table into a cup with a straw and a lid and held it to Beth's lips. Beth drank from it, and it was both the best and the worst of sensations. It was endlessly refreshing but it was also like drinking shards of glass. She sipped a little more of the tepid water into her mouth and let it sit there, helping with the feeling that her mouth was lined with dried-up tissue paper, before letting it trickle down her throat, allowing for only the smallest of movements.

Beth lay back as Sister Carmichael went through the motions of checking her blood pressure and temperature before saying again that the doctor would be with her very soon and that she should rest until then. She closed her eyes again and tried to process what she now knew and how she could connect the dots. Several of which appeared to be missing.

She'd been in a car accident. Where had she been going? Or coming from? She scanned her mind before it suggested to her that maybe she had been coming home from her shift at the coffee shop. Her heart dropped. Her dad was always telling her that she needed to get a 'proper' job, rather than still being at the place that she got part-time work at, while she finished up her photography course at college. Her heart dropped further. She'd been driving *his* car, because hers had broken down again and there wasn't time to get the bus and make her shift on time. Had she bashed up his car? He was going to be furious with her. She clasped her clammy hands to the bedsheets either side of her and tried to stay calm. She wasn't a little kid any more; she was an adult, and she would act like one, Beth told herself. Her parents would be relieved that she was okay. Was she okay? She immediately forced her eyes open and glanced at her feet and watched as she wiggled her toes. Thank God. She was okay. All limbs present and correct.

She relaxed back onto her pillows, her dark hair hanging dankly around her neck, and she listened to the sounds around her. Sister Carmichael was at the end of her bed, talking to another nurse. They were both English. Beth wondered idly if they'd known each other from home before she realised it was stupid to assume all English people knew each other. It wasn't weird to have two English people in an Australian hospital. English people were everywhere in Victoria. She had worked with an English girl herself at the café, though she'd not stayed long before she'd headed up the coast to explore. She remembered envying her and promising herself she'd travel one day too. Maybe when she was better that was what she'd do. That'd show her dad that she had some get up and go. That she wasn't drifting along.

She was just wondering how long it would be before her parents arrived, assuming that they'd now been told she was awake, when a taller, older doctor, who had the definite look of a military man about him, appeared at the side of her bed.

'Well, hello, Beth, good to see you awake. I'm Dr Preston, the ICU consultant. You've been in the wars a bit I'm afraid,' he said, a sympathetic tilt to his head.

Also English...

'Hi,' Beth croaked.

He flipped across his notes before perching on the side of the bed. The juxtaposition of his stiff upper lip way of moving jarred with this overly friendly position, and Beth crinkled her brow in confusion only to wince at the pain this caused.

'Yes. You had a nasty head injury. I know Sister Carmichael has filled you in a little, but I wanted to ask what you yourself recall. Why you think you're here?' He looked at her expectantly.

'Uh... I don't really know. This... I might sound...'

'Ask away. Nothing sounds silly here. Trust me.'

'Are we in Australia?' she asked, fully expecting the answer to be yes. She had been at work, hadn't she? In Melbourne. And yet...

'No... No, we're in Cambridge,' he said, a hint of concern in his voice. 'In the UK.' He sat back, observing her.

'I'm in England?'

'Yes.'

Terror flooded her brain. What the hell? She'd never been to the UK; she'd never left Australia. This couldn't be right. Was she... was she still in her coma and this was some weird shit that her brain was pulling? Like you see in the films, where they wake up and realise their subconscious has been messing with them. She *had* wanted to travel; she'd been secretly saving up for it so she could just announce her departure one day and get on a plane the next. But she'd not done it yet. Had she?

'I'm in England?' Beth asked again, in case she'd not heard right the first time.

'You are. I suspect that you might be experiencing a little confusion. Your head injury was not insignificant, though healing well. You had a bleed on the brain, which has now stopped. This is not uncommon following a traumatic experience such as the accident that you had.'

'What happened? I...' Beth could feel panic rising in her, her pulse fluttering at her skin like a frightened bird trapped behind glass.

'Now, I know it's hard but do try to keep calm. You're in the safest place right now. We're taking very good care of you. We've called your husband who is on his way right now. He'll be here in a matter of minutes I believe.'

'I'm sorry?' Beth said, forcing her voice to find its volume. Now she was *sure* there had been some sort of mix up. Perhaps there had been another car involved, and there was another patient. Because though she could just about accept that she was in England, she knew for sure as hell that she didn't have a *husband*. She... she wasn't even seeing anyone! She just needed her mum and her aunties to pop by and the doctor would have a full explanation of her eternal singleness and how concerned they all were about it and how she'd never be a mum if she kept this up.

'My husband? I don't... I'm not *married*.' She held up her hands to show the lack of a ring and for a millisecond was relieved to be looking at unadorned hands.

Dr Preston looked at her, a wrinkle in his brow.

'Yes. Your husband,' he said assuredly.

Beth shakily blew out air from her cheeks. Clearly, she was not the only confused one here.

'No. No, if you call my parents then we can get this all sorted out.'

Dr Preston smiled at her and made a couple of notes on the paper and clipboard that he was holding. He then hugged it to his chest.

She sank back into her pillow as she looked at him, waiting for him to realise that the error was his. This was all too much. She was in hospital, in England, and the doctors had *clearly* got her mixed up with someone else. It was like something out of the daytime soaps that her dad always gave her an ear bashing about watching. Maybe that was it. Maybe she really was still dreaming, and some weird melodrama was playing out while she slept. Otherwise, she was either in the middle of some medical fuck up or she was losing her mind, and neither of those options held any appeal. But, as she waited impatiently and found the doctor still looking at her, assessing her without saying anything, she got a sinking feeling that this was all too real.

'You need to call my mum. You need to speak with her. I want her here, I *need* her here!' Beth said, trying to sound authoritative despite feeling anything but.

'We've called your next of kin, they'll be here soon.' Dr Preston looked away, towards Sister Carmichael, who nodded and came over to them.

'You don't get it. You've made a mistake. You've got me mixed up here. I'm not married, I... look! No ring!' She waved her hand at them, nearly pulling her canula out as she did so.

'Lovey, we need you to take a deep breath, try to keep calm,'

Sister Carmichael said, taking Beth's hand in hers and holding it, not firmly, just supportively.

'I can't, I won't! This is all bloody ridiculous!' Beth said, starting to push herself off the bed, wincing at the pain she felt all over her body, trying to work which muscles did not want to do as they were told.

'Beth, you need to lie back down. You've had a nasty accident. You're still recovering and you need to let us help you. Everything will become clearer soon enough. But now, rest is what matters most.' She turned to the doctor.

'Absolutely. Take some rest now. We are here for you, Beth. We will get this all straightened out. I promise. I need to make a couple of phone calls, see a couple of other patients, and then I'll be back. But Sister Carmichael will be here.'

Dr Preston nodded at Sister Carmichael and stepped away from the bed.

'Yes. Yes! Call my mum,' Beth shouted after him. 'She'll tell you. I... I may not know why I'm in England, but I know I'm not married. Mum will straighten you out. This... husband bloke too, when he arrives, will take one look at me and tell you the same. I'm not his wife!'

'Okay now, try to lie back.'

'Why won't you believe me? This is... this is ridiculous!' Beth said, twisting about on the bed, getting tangled up in sheets and tubes.

'Beth,' Sister Carmichael said again, her tone now that of a disapproving schoolteacher. 'We do need you to stay calm. You're right, this will all become sorted out soon enough. We'll try to contact your mother so that you can speak with her and when Dr Preston comes back, he will talk you through all that's happened to you and what's going on now with your healing and treatment and all will become much clearer. You've had a bit of a time of it. Things are often a bit confused. What's best for you now is rest. Okay?'

'Okay...' Beth was suddenly completely exhausted, the bizarre scenario taking it out of her entirely. She wasn't sure that she wanted to wait, but what else could she do? It was clear that she was in no state to get up and go anywhere. She did not know exactly how she had come to be in England. She didn't know why the staff here seemed so insistent that she had a husband when clearly that was nuts. So she would just have to let things happen. She'd let him arrive, have him have the same 'who the hell is this' reaction, and then they'd have to take her seriously. Then she could have them call her mum, who could fill in the blanks and it would all work out. This would merely be a funny story one day, wouldn't it?

Beth scrunched her eyes closed and tried to not let the dread that was seeping through her veins completely overwhelm her.

What the fuck was going on?

3

Beth turned her face to the sunshine that was spilling through the large window she was sat beside, the rays warming her face and reminding her of home. Sister Carmichael had introduced her to Sarah, her one-to-one ICU nurse, and the three of them had agreed that her stats were good enough to let Beth out of bed and into an upright chair; get her a cup of tea, to try to give her some sense of control and normality in a situation that was anything but. Beth had hastily agreed, initially believing that once up and about she would be out of the door and away from this madness, but she soon realised that ICU had a high security level; she wasn't in a fit state to go anywhere yet, and also she had no idea where she would go. She was in England, she had accepted that, how or why she couldn't say right now, but she realised that she couldn't think who she might know here. But surely there must be someone, anyone, who knew *her,* and she would have to be patient until they were found. Housemate, travel buddy, employer. Someone would be looking for her. She'd also asked to speak with her mum again but when pressed, Beth couldn't recall the phone number. Who knew phone numbers in the age of mobiles? It would come to her, she knew that, and Sarah promised that she would follow up the suggestions that Beth had made as to how to track the number down. She knew her place of work; they could look it up, call and ask them to pass on a message. It wouldn't be hard.

Beth gave in to the pull of her lashes, closing her eyes and drifting off into a light doze, slumped a little in the upright chair. She didn't know how long she had been asleep for but when she opened her eyes again, there was a collection of people at the end of her bed. Sister Carmichael, Sarah, Dr Preston and a strange man she did not recognise. They were talking in hushed, serious tones.

Finally, Beth thought. This must be the 'husband'. Together they could clear up this misunderstanding and then they'd maybe try harder to get in touch with her parents. Then they could put a plan together; maybe she could fly home. Just the thought of sitting in their garden in Melbourne, a cup of coffee in hand and the scent of the lemon myrtle in the air, made her feel better already.

'Beth,' Dr Preston said as he stepped forward, pulling up a chair to sit beside her. 'Good to see you sitting up, that's wonderful. You're doing really well.' He gave an encouraging smile.

Beth smiled back, but something in his face made her nervous. There was a knot in her stomach that felt as though it wound a little tighter as he spoke. She glanced up at the nurses and this strange man. Why was he still here? Surely he'd pointed out that they had no connection by now. It was weird. Still, the whole thing was weird. Her friends at the café would have an absolute fit over this.

'But we're a little concerned about your memory,' Dr Preston continued. 'So I just want to do a few checks with you, if that's okay?'

'What? Look, I know I couldn't remember my mum's mobile but...' Beth's voice faltered.

'I know. As I said, this isn't uncommon, so we just want to do a little checking to see where we are.'

'Fine,' Beth said, crossing her arms. This was ridiculous, but if she went along with it then perhaps they'd get to the point faster than if she pushed back.

'What is your full name?'

'Beth. Short for Bethany. Masters. Bethany Masters.' She raised a petulant eyebrow at Dr Preston as he noted this down. This was such a waste of time.

'And where are you now?'

'You've already told me that. I'm in England. Cambridge.'

'Not Australia?'

'No. Look, you said it wasn't unusual to be confused when waking up after an accident like mine. So...' She tailed off; she was getting angry. This guy was talking to her like she was an idiot, and she didn't appreciate it.

'Do you recall why you are in England and not Australia?'

Beth paused. She pursed her lips.

'Not yet. No.'

'Do you have any recollection of the accident?'

'I... no.' She looked at her feet. When she'd thought about it, she had assumed that she had been driving her dad's car, but now she knew she was in England, she realised that she can't have been right about that and when she pressed her memory for an alternative, nothing was there. She smiled weakly to herself. At least it wasn't her dad's car she'd bashed up.

'Can I ask you what the date is? Or, rather, what year it is?'

Beth wrinkled her forehead but then winced. She'd not seen a mirror yet, but she knew she'd have a corker of a scar when she did see herself.

'Seriously?'

Dr Preston said nothing, his face neutral as he waited for her to respond.

Beth looked at the others, their faces less able to keep their concern from their expression. A sliver of fear lodged into her mind as she saw them. Something wasn't right.

'It's 2019?' she said, the rise in tone at the end of the sentence the only indication that she wasn't wholly sure that she wasn't in for a horrible shock.

'And who is prime minister? We can go for Australia or the UK, whichever you'd prefer.'

'Um... well, politicians come and go like they're on a merry go round, don't they?'

A polite smile from Dr Preston, but silence.

'Morrison. It's, um, Morrison. And I know you, cos you've got Bojo. I mean, what a joke!'

No one laughed.

'Okay. And then just one more. When did you last see your parents?'

This made Beth ache. She wanted them here now. It felt like a lifetime since she'd seen them.

'I live with them. Or, I do when I'm in Australia. So I guess whenever I was last there.'

'And do you recall when that was?'

Beth blinked hard as though she could force her memories to come to her through sheer willpower. But nothing. She swallowed and as she looked up at Dr Preston, his face a calm and reassuring one, she felt the hot prick of tears at the back of her eyes.

'Something's not right, is it?' Beth whispered, barely able to get the words out. She pushed herself further upright in her chair, wishing she had a blanket or something that she could pull around her. She felt cold. Exposed.

'We think you have something called retrograde amnesia. Sometimes, when the brain experiences something traumatic, like a near death experience or...' He paused, choosing his words carefully. 'Or an accident that causes profound emotional stress, it almost *protects* itself by not allowing that memory to be processed. However, the memory isn't necessarily as precise as it might want to be and sometimes other memories get removed as well, leading to amnesia.'

Beth looked from Dr Preston to the others as she let this sink in. Sister Carmichael and Sarah wore expressions of empathy. The man had the glint of tears in his eyes.

'So, my mind has wiped my memory?'

'Not wiped as such. In many cases, in most cases, this is a temporary condition and as you heal and process the trauma, memories often return. Sometimes in bits and pieces, sometimes all at once. In some cases, most memories return, in others, very few or none do. It's different for each patient. Right now, we're trying to determine the extent of your memory loss. Are you... are you okay to keep going with some more questions?' He tipped his head sympathetically to one side. 'Or would you like to take a break?'

Beth was exhausted, and her mind was spiralling at the news, but she also wanted to know how bad things were, and she could feel the expectations of the others.

'I'm okay. Let's keep going.'

'Good. Great. If you want to stop at any time, just say. All right.' He cleared his throat. 'Tell me about yourself. Your day-to-day life that you remember.'

Beth opened her mouth, the answers obvious to her, and yet she took a breath to start, but then questioned herself and stopped. *How bad is this? How much have I erased?* Still, she thought she'd best just say what she knew, what she thought was her *now*.

'I'm Beth. I'm twenty-four. I live in Melbourne, Australia with my mum, dad, my younger brother and our cat. We live in Altona, Rosebery Street.' She smiled as the image of her family home came to her. She wished she was there now. She was safe there. 'Um, I work at a café called Beans and Brew. I worked there when I was at college, and now I'm there full-time while I save up to travel. Except...'

'Go on?'

'Well, I must have travelled already, mustn't I? If I'm here?' She sounded small, afraid. She didn't sound like herself.

'That's something we can only assume at this stage. We're still trying to tie down some facts.'

'So what does all this tell us?' Beth asked, hanging on to some hope that the memory loss was minimal and as he'd said, temporary. It felt like this was happening to someone else. Which, she guessed, in a way, it was.

Dr Preston turned back to the others, his expression hidden from Beth by the angle of his head. When he turned back, seconds later, she could determine nothing of what he might have indicated to them.

'It tells us that you've currently lost a period of about five years. It's 2024. You don't live in Australia, with your family. You live here, in England. With your husband.'

The man at the end of the bed took a tentative step forward and without thinking, Beth flinched. He caught himself, stopped. Held back. An expression clouded his face. Disappointment? Hurt? Beth's mind was still reeling from what she'd just been told. She didn't have enough focus left to worry about what this stranger might be thinking.

Finally, he took a steadying breath and spoke.

'Beth. *Beth.* It's... you.' He ran his hands through his hair, dark brown with the beginnings of a receding hair line and a salt and pepper fleck to it. 'You had us worried!' He laughed and turned to Dr Preston for his approval. 'Is this okay?'

He looked nervous. His hands were twitching at his side, and he balled them into fists.

Talk to me, not about me!

'Is *what* okay?' Beth said, surprised at how husky her voice sounded as she raised the volume. The raw quality to her voice made her sound... older, like she'd spent a lifetime drinking harsh whisky in nightclubs filled with second-hand smoke. Her anger was clear in her tone.

'I appreciate that this is very strange for both of you,' Dr Preston said. 'It's going to take some time for you both to settle into this. Beth, you've gone through a lot in the past few days and now, the memory loss. It's all very disorientating but we can help you. We're here to help you. Including your husband...'

'No. No, it's not okay. I've *told* you. Again and again. I am *not* married. I don't *know* you!' She turned to face the man. 'You could be anyone! Dr Preston, Sarah, please. I... this is too much.'

Sarah turned to the man.

'Could you give us a moment please?'

The man looked pained but nodded his agreement and stepped away from them. He didn't leave though. Beth was aware of him loitering just out of earshot.

Sarah perched on the bedside and looked at Beth. Her higher position made Beth feel like a child being spoken to.

'I can't imagine how hard this is for you. You've had a physical shock, an emotionally distressing accident and now this. It's a lot.'

'You're not listening to me! He's not my husband. I'm not married. I don't *know* him!'

Sarah reached over and took her hand.

'When the police arrived at the scene of the accident, they took the details of the car you were driving and ran it through their system. Its registered owner is Rob.' She gestured over towards the man. 'They checked the insurance, and the provider has confirmed that the policy has two people on it. Rob and his wife. Bethany. Your ID was retrieved from the scene, your photo ID, your UK driving licence. We know for sure who you are. The police contacted Rob, and he has proof that you are his wife. They have seen the marriage certificate and photographs from your home.'

Dr Preston nodded his agreement.

Beth's breathing became laboured, shallow. This couldn't be happening. This absolutely couldn't be happening. She closed her eyes as though she could block it all out if she just tried hard enough.

'Beth...? You don't have to speak with him now if you don't want to. Dr Preston has already explained that this might be difficult for everyone involved. Your husband—'

'Stop *calling* him that!'

'Rob... knows that things might take time.'

'I need to talk to my mum. Please. Did you call her yet?' Beth shook her head. She wouldn't accept this. This had to be a mistake. She needed to talk with someone she *knew*. She needed her mum. Why wasn't she here? Why hadn't Rob called her if he really was her husband?

'No, not yet. We're trying to get a number for her. The time difference is causing a bit of a delay there. But we are on it.'

'If he, if this *Rob,* really is my husband, then why doesn't he call her for me?'

Sarah looked uncomfortable.

'What?' Beth demanded, aware she was being unreasonable, rude even, to Sarah but unable to stop herself.

'I... it's best that you and Rob speak yourselves. If you think you can manage it? I'll be right here if you want.'

Beth was so confused. She was still feeling drowsy, feeling as though her brain was like unfired clay: soft, malleable and knocked out of shape. She reminded herself that she was being looked after, they were tracing her parents and no one was asking her to do anything other than *talk* to this man. What harm could that do? Surely he'd trip up soon enough if he was lying. Why would he even *do* such a thing?

The smallest of doubt splintered into her mind. She'd lost five years. Could she have embarked on her world trip, landed in the UK, met and married someone in that time? It was... plausible. She shook her head. No. She would remember. She would! Still, if she wanted them to track down her mum, who would sort all this out in a heartbeat, then she ought to show willing at least. She looked at Sarah and nodded her agreement. Sarah turned and gestured Rob over.

'Just take things slowly, both of you. I'll be right over there if you need me.' Sarah walked over to the nurses' station and started on some paperwork.

'I'll be back around later if you have any questions for me then. You're in good hands here, Beth. I promise,' Dr Preston said as he left too.

Rob sat down where Dr Preston had been next to Beth. He was close, reaching his hand out to hold hers. She initially went to move her hand back, but then she let him. She didn't know what else to do. It felt wrong but she couldn't find the right way to remove hers. Maybe him touching her would move something inside her. You know, chemistry and that. She looked at their entwined hands, willing this small act to unlock some of the confusion she was feeling. She noted that he had a gold wedding band on his hand. She looked up at his face. He was staring at her, expectantly. He looked worried.

'Um...' She shifted in the chair, finally taking her hand from him in order to be able to push herself up. 'Do I...? Do we...?' What could she say?

Rob's face fell. Just a second before a kind smile washed over it, like a wiper blade removing rain from a windscreen.

'You really don't recognise me, do you?' he said, a tremor in his voice. His eyes were saying something, but as she didn't know him, she couldn't decipher what it might be.

Beth paused before shaking her head tightly, a slight movement which made the nerves in her neck scream at her. She rested her head back on the chair to wait for the pain to subside.

He seemed thoughtful, clearly working out his words carefully before he spoke. There was a measuredness, something almost gentle about his demeanour.

'Shall I... fill in some blanks? See if anything jumps out at you?'

Desperate for information, even if she wasn't wholly convinced of where it was coming from, Beth nodded. She had nothing to go on right now. Nothing to hang her instincts off. She was blank.

'Okay. Well, I'm Rob. I'm your husband. We've... um... This is so weird. Um... we've been married for nearly four years. We met when we were both working in London. Um...' He stopped. She could see that he was trying to decide how best to tell her what she needed to know. Or rather what he wanted to tell her.

'I was working in London?'

She'd always wanted to try London. People said it was like

Sydney but older, with winding streets straight out of a Dickensian novel. It had seemed impossibly glamorous to her and to know she'd lived and worked there, well, it felt like a tick off her bucket list, even if she couldn't remember it right now. She blushed, looked at her hands, noticing now the cuts and scrapes on them. She looked like she'd been in a fight. 'Sorry. I... this is a lot. I'm... I don't know, I...'

Rob's smile tightened as he tried to keep his emotions in check. This was obviously upsetting for him too.

'You really don't remember us? Don't remember our wedding. Our... life together.' Rob looked away, hiding his full emotions from Beth, protecting her from them maybe. He looked at the floor, trying to keep himself together.

Sarah stepped forward, obviously having anticipated this. She sat down on the end of the bed and twisted her body to face Beth.

'This is a lot to take in, I know,' she said kindly, 'but everyone is here to help you both. We don't tend to tell patients everything all at once because it can be too overwhelming and some people don't like to be told, they want to remember themselves. Does that make sense?'

Beth nodded, feeling dizzy. She moved, the smallest degree, to look at Rob. He was still staring at his feet, but she could see the tension in his shoulders.

'Would *you* like to know anything? Anything in particular?' Sarah asked. She then turned to Rob. 'Not too much information at once. Some things can... wait.' She nodded at Rob, who seemed to understand what she was saying to him. Beth could sense an underlying message in Sarah's words but without context she was clueless as to what they meant.

Suddenly she felt rage bubbling inside her. It wasn't *fair*. These two people, who as far as she knew meant nothing to her, knew more about her own life than she did. She felt like she had been robbed of her independence. They could tell her anything and how would she know if it was true or not? Even those closest to you lie to you sometimes, don't they?

'How about the world in general, rather than you in particular?' Sarah suggested. 'The past few years have been... significant. And they might mean something to you that could perhaps give your memory a nudge.'

Rob exhaled long and dramatically.

'What? Did I miss World War Three or something?' Beth snapped, irritated by her own cluelessness.

'Not far off,' Rob started, his voice hard. He looked at her and she could see his face soften as he did so. It felt... nice to be looked at with, what was it? Adoration?

'What happened? Is everyone okay?'

'Yes and no. We had a global pandemic, like... like the Spanish Flu? You know?'

Beth's eyes widened. 'What?'

'I know! It's called Covid, it's a flu-like thing and, well, lots of people died. Millions. Mostly the vulnerable, the young, the old, the ill. Everyone had to stay home. Countries closed their borders. No one could go anywhere. You had to stay in your own household. Not see anyone else or go out. Everything closed – shops, bars, schools.'

'Jesus... are my family okay?' Beth asked, panicked.

'Yes. Yes, they're fine.'

'Thank God. That's like a horror film. Like, unreal.'

Beth was suddenly overcome with tears. She had wanted to see her family, to hold them, and have them hold her, even before this news, but now? Now the only thing she wanted down to the very fibre of her being was to be at home with them.

'Hey. Hey, babe. It's okay. I'm here. I'll look after you,' Rob said, pulling his chair closer and taking her hand again.

Beth was suddenly grateful for him, even though she did not know him. He was being kind and patient. The sort of man she could see that she *might* have married. She left her hand in his, trying to relax into the sensation of being cared for by him. She was so tired, so emotional. It felt good to hand control over to someone else for a moment.

'When they called me to say you'd been in an accident and told me... told me how injured you'd been... Pooks, my world collapsed. Then they said you'd had some memory loss and that you might not recognise me... but I'm just glad you're alive. I'm glad you're okay, and the rest? Well, we can work it out together.'

Beth didn't know what to say. She was staring at him, trying to picture herself as married. To him. His *wife*. She was scrutinising him to see if any part of his face meant anything to her. Despite his kind demeanour and his encouraging words, he was still someone she could not recollect ever meeting, let alone marrying, and his insistence that they were together in this was starting to piss her off. It wasn't happening to him, it was happening to *her*. Okay, he was affected, but it wasn't like it was equal here.

'I'm... sorry?' she said, trying to change the tension in the air that she felt her silence had created. She was aware of her unreasonableness.

Rob ran his hands through his hair. Something played at the corner of his lips, like he wanted to say something but was making himself hold it back.

'No, no, don't be a silly goose. This isn't your fault.' His voice caught in his throat. 'None of this is your fault, okay?' He squeezed her hand. She took it away.

Why would you say it wasn't my fault? I hadn't said I thought it was. Did... did I cause the accident? Is it *my fault?*

'Did you call my parents yet?' Beth asked, wanting to change the subject.

Rob's face fell.

'What? What is it?'

He bit his lip.

'I was going to but...'

'But what?'

'Well, the relationship is a bit strained...'

Beth sat up straighter, her palms suddenly clammy on the wipe-clean pleather of the chair.

'What do you mean?'

Rob ran his hand over the back of his neck as he formulated his words.

'They don't like me.' He looked sheepish.

Beth said nothing; she wanted his unfiltered explanation for this.

'They... think I stole you from them. When you didn't go back home because we were dating, and then you moved in with me quickly.'

That didn't sound like her. She was impetuous, yes, but cautious and independent when it came to men. She'd wanted to travel the world, so why would she put down roots and why so far from home?

'Why did I?'

Rob started to smile. He laughed and then seemed to realise Beth was serious. His face fell. 'We were in love,' he said, as though that was an obvious answer.

Beth wasn't convinced. She was... she had only been twenty-four; she'd had the world at her feet. She couldn't see why she'd do that. Even for love. She had never been wide eyed about it. Had he really swept her off her feet so spectacularly?

'And...'

Ah. Here's the real reason.

'Well, the lockdowns. Your bar job disappeared. Your housemates moved back with their families and the international borders were closed.'

'I had no other option?' Beth said before regretting it as Rob looked as though she had slapped him.

'No!' he sounded angry then calmed immediately. 'No. It was more that all the usual logical reasons for not following your feelings were swept away. It made sense. In all ways. But' – his face clouded – 'your parents didn't see it like that. And they've never really liked me. Too English, it seems.' His expression soured. 'Never gave me a chance.'

'But they'd listen about this? About me?'

'Your parents...'

Beth's stomach dropped.

'What? What about them? Tell me!'

'You don't talk to them. *We* don't talk to them. Not any more. There was a big bust up about your moving out of London to here, about... about marrying me. They couldn't come to the wedding, and they wanted you to wait. They... wanted you to go back to Australia. You, we, chose not to wait and to stay here. You're not talking at the moment. I haven't called them. I didn't know if you wanted me to.'

Beth struggled to speak as she let this new information sink in. She and her parents had always been so close. Even through her teenage years when she and her mother would butt heads more often than either would have preferred. They were still close then. What on earth had happened? To Beth, it was only yesterday that she was happily living at home and now suddenly, seemingly, she was without her family, the other side of the world, married to a man she did not recognise. Was this a nightmare? Because none of it made any sense to her.

'I... they should know. I want you to call them.'

Row or no row, she *needed* them now and they would come to her. She knew they would.

'Are the borders back open?'

'Yes.'

'So they could come?'

'Yes.'

'So, call them.'

'I don't have their number.'

Beth's eyes widened in shock. What the hell did he mean? 'What? You're my husband and you don't have my parents' contact details?'

'They changed numbers and wouldn't or didn't give it to me. So I've been trying to track them down. It's just taking time and I've been here. And sorting things out.'

'Like what?' Beth's voice was tight and angry, and she sensed Sarah take a step towards them, ready to intervene if needed. What was more important than getting the news to her *family*?

'Like getting the car pulled out of the ditch!' Rob barked at her. 'Sorry. Sorry. I'm tired, it's been a lot to deal with. I didn't mean to snap. I'll keep trying. I'll get through to them, I know I will.'

It felt like Beth had been hit over the head all over again. Nothing made sense and her vision was swimming as her pulse raged in her veins. She was estranged from her family? What on earth would make them do that? Was it them? They were protective and close, sure, but not controlling and demanding. Was it *him*? What had he done to make them hate him so much? Was it *her*? Had she caused the rift by acting so impulsively?

Her last memories were of coffees in the mornings with her parents as everyone got ready to go to work. Discussions over her future and how she ought to be doing something, getting on with her life. Had they pushed her to go so far away, or had they railed against it? She needed to speak with them. She would get Sarah to keep trying. Surely they'd call if they knew Beth was in hospital. She felt like a book with pages torn out, a chunk of the story missing. She was too young to be dealing with all this. Or... at least she felt she was. She had to remind herself that she was now nudging thirty. A grown up. She felt like a child.

'Thank you.' Beth managed to smile at Rob. She wanted to *feel* something, anything that made this whole shitshow seem like it might be okay, but when she did there was nothing. Just a vague sense of unease, of wanting to say the right thing. What even was the right thing?

'So...' she started.

'Yes, Pooks?'

Why did he keep calling her that? She hated it. She said nothing. Now was not the time. 'What happened? With the car?'

Rob nodded while he considered his response. So much responsibility in that answer. What he chose to tell, how he did so.

The gap between her asking and his answer grew. The silence was oppressive. He looked at the floor as he placed his elbows on his knees, put his hands together in the middle. He looked as though he was praying. Maybe he was.

'You're sure you want me to tell you?'

Beth laughed a dry laugh. 'No. But not knowing isn't going to help me, is it? You're my husband. I can trust you, can't I?' As she said it, a flicker of a question came into her mind. The words 'my husband' feeling foreign on her tongue. The hospital had *checked*, hadn't they? Sarah said the police had checked too. This wasn't some total random stranger no matter how much she felt he was exactly that. She reminded herself that her instincts were broken. She had nothing to go on and so she had to trust those who were caring for her.

'Well, if you're sure.'

'I'm not sure of anything,' Beth said, a little strained.

Rob smiled, pained but a smile all the same. It was a nice smile, Beth noted. She liked it. That was good, wasn't it?

A start.

'You know there was a car accident. The airbag didn't deploy, and you hit your head on the steering wheel hard. Broke your nose.'

Beth looked worried, reaching her hand up to her face.

'They reset it, don't worry. I'm sure once the swelling goes down and the bruising subsides you'll look as good as new. And the facial stitching was done by a top plastic surgeon so they assured me that your scars will be minimal.'

It wasn't shallow to be worried about how she looked, was it? That was normal, surely? Beth felt a pang of irritation that apparently Rob had been worried too. It was "in sickness and in health" wasn't it? Not "always hot and never injured".

Focus, Beth.

'A car accident.'

Rob nodded.

'I was driving.'

He paused. 'You were.'

His face was grim. What was he not saying? Had she caused it? Was anyone else hurt?

'Okay...' she said, waiting for him to keep going, but he didn't.

He looked at the floor again. He was clearly trying to work out how not to distress her.

What had she done? Her breathing quickened.

'Were there any other cars involved?'

He nodded. He added nothing else. She was going to have to ask but she didn't know what she ought to be asking. Wondering if certain things might nudge her memories, including places, she turned to him and asked, 'Where? Where was the accident? Where did it happen?'

Rob swallowed. It was obviously hard for him to talk this through. Beth supposed that he had nearly lost his wife and to some extent he actually had, being that she couldn't remember that they were married at all.

'It was the fen road. The one you always hated. The one with the ditches either side.' He looked up for her reaction. Seeing her face blank, he shook his head in disbelief. 'Really? You have nothing?' He sounded almost annoyed. 'You hated that road, and I always downplayed it. I said there was nothing to worry about, but now? This is my fault.' He buried his face in his hands.

Suddenly her heart went out to him, and she reached out. Was this love? Or just human empathy for someone else in obvious pain?

'What do you mean? You weren't there.'

He shook his head vehemently. 'No, I wasn't there but you were coming *from* me. I told you not to waste time taking the longer route. Told you that you were being irrational. Turns out a pothole, a driver behind not paying attention, another driver going too fast out of a junction, and you got shunted off the road and into the ditch. You could have drowned.'

Beth recoiled. Whatever else she might have forgotten, she had never lost her fear of drowning. One day, when she was a young child, she had been at the beach near her home and she had witnessed a young child on a lilo get too far from the beach, the wind just pushing him over the sand ridge out to sea while his parents' attention had been diverted. She looked as the lilo drifted away and had watched as a wave took the little boy from it. He'd bobbed, silently above the water line and then under. She'd told her mum and pointed to him and then panic had broken out.

The screams from the boy's mother had never left her, the desperate attempts to resuscitate him when they'd got him back to shore. The howl of pain when it became clear that those attempts were fruitless. She shivered, suddenly cold. It was the worst way she could think of to go. The ache of missing her parents snowballed inside her and she turned her face away from Rob, hiding into the back of the chair.

Sarah appeared suddenly at the side of the bed, clearly aware that Rob was in need of some support but also that he might be causing distress to Beth.

'Too much too soon,' she said kindly, placing her hand on his shoulder in a supportive way but one that also somehow said *enough*. 'I think everyone could do with a cup of tea. Beth? Would you like a drink? I can get you something soothing, for your throat.'

Beth nodded. This *was* all too much too soon. Everything felt off. The world had shifted off kilter and the room was spinning at the wrong angle. Nothing was in the right place. She felt furious with Rob. He *knew* everything. She had fallen out with her parents because of him. She had been driving the car the route she had been because of him. She didn't want him anywhere near her. Fair or not.

'Actually, Rob.' Sarah turned to him. 'Would you be a dear and go and get something from the café downstairs? I can get you tea, but it'd be that awful machine stuff and frankly, no one needs that.'

Rob rubbed his hands over his face, wiping away tears, composing himself. He nodded. 'I'll be back soon.'

'Not going anywhere!' Beth said, trying to be light hearted but sounding sarcastic.

Sarah watched Rob walk out of the room before turning back to Beth. She tipped her head to one side sympathetically – in a way that reminded Beth so strongly of her mother that she had to fight hard not to burst into tears.

'Love, I just wanted to say that what you're going through and what you're probably feeling is okay. We all use our instincts to get us through things but when you're experiencing memory loss, well, your instincts get a bit wobbly. That's okay. Just take things slowly. You can still trust your gut, about everything.' She looked back at the door. 'About people. You may have to relearn things and fill in blanks, but we're here. You won't be alone. Let's get you back into bed, shall we?'

'Thank you,' Beth whispered, letting her tears creep from the corners of her eyes as she moved back up on to the bed. This was all so much to process, and Sarah's kindness really helped. Beth had a million questions, but she was so tired. She just wanted to sleep and have none of this be happening. To wake up and go back to her life. Except, she didn't know what that looked like. Sleep pulled at her again.

She smiled at Sarah, who patted her hand.

'I'll be here, okay?' she said as she moved away to let Beth rest.

Beth couldn't tell if it had been seconds or much longer when she was aware of a conversation taking place at the end of her bed. It was Sarah's voice, and a man's, she assumed Rob's.

She was going to open her eyes to join them but something in their tone made her keep her eyes closed.

'Look, I know that you want your wife back but it's only her first day with all this. You've had a few days to get used to the fact that things have changed. We have to be patient.'

'But what if she asks? Especially about...'

'Well, then that we will have to deal with at the time. She has a lot to process, a lot to take in, and she's still recovering. As the doctors said yesterday, the swelling has gone down, it's much improved from a physical point of view, but mentally, emotionally, it's too early to say. She's very fragile.'

'I can take care of my own wife. She's all I have.'

'No one is saying you can't, but you can't rush these things. Emotional stress can hamper recovery. Things have to be taken slowly, gently. In their own time. Patience really is key here.'

Rob sighed.

'Look,' Sarah said, 'I know this has had a great impact on you. I know life suddenly looks very different and I know you're dealing with... everything. But you can't rush it. You can't push your way through this—'

'I'm not pushing anyone, I—'

'I don't mean it like that. Look. You're tired too. Beth is sleeping. Why don't you go home, rest.'

'I feel like I'm lying to her.'

'But you aren't. Giving her time to process things is not lying.'

There was a sound like a begrudged agreement.

'You need to process things too. Go. Rest. I'll be here with her.'

'Okay. Will you call me if anything changes?'

'Of course I will. Promise.'

'Thank you.'

Beth worked hard on looking realistically asleep as Rob placed something on the bedside table, and she heard the rustle then gentle squeak as he picked up his jacket from the chair. She knew that she ought to want to talk with him, but he was a stranger to her. She felt guilt and shame wash over her as she realised that her overriding feeling to his leaving was relief. She didn't have to pretend to be someone she wasn't. His wife? She realised that she didn't even know his last name. *Her* last name. Despite Sarah's kind words, she felt utterly alone.

Who on earth was she?

4

'We just need to get you home now. Let's get you back where you belong and then we can work together on... rebuilding things. I can be your memory until you get yours back. We can start again. Let me take care of you.'

Rob pulled his chair closer to where Beth was also sitting. The highbacked, wipe-clean hospital chair was making her feel about a million years old, while her inner fear and anxiety made her feel like a kid. He was right though. She needed to get out of here. She was much better than she had been; her health was much improved, and in all honesty they needed the bed. Rob was being encouraging and supportive and he wanted to help her recuperate in her own home. Everything was fine. Even if it didn't feel it.

'Being home can only help, right? Being in your own space, with your own things. Hospital is disorientating. People coming and going, noise all the time, especially in here.' He continued, leaning forward towards her, making his point.

'Everything is disorientating,' Beth said before she could stop herself. She sounded petulant. She didn't mean to. She caught the flicker of disapproval in Rob's face before he fixed it, pasted his never-ending patient smile back on. Patience she was both grateful for and resentful of. She herself often felt angry, wanting to lash out, and yet Rob's steadiness felt like she wasn't allowed to feel like that, that she wasn't being fair to him when his life had been turned upside down too. Dr Preston had said that some people find their personalities altered. Was the anger she was feeling genuine or a result of some personality change?

'I know, babe, it's been a lot. But we haven't lost everything. We can fix this. You have me. I have you. It's going to be okay. Just tell them what they want to hear and let's get you home.'

He's right. There are always hoops to jump through but I just need to get home.

It had been a complex couple of weeks, moving out of ICU after a few days into a sort of in between ward before this regular, revolving door ward. It was always busy, day and night, and Beth was exhausted from it all. She felt like she was sat down in the middle of a busy train station, watching everyone else get on with their lives, leaving, arriving, meeting their loved ones, while she was stationary, stuck, alone. She did need her own bed, even if she didn't remember it as such. So she had listened to what Rob had told her about now, here, dates, times, important facts. It was her way of showing willing with him, a new connection of sorts in place of any recollection of him as her husband. In that sense he was still a stranger, the man she married. It had almost felt like running lines in a play, with Rob the only one holding the script. She felt she was playing the part of his wife, playing the part of a Beth she didn't know.

Rob had brought in mementos, photos to try to give her memory a kick start. He had brought in items from their early dates: gig tickets, travel receipts, showed pictures on his phone.

One day he'd gone all out in an attempt to remind Beth who she was.

'What are you wearing?' Beth had laughed as Rob had arrived at her bedside wearing a dark grey suit with a waistcoat and a rose in his buttonhole. He was holding a long garment cover bag, a paper bag and a cream covered box. 'What's all this?'

Placing the items down on Beth's bed and pulling a chair up, Rob took her hand and smiled. He looked pleased with himself.

'Today is a special day.' His eyes twinkled. Beth couldn't tell if it was the lighting or if he had the start of tears in his eyes. 'Though traditionally it's me who's supposed to not remember the date...'

'Is it?' Beth smiled. She felt a flickering in her stomach. Almost like... was he flirting with her? And... did she... did she like it? Was this what they were like together?

'It is. Today is our wedding anniversary. We got married four years ago today.'

Beth didn't know what to say.

Rob continued. 'So I thought I'd wear what I wore' – he gestured to his outfit – 'bring what *you* wore' – he held up the garment bag – 'and I've brought the photos and some cake that's the same as we had on the day. New, of course, not four years old!' He laughed.

She was touched. This was so thoughtful. She knew he was hoping that all this might dislodge whatever it was that was blocking her mind, but she wanted that too, didn't she? She wanted this black hole in her mind to find the light.

'Okay, show me the dress!' she said nervously.

Rob stood up and ceremoniously unzipped the garment bag. Instinctively, Beth pictured a strapless, sweetheart neckline, fishtail dress. Something beachy, something both beautiful but chilled. Something you could get married in at the water's edge but also that your gran would approve of. She held her breath and looked up.

As Rob unsheathed the dress and held it up, Beth felt the disappointment pull her stomach over inside her. The dress was white, empire line, with gauze sleeves and lace and beading. It looked like something out of *Lord of the Rings*. She hated it.

If Rob caught her expression, he didn't say anything as he placed the dress back in the bag and set it down.

'Here, let's get a cup of coffee and have some anniversary cake while we look through the photos, mmm?'

Beth nodded. Maybe it looked better on. Sometimes dresses did that, didn't they? Looked insipid on the hanger but amazing on a person. She'd seen enough episodes of *Don't Tell the Bride* to know that. Had Rob picked this out for her maybe?

While he went to get coffee, Beth couldn't help herself and she opened the box with the photo album to take a look while he was gone. Something inside her felt she needed to get her first reaction out while he wasn't there to watch, in case it wasn't what he wanted to see. If she was disappointed or dismayed or just unmoved at all, then she felt she needed to do that without an audience.

She flipped through the pages expecting to find celebratory photos, pictures with friends at least, if not with family. Photos of the two of them glowing with happiness, with her looking radiant in the gown. She expected to look at them and know herself.

She was wrong.

The venue seemed to be a town hall, all greys and beiges and noticeboards on the wall. The main photo of them both was the pair of them stood outside what looked like a grey-blue corrugated iron building, which blended into the grey-blue sky above them. He was smiling widely, his arm slung around her waist, holding her tight. Her expression was... What was it? It wasn't carefree, Beth could see that much at least. Had she been happy? She looked... well, nauseous. Maybe she was nervous; a big day, after all. The dress looked as wrong on her as it did on the hanger. It fell in waves to the floor but looked as though it was swamping her frame. It looked like a cheap satin bedsheet. Catching sight of Rob returning, mugs in hand, she quickly put the book back and tried to reset her expression.

'Right! Here we go,' he said, placing them down on the tray table that stretched across the bed. He tidied away the magazines that he had got for her, placing them neatly in the cabinet beside her bed. He then reached into the cake box and got out two slices of elaborate red velvet cake. Beth wrinkled her nose in confusion. That was their choice of wedding cake?

Rob pulled his chair next to her, leant in and took a big bite of cake.

'Hmm, my favourite,' he said between chews.

Maybe she had let him choose it if he liked it, because she hated it. It looked like blood and tasted like food colouring. Nasty. Maybe it was a keep-him-happy choice. It had been his wedding too, after all, and Beth didn't think she'd have been a bridezilla.

'Tell me about our wedding?' Beth said, hearing the crack of hope in her voice. So far, the only thing the memories had provoked was disappointment.

Rob wiped his mouth on the back of his hand and opened up the wedding photos.

'You looked so beautiful.'

'Hmm.'

'You don't think so?'

'No, it's just, it's not the dress I'd envisioned, that's all. It looks a bit...' She chose her words carefully. He had an emotional connection to the day, and she didn't want to spoil that. 'It's very... floaty.'

'You wanted to be my English Rose. Said I could be your Mr Darcy.'

'Like Keira Knightley?'

'Exactly. And... Well, it was 2020. The world was a bin fire. We got married when we could, where we could and with what wedding stuff we could get. Choices were limited. We just wanted to *get* married, we didn't care about all the rest of the stuff.' He sounded offended.

'I...'

'Look, it's just... you can't really fill in the past few years using *normal* years as a template. Everything was on its head. Things were just... different. And I can fill in as much as I can but you're going to have to trust me on some things. Okay?'

'Okay.' She bit her lip. It must be hard that your wife doesn't recall your wedding day even when it's staring her in the face. She sat up and flipped through a few more pages. There were photos of her, of him, of her and him. Pictures inside the ceremony room. Pictures outside. A taxi with a white ribbon on it.

'Where is everyone else? Where are the guests? Did we have photos of them?'

'We didn't have guests.'

'What?' Beth's eyes widened in surprise.

'I told you. Lockdown. Weddings were cancelled. When they restarted you weren't allowed many, if any, guests.'

'Then who were the witnesses?'

'The staff. It was just you and me, Pooks. You and me against the world.'

'But our families...'

A hint of irritation passed over Rob's face. Beth caught it.

'Look. Yours couldn't come as international borders were closed. I'm not... close to my family and it seemed unfair to have anyone from my side there if yours couldn't be. We decided it was more *romantic* to be just us. It was for us, about us. And like I said, it was a different time.'

'Couldn't we have waited? Married once it was all over? When people could come?'

'We couldn't wait. I... We didn't want to. We were madly in love and decided to just do it. Bring some happiness into a difficult time. And we didn't know when *over* would be. No one did.'

Beth sank back into her chair. She could feel how disappointed her mum would have been not to be at her only daughter's wedding. Is that what they had rowed about? Had she cut her mother out of her life over this? Was life really that different in the past few years? What was Rob not saying? Silently, Beth pored over the photos, looking for details that might give her some clue as to what he wasn't telling her. She could feel his eyes on her as she did so. Sarah had said that her gut feeling wasn't broken, just wobbly, and something about this felt *off*. Why would they rush to marry, so soon after meeting, in the middle of a pandemic, without their families there? It just didn't seem like something she would do. She was a romantic at times, yes, but relentlessly pragmatic too. No rose-tinted glasses about blokes for her.

Despite all this effort from Rob, there had been no miraculous recovery for Beth and she was still missing the years that, for whatever reason, her mind did not want to release to her. There was nothing more the hospital could do. Time was the only healer now and she was heading home with Rob. They were just waiting now for the final paperwork to be done and for her follow up appointments to be scheduled, and then Rob would be taking her home.

Beth wasn't sure how she felt if she were honest with herself. She was mostly just really tired still. She still didn't recognise Rob as her husband; nothing within her felt connected to him, but he knew so much about their life together it had to be true. He knew where she'd studied, what she'd studied. He had information about her life before she had met him, memories that *she* still had, that she assumed she must have told him. He was clearly someone important in her life, even if she did feel like he was withholding something from her.

Even now, he was over talking with the nurses at their station, talking about her being discharged and her ongoing care, *without* her. She could tell from their body language that there was a tension there. His shoulders were hunched; the ward sister was holding her clipboard just a touch too tightly. From years working as a waitress, a barista, a barmaid, she was good at reading people, and something wasn't right here. But what? The nurse looked over at Beth, and was that pity on her face? Sorrow? For what? For her missing memory or for something else? Something that everyone but her knew? It felt like she had walked into a room and everyone had stopped talking.

She had nothing to pin her life on outside the hospital walls other than Rob, so, a bit like a bungee jump or a skydive, she decided that she had to trust in the situation, close her eyes and jump and just hope to God that she didn't hit the ground. Maybe once at home, she could do a little digging, find out what was between the lines of what people were telling her. There was something, she just knew it. She could *feel* it.

'Beth. Okay, so we're all set.' The ward sister was holding a bunch of files in her hands. 'Paperwork is all done. A community nurse will visit you in a couple of days to check that you're settling in okay, but you can call us at any time if you want to. All the details are in here,' she said, indicating to the files before handing them to Rob. He took them and put them the bag that held all of her personal belongings. She really was going... *home*. She desperately tried not to picture Australia when she heard that word, but it was proving difficult. Apparently home *here* was in some village outside Cambridge. Out in the country, not the big city she was used to, suburbs or not. She willed the tears that were forming at the back of her throat not to fall. She didn't want to seem ungrateful, to anyone. She was here, alive. From what she had since learnt of the accident, that was not a foregone conclusion.

'Thank you. To you, to everyone here and in the ICU. You've all been wonderful.'

'Our pleasure. Just remember now, take things easy, don't push yourself, and if anything you remember is... distressing or upsetting to you, you can always call our counsellors, okay? We're all still here for you.'

Beth nodded. She couldn't say any more without crying. She felt like a kid on the first day at a new school, going into an environment unknown to her, where she couldn't control how things would be, she didn't know how she was going to feel. But now, she also couldn't go home at the end of the day to somewhere she felt safe, with people she knew. Despite all efforts, both from Rob and from the hospital, they'd not been able to contact her family yet. It felt like forever despite only being a couple of weeks and she felt cast adrift in the enormity of the world. Apparently her dad had retired in the years Beth was missing and her mum's work wouldn't pass out information, understandably. They'd said they had passed on the message, but Rob had said that the receptionist had sounded bored when talking with him and he wasn't convinced that she had done so.

Beth had asked Rob to contact Beans and Brew, but they had closed down, a casualty of the pandemic apparently. Small businesses had folded under the pressure of enforced restrictions. Once in the new ward, she'd asked about getting a smartphone, but it had been agreed that perhaps that would not be wise just yet. Too much to wade through, an assault on her brain when she was still fragile. Instead she had agreed that she would wait until she was discharged. Then she'd contact some of her friends back home in Australia to try to get a message to her folks. It wouldn't be hard, she assured herself. This scenario wouldn't be for long.

She knew she *ought* to feel safe with Rob and that it wasn't his fault that she didn't quite yet. Or at least, she didn't feel *unsafe*, just more that she couldn't really tell him anything she was thinking. She was worried she'd say the wrong thing and upset him. Surely, if they had been married, they'd be able to tell each other anything? Wasn't that what marriage was supposed to be like? Or was she being naive? Maybe she'd learnt about adult relationships in the five years she was now missing and now had lost all of that wisdom. Wise or not, for the second time in her life, it seemed that she had nowhere else to go than to be with Rob.

'Okay, babe. Let's go,' Rob said, walking over and holding his hand out to her. 'I booked a cab as I wanted to be able to sit with you rather than drive.'

Beth took a sharp breath inward. She'd not considered that being in a car again would trigger something in her. After all, she didn't remember the accident at all. Rob was being thoughtful and considerate of her feelings, thinking of things *for* her. That was a good sign, wasn't it?

'Okay.' She stood up and walked with him to the door and out into the next part of her life.

Her life after.

5

Rob opened the door and they stepped inside the house. A new build on the edge of a village. The air inside felt stale, as though it had been shut up for weeks. Beth stepped into the small, boxy hallway that led immediately to a fairly spacious living room. There was a cream sofa facing a large TV, with a matching chair pushed up against the window, which was large, letting in the mid-afternoon sunshine. If you were to carry on straight through, you could see a kitchen diner. If you turned left, there were stairs, which Beth assumed led to the bedrooms and bathrooms. Despite assuming this, when she tried to picture what was upstairs, nothing came to her.

'Let me get in,' Rob said, coming up close behind her and stepping round. 'Welcome home,' he said, awkwardly waving his arms around the room. If he was aiming for light and breezy, then he failed. It came out weird and stilted.

Beth walked into the room and looked around the space. The walls were bare, no pictures or mirrors. The effect was to make the room feel flat, almost TV set-like. As though the walls were fake, with an audience watching from the other side. She felt exposed. She knew Rob was watching for her reaction. But she felt nothing. She sighed as she realised that being 'home' had not sparked anything in her. At least, not immediately. Perhaps she had expected too much; perhaps she had watched too many soap operas where the mere sight of a framed photo or a favourite chair brought everything rushing back.

'I'll pop the kettle on,' Rob called from the kitchen, where he had gone presumably to give Beth some space to re-acquaint herself with her home. It was somehow smaller than Beth had imagined, despite feeling as though she'd never stepped foot in this building before. This room felt *alien* to her. It smelt... clean. Too clean. As though Rob had done a hurried clean-up of a man-alone-with-too-much-else-to-do level of mess. Beth imagined abandoned cups of half-drunk tea. A collection of beer cans left on the coffee table. Pizza boxes. Was this a memory of Rob and his untidiness? A relic from his single years when they met, or was Beth filling in what she thought Rob might be like? Making him as messy as her brother was, as he was her only frame of reference. Well, whatever the reason, the room was clinically tidy and there wasn't a speck of dust anywhere. In fact, as Beth walked from the living room to the stairs, to the bedroom, where she pushed back a flutter of panic when she saw the bed, the only bed, a standard double bed, she noted that there wasn't a lot of anything in the house at all. Very minimalist. If it was supposed to jogging her memories, it wasn't going to be doing it with photos, or knickknacks or décor. There was none. Like it had been stripped of all personality ready for a sale. At *home*, her room had been covered in photos, postcards of places she wanted to see. A world map on her wall, on which she'd plotted her trip across the globe as she lay in bed. Her room had a collection of mementos from her childhood. Was this here her new style? Was she a minimalist now, through choice or the practicalities of world travel? Was Rob less of a clutter sort of guy? Or was this the space of someone not planning on sticking around too long? Had they planned to go back to Australia together? Maybe they still could.

Hearing the sounds of Rob bustling about in the kitchen, Beth looked further around the bedroom. Maybe there was *another* bedroom, she thought hopefully, though she couldn't think where it would be. The house was small. But if not, she needed to be prepared for Rob to expect them to both sleep here. She felt cold at the idea, at the thought of being physically close to him. Something was niggling at her about it. She couldn't tell if it was just that with her missing years, their age gap was bigger than it was in reality and that was why the idea of being close to him felt off. Surely she would have fancied her husband? He couldn't have been so different in only a few years, could he? No one changed that much, did they?

She got her answer as she walked into the small shower room off the side of the bedroom, where she came face to face with a huge wall mirror.

'Wha...' she gasped, putting her hand to her forehead.

In hospital, all the bathroom mirrors were small, in badly lit rooms, and so much had been going on that she had barely paid attention to what she looked like. But here? The large, clear, well-lit mirror showed her *everything*. Every line on her face that had not been there the last time she remembered. In her head she was twenty-four, sun-kissed with beach-tousled hair. Carefree. This was not who was looking back at her. She was pale. Pasty. She had dark circles under her eyes, the beginnings of fine lines on her face and a large red scar running down her forehead. Careworn. Though she knew it wasn't the case, it *felt* like she had aged overnight.

But, despite all this, Beth knew *herself*, didn't she? Sociable, chatty, always happy to go to a party or to the beach and grab life by the horns. The sort of person who hops on a plane and heads off into the sunset. And she knew that she liked things, pretty things: photos, reminders of the stuff that she'd done and the places she'd visited.

From talking with Rob, she knew already that she'd been a traveller, had been working her way across Europe, getting bar jobs and agricultural work as she went, before landing in England and then meeting him at the bar where she was working at the time. And yet, here, there were no photos. No mementos or items she'd collected. There was a single photo of her wedding day when it had just been the two of them. Surely there were other people in their lives besides each other? Circumstances might have kept people apart, she could accept, but it didn't erase them entirely.

Where were her family? Rob had said that they'd rowed about her choice to stay in the UK, to get married while no one could go. Had they felt abandoned by her? Had she felt that they didn't understand her new life? It must be hard to have your child so far from you, she supposed. Had they even ever met Rob? Was he as much a stranger to them as he was to her now? Was that why they hadn't called back?

Why hadn't they called? She could ask Rob to let her try this time. She could track down her brother, maybe; he'd be more online than her parents. He'd be easy enough to find, surely. She glanced again at this new reflection of hers and headed back to the bedroom. She was suddenly overcome with weariness. She sat on the edge of the bed and fought against the urge to lie down and curl up and sleep. She needed to stay alert. She didn't know why but she just knew that she did. She didn't want to miss something, anything, that might hold a clue to unlocking her mind. That and she couldn't relax here. It may be her home but it didn't feel like it, and Rob might be her husband but she didn't know him.

'Here we are...' Rob announced as he walked into the bedroom holding two mugs of tea. 'I wondered where you'd gone.' Beth's stomach dropped further as she took one from him. She would never have bought these mugs. They were pink for a start, matching with red polka dots. Twee. She'd always hated country-cottage-style stuff. She couldn't imagine Rob had bought them either. So who had? Who *was* she? Minimalist or kitsch? Something else? It was all too confusing.

'You okay?' he asked.

'Yeah. Yeah. Just trying to get my bearings. Settle in, you know.'

'Anything?'

Beth shook her head.

Was she imagining things, or did he look relieved?

'So...' she said, trying to work out what to ask. She put the tea down. It didn't have sugar in it. She took sugar, didn't she? 'How long have we lived here?'

'Um... a couple of years.'

'Really? It seems...'

'What?' He looked at her over the edge of his cup. It made him seem stern.

'Well. Sorta empty?'

He coughed. 'Ha! No, you're an absolute hater of clutter. Said that living out of a backpack meant that you started to hate unnecessary stuff. I... I used to worry it was because you had one foot out the door, back to Oz, but you eventually convinced me it wasn't. Less to tidy, you said.'

Beth nodded. It was plausible, she guessed, even if it didn't quite sit right with her. She supposed that this part of her had been formed during the time her memory was missing, and people changed, didn't they? Travel broadened the mind, after all. Maybe travel had made her a minimalist. But home was where the heart was, wasn't it? Maybe this had never really felt like home to her.

They sat in uncomfortable silence, sipping at their tea. The air crackled with the questions both wanted to ask but couldn't bring themselves to do so.

'Rob?' Beth eventually said, quietly.

'Yes?'

'Did you try again? To call my folks?' Beth felt nervous, her hands scratching at her neck as she prepared herself for news she didn't want to hear. With the suggestion that she had fallen out with them still smarting, it felt almost a betrayal to keep asking Rob to call them, but she had to force the issue. She wanted nothing more than to be with her mum, have her looking after her. That would make everything all right. She knew it.

Rob cleared his throat. 'I am trying.'

Beth felt her stomach drop.

Rob must have seen it as he hurriedly continued. 'I tried the number we had again but still nothing. It just rings and rings.' He bit his lip.

'I thought you said they'd moved, and you don't have the new number?'

'I... well, yes. But I called the old one in case the new house owner knows where they've gone, or if they ported the number maybe.'

'Can you do that?' She'd never really got landlines. They seemed so archaic.

'I don't know, Beth! I'm just trying, okay?'

'Sorry. Sorry. I just really want to talk with them.'

'I know, Pooky, I know. Look. I've emailed your mum's office.

Told them it was urgent and asked them to call me. As soon as they could. I... I've yet to hear back but I'm sure they will call. Even... even with how things are. How things were left.'

'What do you mean?'

'Nothing.'

'No, what?'

'Just the wedding and stuff like that.'

But we've been married four years. Surely things have worked themselves out? That's enough time for frayed tempers to cool and for hurt feelings to recover. Isn't it? Is there something else he isn't saying?

'How bad was the row?'

'Well, it wasn't great. Things... were said. On both sides.'

'Oh.' She knew how she and her parents had fought when she was a teenager; she knew how vicious she could be. Had she said something unforgiveable?

Beth felt the strain she knew her expression was showing. Why would her family have rejected her? She needed to change the subject before she lost her composure entirely. She sniffed, shook her head lightly and grabbed another subject out of the air.

'And where do I... where did I work?' Beth suddenly realised she'd not asked about this. There had been so much to catch up on with Rob, and her family. She'd not even had time to think about her job. Did she still do bar work? Rob had said the hospitality sector had taken a battering, but she must have been doing something. Surely it would have been a major part of her life before the accident, what she had spent most of her time doing. She'd have colleagues, friends, even. Why had they not come to see her? Did she have friends back home who'd been wondering why she'd suddenly gone quiet? Apps and platforms switched so quickly, didn't they? How had she kept in touch?

She couldn't recall. And all their numbers were on her phone that had not survived its dip in the fen waters. She'd have to ask Rob to get her a new phone and she could start to track people down. She could hear her mum in her mind, saying how a paper address book never let you down...

'Well, you did hospitality stuff mostly. A bit here, a bit there. Work was patchy for a while, and you sort of fell out of it. It was fine though, as I was happy, am happy, to support us both. You... you said you wanted to be a photographer, so you were working on that. Building a portfolio.'

Beth's forehead wrinkled as she thought. She had always wanted to be a photographer and this meant that there would be lots of photos. She could look through them, literally see the world through her own eyes! A feeling of lightness fluttered inside her.

'This is great news, isn't it?' she said.

'What is?'

'My portfolio. I can look through it, see what I took, what I focused on.'

'Ah.'

'What?'

'Well, I don't know whether to tell you...'

'Tell me what?'

Rob looked pained but also as if he had been preparing for this. Beth hated this feeling, knowing that he knew something that she did not, and he was working out how to present it to her. No one person ever had the whole truth, did they? True was different to different people. She would only ever be getting *his* version of *her* truth.

'There was a tech glitch, and the hard drive of your computer failed. You'd not set up a backup. I'd told you time and again to do that but...' He shook his head in exasperation.

'They're gone?'

Rob nodded.

'You sort of lost enthusiasm after that. It knocked you for six a bit. But it's okay. We'll start again. You can. We can. It's early days, Pooky,' Rob said, an almost desperate look in his eyes. 'We'll figure this out. We just need to start over. That's all. Just take this as Day One. Pooky and me, take two,' he said as he patted her knee affectionately and then left his hand there, on her skin, as he picked up his cup again and sipped calmly from it. Beth suddenly couldn't breathe properly. What did this reaction to his touch mean?

It felt like fear.

How had she got here, in this house that she did not recognise, with a man she did not really know, the other side of the world from her family who apparently did not care if she was alive or not? Maybe, if she was as impulsive and selfish as Rob was unwittingly painting her out to be; maybe her family were pleased that she'd left. Maybe this was why no one had visited her. No one really believed themselves to be unlikeable, but surely if she truly only had one person in the whole world who cared about her, then maybe she was. She'd never kept new friends long despite always being up for hanging out. She found it hard to connect and lots of her friends had moved for uni, or had made new friends, leaving her behind. She was older than the others at the café and her childhood friends all had new friendship groups. Maybe she was the problem, after all. Maybe she deserved this solitude. Maybe the accident had been karma for always putting herself first.

Rob said nothing more but spread his fingers over her knee, almost absentmindedly, stroking his fingertips over her skin in a repetitive, circular motion. It felt like something he was used to doing. It felt like an invasion to her. She wanted to scream and yell at him to stop but something in her told her not to rock the boat. She suddenly felt very cold. The hairs on the back of her neck were prickling. Her body was telling her something but what she couldn't say other than to stay silent. To not upset him by rejecting this affection. After all, he was all she had.

6

'Why don't you take a nap? I've got to pop out to do some work. You could rest while I'm gone, make the most of the peace?' Rob said as he moved about the house getting ready to go to work.

'I am really tired still, but I can't get comfortable. I guess I'm used to hospital beds now,' Beth said, although the main issue was that she couldn't relax enough, lying in bed next to Rob, to really sleep deeply. He hadn't tried anything intimate yet – he was being respectful of that for now – but surely it was only time. She was his wife, after all. In bed she could feel the warmth of him radiating towards her, and the sound of his breathing set her teeth on edge. When she'd been awake long enough to worry that this was another sign of her temper, it then led to her worrying that she'd had some alteration to her personality. It happened, didn't it? What if she was now irrationally angry about everyday things? Could she really trust her own feelings?

What if Rob left her? As much as she was terrified that she didn't know him, he was the only one looking after her. Without him, where would she be? She had no one else. In the depth of the night, in the hours where the world was quiet and black and lonely, she had spiralled into a total panic about her whole life and what a literal car crash it seemed to be. In her head, she was still in her early twenties, a time when you could go anywhere and do anything. You could pick up jobs, friends, somewhere to live, a life, almost as easily as getting a cup of coffee. Now? She was alienated from her family, no career, no job. She was nearly thirty with no work experience or contacts, a literal dependent on Rob, who apparently was her visa sponsor. And where were her friends? Did she even have any? She had lain there, as the pale light of morning had finally dawned, and inched across the room as the sun rose, and worried about pretty much everything.

But she had made a plan. She was going to get online and do some research. Into herself, her past, the accident. Everything. Anything to help nudge her mind into remembering. She was driving herself nuts not knowing. All that experience that she and her friends had cyber-stalking potential dates was going to come in handy. She was going to find out everything about herself. She would fill in the gaps in her mind with her own digital footprint.

'Why don't you take some of your painkillers? They usually make you sleepy, don't they? The docs said you could take them as needed?' Rob suggested, not looking at her while he packed up his work bag.

He'd not left her side since they had arrived home. She assumed he had things to do, places to be, and yet he had spent all his time with her. He'd made lots of phone calls, tucked away in a different room so as not to 'disturb' her, but it made her feel like she was in the way. She ought to make him feel like he could go.

'Maybe. Though I don't think I'm supposed to use them for that? I did think I'd maybe do a little research though. You know, online? Do we have a laptop somewhere?'

'Hmm?' he replied almost absentmindedly. 'I need to take this with me,' he said, gesturing to his bag. 'And besides, it's a bit soon for that, isn't it? I ought to be with you. In case you need something? I think sleep is a better idea for now.'

'I... I was going to try to track down my brother.'

Rob grunted. 'Let's do it together, this evening, eh? He'll be asleep now so if you did find him you wouldn't get a response anyway, would you? A few hours won't make a difference.'

Beth sighed. She could feel her toes fidgeting and made moves to make herself stop. She was jittery. Maybe she did need a nap. She felt wired.

'That makes sense, I guess. Thanks.'

'Your meds?' Rob repeated at her, raising his eyebrows.

'Oh. Yes. Okay.'

Beth walked to the kitchen where the box with all her medication was sitting, organised, on the counter. She hadn't done this; Rob had. He obviously had a 'place for everything and everything in its place' mentality as the house was spotless. The tea, coffee and sugar containers were in a neat row, arranged so that the lettering read in a straight line. The sugar one was empty as she'd learned by their second cup of tea that Rob didn't believe in adding sugar to things. The cupboards were the same, with the items all lined up, looking like they were still in the store to some extent, and the hand towel and tea towel were neatly folded and hanging on a rail for that exact purpose. It was another thing that made Beth feel ill at ease, unable to feel properly at home, for fear she would mess up the aesthetic. Rob hadn't said anything about it, or even tidied up around her, but Beth just got the feeling she ought to toe the line. Her instincts on that were working, at least.

She didn't actually want to nap though, and the idea of using painkillers to sleep sounded like a slippery slope to choose, so she went through the motions of taking the medication but left the pills in the packet. As an afterthought, she hid them in her pocket to dispose of later. She didn't want Rob to know she was sneaking about. Why did she feel she needed to? She couldn't say. Maybe this was a symptom too. She made a mental note to ask when the nurse came for the checkup tomorrow and then she put the kettle on. As she did so, she noticed Rob's phone sitting on the counter. Without thinking, she swiped open a kitchen drawer and put it inside, then closed the drawer again.

'Do you have time for a cup of tea before you go?' she called into the other room where Rob was picking up his coat.

He wandered into the kitchen, a wry expression on his face.

'You don't want me to go, do you, Pooky?' He smiled. 'Don't worry, I won't be long. There are just some things I need to do. Places to be, that sort of thing.'

'It's okay, I was just making one for me, so wanted to offer one to you too.'

Rob's face changed, a question forming. 'Why? If you want to nap, why add caffeine and tannins into your system? Unless you were having a herbal tea? That'd be better for you, anyway, wouldn't it?'

His expression made Beth realise that this was not a question but an instruction. He reached past her, into the cupboard, and took out a packet of herbal tea, handing it to her. She nodded slowly as she took it from him, seeing his face revert back to smiling as she did so. Was this their dynamic? He told her what to do and she did it? She'd never been one to be told what to do. Especially not by a boyfriend. *Husband*, she corrected herself. She recalled an ex trying to order her a salad on a date once and she had very pointedly cancelled the order, ordered a huge burger and chips, eaten it all, paid for herself and left. She did not take kindly to this sort of interference. She'd make the other cuppa once he was gone.

'Okay, well, why don't you pop yourself on the sofa. I'll get you a blanket and you can have a sleep. Like I said, I won't be long.'

Beth did as she was told, abandoning the tea altogether. Rob followed her and tucked her up under the blanket as he'd promised. Part of her felt like a cared-for child as he did so, and she smiled at him to show him that. She had to stop assuming the worst of things. He paused and then leaned and kissed her on the head. Then he looked back at her, perhaps for reassurance that it had been okay to do so. They were still teetering around each other. Perhaps he felt like he was sharing his home with a stranger too. He continued getting his things together and Beth felt like he was waiting for her to sleep, and so she closed her eyes and tried to slow her breathing, to look as though she was. After a while she could sense him standing near her, probably checking if she was asleep.

'Beth?'

She didn't respond, merely shifted her body as though she was getting comfortable and then stilled herself again. Then, a few moments later she heard the front door open and close, and in the distance if she strained to hear, a car start up and drive away. She waited, still, eyes closed, until she was sure that the atmosphere had changed around her and she was alone.

Sitting up, Beth took a moment to shake off the beginnings

of sleep that had started to settle on her. She was still so tired and, at that moment, decided she would take a quick look at the phone she had hidden and then actually try to nap. Not only would it be good to rest, she also felt it would look better if she was asleep when Rob returned. Like she had not been lying to her husband if she did so.

Noting Rob's attention to detail, she looked at where she had been lying and how the blanket had been draped. It was one of those handmade crochet ones, which had different sides depending on which way it was draped. Who made it, she wondered? Then she stood up and walked back into the kitchen and retrieved the phone from where she'd put it. What had made her do that? It had almost felt instinctive, which, given her complete lack of instincts at the moment, felt significant somehow.

She turned the phone over in her hands, at first surprised at how it didn't look new to her. She had assumed that new technology would look strange to her somehow. She touched the screen, and it pinged into life. The lock screen – dammit. She swiped upwards and it asked for a pin. She put it down while she thought for a moment. People were awful at pins and passwords. Her brother was always giving her hassle about hers. Birthdays, important dates. She realised she didn't know Rob's birthday and so she picked up the phone and tried hers, one way, then mixing up the numbers. Nothing. Her heart dropped as she worried that this was as far as she was going to get without asking Rob directly. She realised that the only other date she knew was their wedding anniversary; four years, just the other week. She typed it in, not expecting anything, but then the screen came to life. Result.

Her knees were suddenly weak beneath her, and she moved to the dining table that was next to the kitchen area and collapsed heavily onto a chair. She had the online world at her fingertips. What did she want to know? Where should she start?

She googled herself – Beth Masters.

The first hits were random people who weren't her: professional websites, social media accounts. Lots and lots of people who weren't her. She tried Bethany Masters and a few more options popped up but it was the same name as a fairly successful mid-level sports player so there was page after page of their results. Beth slammed the phone down in frustration, wishing she had a more unique name. Like her friend, Shawnean. She typed *her* name into the search engine and looked. There she was! On Instagram. It was a private account, but it was her all right, the photo old enough that Beth recognised it from home. She put in the name of her oldest childhood friend, and they popped up too. They were all there, waiting for her to reach out. That was all she had to do. If she had her own account then she could message Shawnean or whoever she followed, couldn't she? And she knew that from there, they could reach her family. She checked for her brother; he wasn't there. Maybe he'd be on another platform, maybe Instagram wasn't his thing. She then searched 'Bethany Masters Instagram' to see what came up, and there she was; she did have an account! It was also private, but if she could somehow work out how to log in then it would all fall into place. And if she could work out Rob's password, then surely she could work out her own. Nothing popped into her head, old password or new, but she was sure it'd come soon enough. She hugged the phone to her, smiling. It was something, a start. She felt less alone already.

She checked to see if Rob had anything else of use on his phone but it had barely anything on it. It was stripped back. He'd already been a bit sniffy about smartphones making people dumb when she'd asked after hers, so this didn't surprise her. She'd log onto her accounts when she could use the laptop or get her own phone set up again. It was fine.

Beth was about to check for other social media sites when a realisation registered with her. Masters was no longer her name. It hadn't been for four years. Her name was now Logan. There could be a whole lot more to find out. She put it in and hit search.

Nothing came up that was about her. She tried Beth Logan, Cambridge. Nothing. She seemed to have become a ghost once she'd left Australia. Even with her travelling, surely there'd be *something* there, or was that just what she wanted, what she *needed*? A past version of her waiting to tell her all that she had forgotten.

Frustrated, she typed in Beth, Fen Road, Accident and the date she knew it had happened.

The first thing that came up was a newspaper headline from a local paper.

Mother & children in tragic fen road car accident

Beth's breath stuttered as she opened the tab to read more. Oh God. Rob had said that there had been another car involved in the accident. She'd asked if anyone was hurt; had he answered? The first few days were so hazy that she couldn't remember much, if anything, other than the shock of finding out she was thousands of miles from home and married. Everything else was a blur.–Her eyes scanned the article, trying to register the words and failing, having to keep reading again and again. But there it was, in black and white.

A local mother was involved in a near-fatal accident on White Drove Road this afternoon. Witnesses say the car in front braked erratically, causing a collision with the car behind. When a third vehicle became involved in the incident, a car was forced off the road into a drainage ditch. Emergency services attended the scene, and the women and two children were taken to Addenbrookes Hospital, along with the other driver.

And that was it. The rest of the article had been updated with quotes from the local politician about the state of the roads and how the funding had been cut, and that the council was struggling to keep up with appropriate road maintenance. The photo with the article merely showed the road. There was nothing to confirm that the piece had been about *her* accident, but it was too much of a coincidence to be anything else.

Hands shaking, Beth scanned through other news sites, all loudly proclaiming the person involved as a mother of twins. The doctor had said that her accident had been 'traumatic'. Had she really hurt someone? Oh God, what had she done?

Frantic now, Beth reopened the first article and scrolled to the bottom. She always used to read local news pages public comments for the sheer amusement factor, but now she was far from entertained. Amongst several complaints about the council, the 'clowncil' and the government in general, were comments from people who claimed to have witnessed the accident.

Poor little toots. They were so pale when the paramedics got to them. I hope they were okay.

I hope they're all okay. It didn't look great from what I could see.

The first car just slammed on their brakes. No warning. Absolutely shocking driving. Reprehensible.

RIP.

Beth threw up a little into her mouth and then gathered herself, dizzy and light-headed, to the bathroom where she spat it into the sink. Holding on to the sides of the cool, pale porcelain for steadiness, Beth looked up into the mirror. What had she *done*?

Why hadn't Rob said anything? Why hadn't anyone? Was this what Rob and Sarah had been whispering about? Why she'd felt sometimes that Sarah was struggling to look her in the eyes? Those poor children. Were they...? Did they...? She couldn't bring herself to finish that thought. No. No! The article said *near*-fatal, didn't it? Would the news be updated if they had... She swallowed. If they had died? One comment said RIP. Did they know? Or was it just someone being dramatic in the comments for their own self-importance? Had she caused death by dangerous driving? Would she be going to court? Would she be going to *prison*? Surely the police would have visited her by now though if that were the case? That thought calmed her a little. Surely the authorities would want to have a word with her? Were they waiting for her to be discharged? Was her suitability to be interrogated one of the things the follow-up appointment was to check? How did things like this work in England?

Her breathing was way too fast now, and she was feeling wobbly. She slipped down onto the tiled floor and let the coolness seep into her. She was hot and clammy and in a state of shock. Her worst fear had come from watching a little child drown. Had her own behaviour, her reckless driving, caused the death of another? Her breath became ragged as panic overtook her. This couldn't be happening. It couldn't.

Was that why Rob seemed distant with her? Why he was withholding something? Was that why her family wouldn't call back? Did they know? Was that why no one else had called, or had visited her? Why Rob had said it was just about the 'two' of them, about rebuilding a life?

Had she killed someone?

A piercing pain suddenly radiated across her skull. She had to take a sharp intake of breath to calm it. It pulsed across her skin, heat flooding her scar where her forehead had taken the brunt of the force. She breathed out slowly, forcibly. No matter how many breaths she took, she could not ease the terror nor the guilt that was cloaking her, dragging her down. She wanted to die. Now she understood why everyone was keeping her at arm's length.

Fighting against the panic-flooded thoughts, Beth tried to tell herself that she didn't *know* anything for sure. No one had told her, no one had mentioned anything about children. The police hadn't been to see her. She would ask Rob; she would have to ask him. How, she didn't know. How did you ask if you'd killed someone? Where did you even start?

Beth swallowed down tears as she gathered herself from the floor, slowly stood up and returned to the kitchen. On almost automatic pilot, she picked up Rob's phone and deleted the search terms. This was why he didn't want her to look. He was protecting her; she could see that now. He would be so angry with her for going against what he'd said. She then returned to the sofa, stuffing Rob's phone down the side of the chair he had been sat in this morning, before curling up and pulling the blanket back up over her and closing her eyes. Perhaps this was all a hallucination, a bad dream brought on by the medication, the stress of being home suddenly with the stranger she was married to. Maybe when Rob returned, and Beth woke up, none of this would be true.

She wouldn't be a child killer.

7

Rob had been home a good ten minutes now. Beth had tried to go to sleep as she'd planned but her whole body and mind were wound up, destroyed, exhausted by her discovery. Everything hurt. Her head ached, pulsed with the stress, which in turn made everything feel heavy and distorted, as though she was trying to walk underwater. She'd been lying on the sofa, exactly where Rob had last seen her, when he'd opened the front door and quietly crept in. She'd heard him place his bag on the floor and his keys on the table. She'd heard the rustle of cloth as he took off and hung up his coat. Then she'd sensed him standing over her, watching.

What did he see? His wife? Or a woman who didn't know him but had done a terrible thing? How alone he must feel. How alone she felt.

She felt ashamed as well as broken. Ashamed of what she had done. Ashamed that she did not remember any of it. Ashamed that her own needs were making him push his own away and ashamed for how she did not feel any connection to him at all. Ever since she had woken up she had distrusted him, pushed him away, questioned his motives. When he had been standing by her, supporting her despite what she had done. He could have washed his hands of her and walked away, but he hadn't. He had stayed by her side. For better, for worse.

'Beth?' Rob's voice came quietly from the side of the room. 'Beth? Are you awake? Pooky?'

Beth took a moment. She wanted to bombard him with questions, ask him outright. But then he would know that she had hidden and used his phone. She was on thin ice here; she didn't need to make him angry with her. Over anything. She would need to be subtle.

'Hmm?' she said finally, opening her eyes and pushing herself up to sitting.

Rob came to sit on the coffee table in front of her, reaching his hands out to hold hers. Beth felt he was in need of comforting somehow and so she let him touch her, despite the fibres of her being not wanting him to. She was dirty, wrong. She was a killer.

'Hey,' he said. 'Good rest?'

'Yeah.' She nodded. Truthfully, despite being bone tired, adrenaline was coursing through her body, making her feel jittery. The very opposite of rested.

'Good. Good. Well, I got done everything I needed so I can focus on you again.' He smiled.

Beth tried to read his face. What must he be going through?

'What about you?' Beth finally managed to say, her voice wavering.

'What about me?'

'Just, this must be hard on you as well. You must be exhausted too?' Beth's voice broke as she spoke. Could she tempt the truth from him? Or would she have to confront him with what she knew? What *did* she know, really? She knew something felt like it wasn't right and this explanation, the consequences of her actions, felt like the reason.

He nodded. 'Yeah. But I'm just tired; you're tired and healing.'

'It's not a competition.' She smiled weakly.

'No, I didn't mean it like that.'

'No, I know you didn't.'

'I'm not trying to be the victim here.' He was suddenly defensive.

'No. That's not what I meant, I...' Beth flinched. Was he disgusted with her, acting like the trauma was hers alone? This was going wrong; how were they arguing? She'd just been trying to be nice. Maybe his anger at her was sneaking out of him against his best efforts.

'Sorry, sorry,' he said, running his fingers through his hair. He visibly reset himself, closing his eyes, clearing his throat and rolling his shoulders. When he re-opened his eyes, a totally different expression was on his face. Kind Rob was back. How did he do that? What seemingly limitless pool of patience was he drawing from to give her such attention when she was the reason for all of this mess?

'Look, why don't we go for a walk? It's a lovely day and you've not been outside properly since the accident. Fresh air cures everything, right?'

'I...' Beth was shocked at the sudden terror that rose in her. She couldn't breathe, like someone had placed a black bag over her head. She couldn't go outside, she couldn't. What would people say? Did everyone *know*? What did she think was going to happen? That people would hurl insults at her from the street like some medieval punishment? Wasn't this one of those English villages where everyone knew everyone else's business? Maybe she deserved it. And perhaps, if they did, then she and

Rob could at least be honest with each other. She steeled herself. She could do this.

'Yes. You're right. Maybe a walk would be good.'

Rob nodded and moved to pick up his things. Beth went into the bedroom to find a jacket. It still felt so odd knowing that these clothes were hers but feeling no connection to them. They were clothes for the wrong country, the wrong person, the wrong life. They were *older*, sensible. Jeans without rips. Shirts instead of T-shirts. Classics. Breton tops and flat shoes. Not her at all. Where were her favourite vintage Levi's, or her bike shorts? Where was her oversized plaid jacket? She could do with it here; it was cold. These sensible, older clothes felt like they belonged to someone else. Putting them on felt like putting on a costume. She looked at her practical jeans, her black and white striped rugby top. They hung heavy on her. Tears pricked at her tired eyeballs, tears for a life she did not feel belonged to her. She should have been the one to die in that crash.

Taking a deep breath, she returned to the living room to find Rob, who was checking his watch and holding the door open. He gestured through it.

'Shall we?'

Rob looked around the room and started patting his pockets.

'Have you seen my phone? I think I left it here...'

Beth's stomach dropped.

'No, I... I haven't seen it.' She couldn't look him in the eyes. She hoped he wouldn't notice. All these lies, all these half-truths. No wonder she felt so distant from him. 'Where did you last have it?'

'I don't know, do I? Otherwise I'd know where it was!' he snapped. He was starting to look panicked, an overreaction,

Beth thought, for someone who didn't seem to like mobile phones.

He started pulling the cushions off the sofa into a pile behind him. Then the chair.

'Ah! Found it.'

'Oh. Good.' Beth wanted to offer an explanation of how it might have got there but decided that it might make her look like she knew something, which of course, she did. So she stayed silent and put on her jacket. Rob was all she had for now, until she knew if her family really had abandoned her or if they would reconcile, and she already felt like he had one foot out of the door. She couldn't quite put her finger on it. He was kind, attentive, always there, always checking what she needed, and yet his mind clearly wasn't always there too. What they really needed to do was to sit down and talk everything out. She needed to know everything, however awful, and how he felt about it all. She needed to work out how *she* felt about it all. Then it might feel real to her and, once they had everything out in the open, they could move forward, together, or perhaps not. Tragedy often pushed families apart, didn't it? She needed this to bring hers back together. She needed to talk with Rob and then message her friends, track down her brother.

She would make them talk, but right now she felt so wobbly, all she could focus on was putting one foot in front of the other and not falling. Was this recovery or was this her guilt? Did her body know what her mind did not?

The coolness of the air hit her face as they stepped onto the street, and it felt wonderful. It reminded Beth that she was *alive*, though she immediately remembered that those children were not and the guilt she felt almost floored her. She held her breath until it hurt.

One step a time. Just one step. That's all you need to do.

As they started down the road, towards the centre of the village, Rob walked beside her and took her arm in his. At first Beth jolted at his touch but then she felt relief. He didn't hate her. Whatever they might still have between them, however they would move forward, it seemed that he didn't hold her responsible. She just had to get him talking. She had to put aside this mistrust of him, born of what? Of nothing other than her lost memories? She had to let her walls down. What other choice did she have?

'Careful now,' he said as they crossed the road, him looking nervously in both directions before starting into the road. He gripped her arm tightly, leading her into the shade of the trees and a path which led towards what looked like a duck pond. In another life, Beth could see how she might have fallen for this chocolate box version of England. A handsome man on her arm as they strolled through this pretty old English village, passing gorgeous little cottages, quaint and dainty in a way Australia never was. They passed a man walking his dog and Beth willed herself to look at him, to see if there was any recognition in his face. If there was, he concealed it. Most likely he didn't know. Not everyone would, Beth reminded herself.

They walked in silence at first, in a strange state of both knowing each other too well for chit chat, but also not knowing each other at all. They stopped at a bench by the pond and without speaking, they sat on it, looking outward at the ducks, who swam over towards them in hope of being fed. Rob looked at his watch but then back out at the pond. She could feel his tension as he sat beside her and Beth suddenly felt a million years old. How was this her life now?

'Sorry. I know this is difficult for you too,' Beth said, holding an olive branch out.

He said nothing but squeezed her arm. She squeezed back,

hoping some affection on her part, albeit forced, might help with what she needed to ask.

'I need to know more. About the accident,' she blurted out. So much for subtle.

Rob sighed lightly and turned to look at her.

'Here? Now?' He hesitated. 'What do you want to know?'

Beth was surprised. She had thought he was going to refuse. He was being to the point. So she should be too.

'Was the accident my fault?'

Rob drew in his breath. He wouldn't look at her. 'Sort of.'

'What do you mean?'

'You did an emergency stop for whatever reason.' He waved his hand the air, indicating randomly. 'The car behind ran into you like a ton of bricks. Flung you across the road where the third car hit you.'

Beth gasped. His direct choice of words felt like he had tightened something around her neck.

'Why did I do that? Why did I brake?'

'I don't know, Beth. Why did you?' Rob said, a slice of anger in his tone. 'The police are hypothesising that perhaps you were trying to avoid a pothole and maybe braked without looking. But no one knows. Apart from you. And you can't remember.'

The accusation hung in the air. He *was* angry with her, and with every right. What had she done?

'The police?'

'Yes, Beth. It was a three-car accident with casualties. The police have been involved.'

'Why haven't they wanted to speak to me?'

'They did. They... do. We... we thought it best if you recovered a bit first. To see if your memory returns. They're being very understanding. For now.'

It felt as though something heavy had just sat on her shoulders, pushing her down towards the ground.

'Was...' She had to ask. She needed to know. Keeping this inside was too much. 'Was anyone else... hurt in the accident?' She looked at the ground, her heart pounding in her chest. She couldn't ask exactly what she wanted. Not yet.

She felt him tense further.

'Yes.' He didn't even pause.

'What? Who?'

'I don't really want to do this here, Beth.' He looked around but there was no one about. It was midweek and everyone was getting on with their own lives. Like nothing had happened. Except it had. It had happened, it was her fault, and lives had stopped in their tracks because of it.

'Look, it wasn't your fault.'

'But you just said that the accident *was* sort of my fault! Who was hurt, Rob? Tell me.'

He bit his lip and turned to face her. He took her hands in his. His expression was one of regret. For what had happened or what he was about to tell her? No one likes being the bearer of bad news, do they?

'The car behind you had two children in the back.'

Beth froze. Once he said the words, she wouldn't be able to pretend that she might have been wrong. In a millisecond her life would be changed forever; *she* would be changed forever. It had already changed though. She just didn't *know* it yet.

'And?'

'And they didn't make it.' Rob wouldn't look at her. Couldn't look at her.

'What?'

'They didn't make it, Beth.'

'But... their car hit *me*. That doesn't make sense...'

Why was she arguing? It wasn't like she could change the outcome if she just threw logic at it, was it?

She felt cold. The hairs on the back of her neck rose as her body went into fight or flight. Her whole world was collapsing in on itself. *Now* she could see why her brain had denied her this knowledge – because it would destroy her. Even if she could claw her way out of the dark hole that she felt she was falling into, she would forever be responsible for the death of two children. She felt the acid buzz of bile at the back of her throat and gulped in the clean fresh air to stop it rising any further.

'Pooky.' He was still holding both her hands in his. 'We will get through this. You didn't mean to; it wasn't your fault. It will be okay. I'm here.'

'How? How will it be okay? How was it not my fault if the *accident* was my fault? The police want to talk with me.'

'Look. Yes, you braked hard. But the car behind you was too close and the driver was... distracted. The children weren't properly strapped into their car seats. They... they had winter coats on.'

'I don't understand. What difference does that make? Coats or not?' All the paraphernalia to do with children was a mystery to her.

'The coats were puffy, you see.' Rob suddenly sounded like a kindergarten teacher, explaining a basic principle to a small child. 'And when the car seat harness is tightened against it, it's not tight enough. In an impact scenario, the air in the coat gets compressed, which loosens the harness against the body of the child and... well, then they don't work properly.'

Beth turned to the side and vomited. She knew what Rob wasn't saying, about what had happened. Dear God, those poor kids.

'The third car was going too fast and didn't stop at the junction. It was a little bit of everyone's fault. Not just you. They think you hit a pothole, swerved and hit your brakes to avoid the ditch. I think... I think it was just a horrible combination of a lot of different mistakes. One of those things.'

'One of *those things*? Children died!'

Rob looked around, embarrassed.

'Okay, keep your voice down. This is why I didn't want to do this here. I didn't think you would be calm about it.'

'How could I be calm? Those children's deaths are my fault.'

'No. No! I won't have it. The police are still talking to witnesses, and they know you've no memory. If it was as clear cut as you're saying they'd have already been around to see you and they haven't. See? It's not your fault. None of it is, Pooks. *You* were hurt because the driver airbag didn't deploy properly. It was a manufacturing flaw. We were supposed to get a recall letter so that we could get it replaced but...' He shrugged as he let go of her hands.

'But what, Rob?'

He didn't reply. He didn't look bothered. How was he not bothered?

What was he still not telling her? This didn't add up; something wasn't right. She would have to pay for this; she surely couldn't just walk away scot-free? Beth felt like he was trying to protect her, but from what? And how long did he think he could manage that? Even without half the information, Beth could see that wasn't going to work.

How on earth would they ever survive this?

8

Beth couldn't say how long they had sat in silence after what she had learned. She was reeling from having Rob confirm what she had feared. How had he kept this from her? How had everyone? If she had not seen the newspaper article, would he ever have told her? She knew that wasn't fair. How would you even start with something like this? But still, he was being cold about it. Separating different elements into different boxes, in a way that Beth couldn't do.

Rob checked his watch again.

'Are you waiting for something?' Beth asked, indicating his watch. 'You keep checking the time.'

'No,' he said breezily.

'Oh!'

'What?'

Beth scanned her memory. The days had merged. She wasn't really sure what day or time it was as she had nothing to pin the days to. She had slept and pottered about and slept and it didn't matter if it was day or night, weekday or weekend. It was just... time. But she realised now that she had not had her checkup. Her medical team were supposed to be sending out someone to see how she was getting on.

'Are we expecting my follow up appointment today?'

'Eh?' Rob screwed his face up.

'With the nurse?' Beth's stomach churned. Something wasn't right. They'd said the nurse would come round the next day. But she'd been out of hospital longer than twenty-four hours, hadn't she? Rob was right that her painkillers had made her woozy; had she had the appointment and not remembered it? The doctors had said that new memories might not stick too well either, and Beth supposed that her ongoing healing, plus tiredness and the medication, might have caused her to forget. But Rob wouldn't have, surely? Was he trying to hide her away from all the authorities, medical or legal, somehow hoping this would all blow over when clearly it wasn't going to? Had he somewhat lost his mind?

'Oh. Oh! Yes. God, yes, you're right. It's Wednesday today. The days, they all run together right now.' He checked his watch again. 'Sorry. But not to worry, we've time. We can loop round the pond and still make it.'

Why is he all jittery? And 'loop round the pond'? She looked out at it. It was large and she could not clearly see its outline. *That would be a long walk, wouldn't it?*

'Are you sure? I... I don't know if I've got the energy for that far today.'

'Got to build up your stamina.' His optimistic manner had returned. He insisted on her sleeping, on making sure she got her painkillers, on making sure she ate right. He obviously wanted her back to health. Maybe he thought he could get his old life back with her. He couldn't though and not only because she had no memory of it. What she had done had destroyed their life from before.

Beth's stomach felt heavy. She wanted to offer him something, anything.

'Yes, but not all at once perhaps? Let's get to the corner there and turn back? Make sure we're back on time.' Beth had a million questions that she wanted to ask the nurse. When the police came for her, she wanted to be able to co-operate with them. That was the right thing to do. But was there anything that she could do to help get those vital memories back? Memories that might either condemn or exonerate her.

Rob cleared his throat.

'Come on, if you don't try you won't know.'

'I just don't think I can.'

'You've not tried,' he pushed. 'We could just do fifteen minutes, see how you go. That's all we need to do.'

'No.' She felt bad being so obstinate, but this didn't feel right.

He sighed, his irritation clear to see.

'I want to go back. I need to go back.' She could hear herself pleading. She didn't want to have to go back without him. She felt as flimsy as a fallen leaf, as though the slightest breeze would send her floating over the water. She needed Rob to steady her.

He tapped his foot on the ground as he sighed again, more deeply. She had disappointed him. She took his arm to make him come with her. He yanked it back.

'Don't manhandle me, Beth!' he snapped at her. 'I'm just trying to help you. To do what's *best* for you. I know what's best!'

Something in his tone unlocked something in her mind. She'd heard that tone before. *Don't talk to me like that!* She couldn't figure out if he was being possessive or protective. Did he want her better or just doing whatever he told her to do? She had not expected this; this feeling in the pit of her stomach. What did he want? In her head there was a flash, a minuscule moment of something that called at her. Like a recollection was knocking at a door but she couldn't quite get it to open. But it was there, waiting for her. It had left a *feeling* in its place, to remind Beth to come back to try again.

'Fine. Let's go then,' Rob said, failing to hide the sulky tone in his voice, or perhaps not even trying to. Maybe he wanted Beth to know of his disapproval.

Slowly, steadily, they walked back through the village to their street. Outside was a car in the visitor's spot that hadn't been there before. As they approached, a tall sturdy-looking figure got out.

'Beth? Rob?' he said.

Rob nodded but said nothing.

'I thought you were out! I've been here nearly ten minutes calling your phone.'

Rob patted his pocket. 'I must have left it in the house.'

But he looked for it just before we left? Why would he then leave it behind?

'We only went for a walk. Get some fresh air, and she's not as fast as before,' he said. Beth noticed the shifting of blame despite it being her who insisted they return.

'Right, right. Well, I'm David, your community nurse.' He flashed his ID card at them. 'Let me help.'

David joined them and offered Beth his arm as Rob moved to open the door to let them all in.

Once back inside, David helped Beth to the sofa.

'I'm glad you're here. I called yesterday as agreed but no one answered the door or phones,' David said.

'Oh. Sorry. I must have misremembered the date of the appointment. And... I left my phone here, down the side of the chair. It must have been on silent.' Rob rushed out the excuse.

That was this morning, Beth thought. *Wasn't it?* Was she confused? So much had happened, had changed. She had felt hope, then despair. Then, what? Anger?

'Well, I'm glad you're here now. I was going to have to escalate it otherwise.'

'Escalate? To whom?' Rob sounded flustered. He looked at Beth. 'It's not like we're a flight risk!' he joked, laughing a little too loudly.

David looked bemused.

'No. No, just we need to check in on Beth, see how she's doing, if she's settling back in. How are you, love?'

'She's good. She's still sleeping a lot. Confused, you know.'

David smiled a wry smile at Rob before turning his whole self to face Beth.

'*Beth*, how are you feeling?'

'Like I said, she's tired. Sore. But I'm looking after her,' Rob interjected.

'Right. Good. Glad you are, Rob. I'm sure you're doing a wonderful job. Might you rustle up two cups of tea and whatever you want for yourself, Rob? One sugar for me. Thanks,' David said, dismissing Rob from the room.

Rob looked affronted but then went to the kitchen anyway. There were sounds of him filling and turning on the kettle.

'I'm not sure I can approve of all this,' David said, turning to face Beth, an expression of exasperation on his face. It was tinged with kindness but a telling off all the same.

'Oh, Rob is just protective, that's all.' Beth was surprised to find herself making amends for Rob's rudeness. Usually, she would call that behaviour out.

'By taking you on a hike? You've been out of hospital two days. *Two.* Bed rest and gentle exercise, you were told. Not a long walk. You look worn out.' He got out his paperwork and spread it on the coffee table.

'Now, as I said, I'm David. I'm here to see how you're doing, to answer any questions and help get you back on your feet. You've been through... a lot,' he said, looking around the room as he did so. 'I'm also here to see that you're not overdoing things. So, clearly it was good timing that I stayed to catch you, but you *must* try to be available for your appointments, my lovely, as my schedule doesn't have much room in it. It was only due to a cancellation of an appointment today that I could come back here.'

Despite his authoritarian tone, Beth immediately felt safe with David in a way that right now she realised she did not with Rob. She relaxed and let herself be cared for. She noted that she tensed when Rob returned to the room.

'Your drinks. This one is yours, Beth,' Rob said, handing them each a cup.

David nodded a thank you in Rob's direction and went about checking Beth's blood pressure, temperature and asking basic medical questions. He asked about her memory recall, retention of new memories and if anything had come back to her. Some questions felt pointed in a way Beth couldn't tie down. Every time Rob tried to intervene or interrupt, David would politely wave him away, insisting that Beth herself answer. Beth could feel Rob's irritation growing and, as it did, so did her anxiety. He would be angry. Why did that make her so nervous?

'So, *Beth*. Is there anything else I can do for you? Physically you're doing really well, I'm happy with how you're healing, but, well, you weren't in a great way in yourself when I arrived, were you, and now, still, you're not. Well, not calm. You seem agitated, though this is not unusual for patients with brain injuries.'

David checked through his notes again, pausing at one point on something, but keeping his face neutral. 'Is there anything you wanted to discuss?'

Without looking, Beth could feel Rob hovering at the edge of the room. She could *hear* him in her mind without him speaking. *Not. A. Word.* She crinkled her nose. Where had that come from? What was her subconscious trying to say?

'I guess...' She wrung her hands. 'When might it be likely that I start to remember things?' *To know with my own mind what it's trying to tell me.* 'Is there anything I can do to help with that? Like, snippets of things keep popping into my mind, like an inner voice. Is that memory?'

'Like what?' Rob asked.

David ignored him.

'I know how disconcerting it must be. You've lost a large chunk of time, some significant years. But your body and mind are healing at their own rate. The best thing you can do is to immerse yourself in your life, look at photos, talk about things, every day. Smell is a particularly interesting thing – it can nudge memories you didn't know it could. Have your mum's cooking. Sniff your favourite flowers. Things like that. The mind is a strange beast. It knows what to do. I'm afraid that being patient with yourself is the best thing you can do.'

'I can help with most of that,' Rob said, coming to sit with them from where he had been standing. 'Not with the home cooking, I'm afraid. Your parents still haven't called. I... I don't know what to say about that.'

'Oh. Oh, I'm sorry,' David said, his tone softening. 'Families are tough sometimes and often they don't react well to stressful events such as this. Make it about themselves rather than about the patient. Seen it far too many times, I'm afraid. Still, you've got your husband. He can help fill in some details. As and when you're ready, of course, and remember that you have access to the counselling service, and I really *do* recommend you make use of it.' He looked at her with such concern that Beth had to fight hard not to cry. She seemed to have lost so much, and her feeling was growing that Rob, who was all that she had left, was not what he seemed. But based on what? She couldn't pinpoint what it was quite yet, just that she didn't think she could fully trust him, and something inside her was telling her that she ought not to.

'Thank you,' Beth managed to say. 'Are we all done?'

'Oh, of course. Yes, we're done for now. I'll be back on the twelfth, same time.' He turned to look at Rob. 'Don't be going on any more hikes! Gentle, gentle. We'll get you back up and running, don't you fret.'

As Rob moved to clear away the cups, David quickly turned to Beth and said in a low voice, 'And of course, if you want to have an appointment away from here, we can arrange that too.' He looked at her pointedly, waiting to catch any response that might tell him if there was anything she couldn't say out loud.

Beth nodded to show that she understood what he was saying. She didn't though, did she? Rob was trying to protect her. That was all. He was invested in getting his wife back.

'Thank you. I appreciate it,' Beth said.

'Okay, well I'll be off then. I'll see you soon, lovey.'

David packed up his things and made his way out.

When Rob closed the door behind him and turned back to the room, the atmosphere was stilted. Beth felt that she had somehow done something wrong and yet she didn't know what. Whether it was how she'd been with David, letting him push Rob out of the appointment, or the accident, the children, or something else. She hadn't done or said anything untoward, had she? David had been dismissive with Rob but that wasn't her fault. He'd suggested that Rob ought not to be there but Beth hadn't asked for that, had she?

She opened her mouth to speak but couldn't work out what to say, or even what she wanted to say. She was exhausted suddenly and craving the oblivion of sleep, which was nudging at her eyelids. There were too many strands running through her mind for her to tie any of them together into a coherent thought. But, wanting to be a peacemaker, wanting to find some peace for them both, Beth simply asked, 'How are you holding up?'

'What?'

'How are you? I know all the focus has been on me, on the accident, on my recovery, on my needs. But what about you?'

Rob smiled the briefest of smiles, a flash of kindness that lit up his face. He had a nice face when he smiled. Beth felt she had done the right thing. After all, no scenario was only about one person, was it?

'What about me?'

'Are you... angry? With me? About... the accident?'

Rob breathed slowly out of his mouth. He rubbed his hands over his five o'clock shadow. Then he sat down opposite Beth and took her hands.

'Am I angry? Yes. Yes, I'm angry. With you? Yes.'

She *knew* it. She *knew* something wasn't right between them.

'For... for what?' Beth whispered. This was it. He was going to tell her that her poor driving, her bad decision or whatever had made her slam her foot on the brake, had destroyed everything for them both.

'Everything,' he said quietly before raising his voice suddenly. 'I'm angry at you for everything!' He slammed his fist down onto the table in front of him with a loud crack. 'My life is falling apart! I... I had a plan. I knew where I was going, I was getting what I wanted from life, and now? Now? Half of everything is... gone.'

'I'm sorry, I...' Beth recoiled. This explosion was not what she was expecting.

'No. No... I shouldn't have yelled.' He shook his head, breathing out a long breath, his rage seemingly spent in a second. 'It's just hard.' He smiled. 'You don't know me, do you? You have no memory of *us*, of our life, and so I'm grieving you, but you're *here*, and yet you're not here. But you might come back. What do you know? What don't you know? All this guessing is driving me mad. I'm trying to protect you from all of this and I don't know how! I don't know what to *do*!'

'You could just... tell me what I need to know?' Beth said, reaching out to him. She could see his inner turmoil, feel it echoing the tangled confusion she herself felt. They were both drowning. Would they rescue each other or would one pull the other down with them?

'I could.' He nodded. 'I could.'

'So tell me. What our life was like. You've told me how we met, how we got married. But tell me what our life was like. So we can... get back to that as close as we can?'

'We can't. No one gets to go backwards. We only get to go forwards.'

'But we could go forwards... together? Rather than this weird, I don't know, this dancing around each other we're doing. I know you feel it. I feel it too. It's... odd. I don't like it.'

'Yeah. Neither do I.'

They sat again in silence.

Rob then stood up. 'I need a shower. I need to think.'

'Oh. Okay.'

'Do you think you could make us some food while I'm gone? Just a sandwich or something? All the stuff's in the kitchen.'

'Oh. Okay. Yeah. Sure.'

'Great,' Rob said as he picked up his phone and headed into the bedroom to get changed.

Beth didn't know what to do. They'd been talking, opening up, and then Rob just pulled the shutters down as if they'd been talking favourite ice cream flavours. What the hell was going on?

9

Beth was looking through all the drawers in the kitchen when she heard Rob start the shower running. She'd thought she would instinctively know where things would be kept but it was like she'd never been in a kitchen before. Things were in places that her brain could not decipher, and it took an age before she located what she needed to make Rob his sandwich. Beth wanted to feel hungry herself, but she felt mostly empty. Her stomach ached but not for food. Her appetite for anything had gone. She'd make one for herself all the same, in case Rob was offended by eating alone. He seemed on edge after David's visit and Beth had no desire to see his temper erupt as it had done earlier.

At least I've remembered how to make a sandwich, Beth thought as she spread mayonnaise over the sourdough bread that she'd found on the countertop, adding the pre-sliced cheese that was in the fridge, before laying on tomatoes and basil leaves. It reminded her of the simple times working at the café, and she longed for it.

Bending down to find where the plates were in the lower

cupboards, she reached around a corner without looking and her hand landed on something that felt... strange. Pulling it out, she found she was holding a mobile phone. It had been sitting in a stack of bowls pushed right to the back of the cupboard. She held it up and stared at it. What on earth was a phone doing *there*? Whose was it? Rob had *his* phone, which seemed almost permanently attached to him. Did he have another? Was this an old one, just randomly stuffed in a drawer and forgotten? She couldn't gauge its age because she had no frame of reference. Phones went out of date so fast, five years could be everything and nothing. Was it hers? It didn't look water damaged but maybe Rob had hidden it so as not to upset her with it. If so, she ought to put it back. But...

Listening out for Rob and hearing the sounds of the water still running, Beth found the on switch and turned it on. She waited while the screen came to life. Her hands were clammy as she held it. What if she could use *this* phone without Rob knowing to look things up, to contact her family, her friends? Every time she tried to ask him about a computer or her phone, he dismissed it or changed the subject. Protecting her maybe, but she was not a delicate princess who needed shielding. She was a grown woman who could take responsibility for her actions and whatever consequences were coming. She would do that. It was the right thing to do. But still, she wanted to speak with her family; she needed them. She would tell them what she had done and they would forgive her. They were her *blood*. Whatever had happened, they would not push her away, even if she had done so to them... would they? A knot tied itself in her throat.

The light of the screen flashed on and Beth felt something flicker in her stomach. The lock screen stared at her but this time it did not request a pin. It had the fingerprint recognition icon at the bottom, which always looked to her like a slice of the inside of a tree. Defeated, she placed her fingertip on the icon anyway, only to be surprised that it unlocked. Her fingerprint worked! This *was* her phone! Her heart leapt into her mouth as she went to the app list and opened her Instagram, hoping that she wouldn't have to log in, that there wasn't some time delay that meant you had to re-enter your password. She'd always used it daily, so she'd never even thought to check. Her breath stuck in her throat when it opened up and there she was. She immediately selected her own profile and suddenly there was her life, in pictures, like a flood in front of her.

At first, she was overwhelmed. She didn't know where to start – photos, DMs? Anxious, wanting to take her time but also aware that Rob would be out soon, she flicked further down the screen. Why did she not want Rob to see her do this? Why would he be mad? If it was an old phone then it wouldn't be connected still, would it? If it was her current phone, then why didn't he just give it back? A smile crossed her face – maybe this was a new phone, and he wanted to get it all set up ready for her, even with the social media apps that she knew he hated, as a surprise? Had she spoiled his surprise by finding it? She didn't think he'd like that; she ought to put it back. But...

Just as she considered this, an image popped into her mind: Rob, raging, his face flushed puce as he threw a phone angrily across the room, smashing it.

'You care what *they* think, eh? But not about your *husband*? You disgust me. You attention whore.'

Beth nearly dropped the phone in shock. Where had that come from? Was that a memory or was she predicting what he would be like now? She tried to replay it again in her mind, to make the scene continue, but it was gone. All that was left was a bad taste in her mouth and a pressure in her stomach as she tried to work out what that was.

Looking back at the phone, needing some Insta-happy content and the dopamine it provided, she flipped through her posts. They were mostly of her and Rob. On holiday, at gigs, out and about. There were photos of them together, very cute and couple-y. There were arty shots of Cambridge. Posts from bars, restaurants, walks in the country. Further back there were images of London. But no people. No one was tagged and no one had commented. No interaction whatsoever. Tears pricked at the back of her eyes. It seemed she really had been cut adrift. Or perhaps she had done the cutting. Still, it hurt.

She heard the sound of the shower turning off. She didn't have much time, and looking through this had incited more questions than answers. She opened the DMs. Empty. What? Had she deleted her messages? Had Rob? Surely there would be *someone* here?

Beth flicked to her followers/follows. Zero followers. None. She apparently followed Rob and about three cafés, art galleries and some random account about Aussies overseas. This wasn't right. This wasn't *her* profile surely? She'd not become some online idiot, had she? She had posts about trips to the market, or a day by the river. One about baking some complicated bougie dish, and it just didn't sound like her. At all. She didn't recognise her life now and she didn't recognise the person that this profile belonged to. People showed off online, didn't they? Though with no followers, showing off to who? Something just felt wrong.

Beth found herself scrolling back through the posts. No comments, no likes. A profile that had almost no impact on the world it was put out into. No comments from relatives with bare knowledge of emojis commenting thumbs up. No friends being supportively envious about this wonderful holiday they'd been on. It was like this account was existing but nothing more. Dormant despite having regular new content.

It didn't make sense.

Looking back as far as it went, Beth wanted to see if there was anything from her time back home. She and her friends from the café would spend quiet shifts swapping memes and commenting on each other's posts, but those weren't here. She only found a smattering of photos from Australia, all vague and almost like they were professional shots from Tourism Australia – but then she saw it. Evidence that something was amiss. It was an image of her snuggled up on the sofa, some cosy movie night or something. 'Cuddling up under the duvet', it said. No. That was wrong. She'd never say *duvet*. It was a *doona*. And cuddling up? No, *rugging up*.

She didn't write this. She hadn't written it.

She checked the date. It was posted a week ago. She checked another post and another, over and over. They had all been posted in the past few days. What the hell was going on?

Beth felt the prickles of ice as they travelled inch by inch up her spine until her whole body was trembling.

Rob.

This profile had been put together by Rob. Had he done it for her? Or was she not meant to ever see this? Was it his? To create a world where she only had eyes for him? Was he planning on using it to tell her of a life that wasn't actually really hers? Why would he do that? Was he having some sort of breakdown, caused by the stress of recent events? Did *he* need help?

As Beth thought through the implications of the phone she held in her hand, she suddenly felt as though she was going to pass out. The fingerprint sensor. It had worked. Was this an old phone of hers? Or had he managed to set it up with one of her fingerprints while she was sleeping? She had been sleeping a lot, she knew that. She shuddered. The idea of him creeping around while she was unconscious and vulnerable made her want to be sick. Her throat contracted but she pushed it away. What in the ever-living fuck was going on?

Her heart raced in her chest as her mind struggled to work out the why and the what as to what this meant. She closed Instagram and scrolled through the rest of the things on the phone. No phone history. No search history. No photo roll. Nothing. She pulled up the contacts list. Rob. 'Mum' but a number that when she hit dial just gave a 'number not recognised' tone of a non-existent number. 'Home' – she called it and immediately hung up when the landline in the hallway trilled into life. There was a doctors, a dentists, a hairdresser. Random names that didn't register with her and weren't listed in the phone calls. According to this phone, she lived and breathed her 'hashtag blessed' life with Rob and no one else. It was possible, of course, that they'd met, fallen madly in love against her family's wishes, her family and friends at home disapproving of her staying here, but would she really leave everything, and everyone, for him? She knew of herself as sardonic, cynical, worldly. This did not seem like who she would be. She was not a Stepford wife. Not then, not now, not ever.

Were they that in love that they had shut out the rest of the world entirely?

And if that was the case, why did he scare her?

As this thought entered her mind, she heard a flicker of a conversation in her ear, from somewhere she couldn't place, in a voice she knew from her soul.

'Don't do this, love. Trust your gut. Come home. Come home to us.'

And without warning, tears pricked in her eyes, her nose

stinging as she struggled to keep calm. That voice. That tone that only a mother can use, the one that says 'I love you, I know you, I am your home'. Her ma. She suddenly missed her with a ferocity that winded her. What she wouldn't give right now for a whole-hearted hug from her mum. One that shut out all the world's difficulties with the sheer strength of love it contained. How had she and her parents fallen out so badly that they wouldn't call her after such a horrific accident? They wouldn't abandon her. She just *knew* it.

Unless...

Unless they didn't know.

Unless nothing, *nothing*, that Rob had told her from the moment she had woken up was true. Unless he was lying to her about *everything*.

Her mind was reeling trying to piece together anything, everything, that had happened from the second she had woken up in the hospital. What changed if she assumed that Rob was *lying* rather than telling her the truth? What might it mean for them, for him, for her? The hospital must have done checks as to his veracity as her husband. She didn't doubt they were really married. He knew too much about her, and she didn't think the photos she had seen of them both were fake, though she supposed they could be.

The little flickers of recognition that she had been having of them together, like a holiday slideshow that had shuttered into her mind and was then replaced almost immediately with darkness, came back to her now. None of them had been exactly happy memories of a balanced, loving relationship. Beth wondered now if the nervousness she felt around Rob was not based on the fact she did not *know* him; in fact, quite the opposite. It was based on the fact that she *did* know him and what he was really like.

His face came to her mind, his expression twisted in anger. He was insecure, prone to anger, quick tempered, possessive.

What lengths would he go to in order to keep her his and his alone?

Would he even lie about the children? Had they actually died in the crash or not? If they hadn't, and that was entirely fabricated by him, that would explain why the police hadn't been chasing up to speak with her. Why there had been no mention of it by anyone, none of the professionals she had seen since she had woken up? The newspaper report said *near* fatal. Nowhere, other than from Rob's lips, had she learnt that the children had died.

Blinking hard to try to stop her brain from panicking, Beth deleted the call history, closed all the tabs on the phone and put it down on the counter. She tapped her fingers against its dark screen as she did so, echoing the rapid heartbeat she could feel inside her. She was beyond vulnerable. She knew that now. She just didn't know what he wanted. Or why.

Beth quickly shut off the phone and put it back exactly where she had found it as blind terror started to flood her brain. Rob wandered into the room, smiling benevolently as he towel-dried his hair, another towel wrapped around his waist. His body was glistening with drops that slowly trickled their way down his exposed chest. It felt as though he was trying for movie-star charm, all barefoot and supposedly bedraggled, a winning smile with beaming white teeth. The effect sent chills through her. Who *was* this man?

She was trying to paint a façade of comfort, of trust, on her face while beneath the surface she was scrabbling to tie together too many threads. Was Rob losing it? Was he using her memory loss as a chance to reform their life together? To form it into how he wanted them to be rather than how they were.

How would he be able to control the narrative to keep this up? Especially as she healed, as her own memories came back to her, he wouldn't be able to explain this version of events he was creating. Beth would need to have no contact with anyone from their life who knew the reality. He would have to be her only source of information. Her only source of truth. The only person she spoke to.

He came and stood beside her, draping his arm around her. His skin smelt warm, with waves of his soap fragrance filling her nose. He was warm and damp. Beth's stomach retracted. Not with desire but with nervous anticipation. Her senses were warning her of something, even if her memory could not provide her with the details as to what. Being this physically close to Rob in such a state of undress made Beth nervous. She was beginning to realise that they were not the happy couple that he seemed to want to make them out to be. And perhaps they never had been.

Aware that the silence was building uncomfortably, Beth said, 'Your food is ready,' hopefully in a way that would placate him. She was painfully aware that they were alone. She was smaller, weaker and without anywhere or anyone else to go to.

'The best. My wife.' He squeezed his arm around her before dropping it and moving away.

She nodded tightly, her smile still holding despite the waves of revulsion that were now flooding through her body.

She was utterly terrified. She realised that she had no memory, no contacts, no idea where her passport was. Did she have any money of her own? Did she have any friends? Anyone who could help her? She wasn't well enough to run anywhere and this village was miles from anywhere anyway. She could call the police, but what if he *had* been telling the truth about the children and they thought she was insane? It's not like it'd be the first time a woman wasn't believed over the word of her husband.

It was just her, and just him. In this house. Alone.

He was either trying to rebuild a life that they hadn't had, a weird sort of chance to start over or he was creating a fake sense of safety before delivering her punishment for what she had done. Was he toying with her? And if so, why?

As she watched Rob walk back out of the room to get dressed, she placed her now shaking hands on the countertop to steady herself.

She knew nothing, but she did know this.

She was in danger.

10

Beth barely slept that night, terrified for what she *felt* but didn't know. By the time morning came, however, she had formulated a plan. Her rationality had returned with the dawn, and she decided that she needed more information, something that could corroborate or dismiss the rising panic she had about her and Rob's relationship. She knew that the walls of this house were thin – she could just about make out what shows their neighbour was watching when his TV was on. He seemed to be a twenty-four-hour news person, as Beth could hear the serious tone of voice as it drifted through the walls on a twenty-minute or so rotation. So she figured if she and Rob had had the screaming rows that her mind seemed to be remembering, then surely they would have heard? They would know *something* of the inner details of their lives, even if in normal circumstances they wouldn't say a word. The village was small; everyone talked, didn't they? She was pinning her hope on finding out enough in order to make a decision as to what the hell she was going to do. Also, it occurred to her that they would have a phone, and she might be able to convince them to let her use it.

Maybe Rob hadn't been telling the truth; maybe her parents hadn't moved, perhaps they were still in the house she could see in her mind's eye, and she knew that her parents' landline hadn't changed in all the years of her life that she *could* remember. Rob had been chasing a mobile number. Or at least he said he had been. But maybe they should have been calling a landline. A lot of maybes for sure, but nothing else was definite either so what difference did it make?

She decided to play wife that morning and get Rob out of the house as soon as she could so that she could put her plan into action. He hadn't said she *couldn't* go outside, just inferred that she *ought* not to. She could act dumb if he found out and asked. She got the feeling he liked his women dumb.

'Did you enjoy your breakfast?' Beth said as she tidied the washing up away.

'Yes, it was great, thanks, babe,' Rob replied, a big smile on his face. 'A great start to the week. I love eggs in the morning.'

'Glad I can still be of some use,' Beth said, not quite keeping the tone of disappointment out of her voice.

Rob jumped up from his seat at the table and came to her.

'Hey, hey, now,' he said gently as his arms encircled her and held her to him. 'None of that. You're not useless. And anyway, I don't love you for what you can *do* for me. I love you for who you *are*. Okay?' He stroked her hair.

Beth felt herself relax into him for a moment. She so wanted to believe him. She really did. But... who was she really? He seemed to love this docile, domestic version she was playing, and yet she knew that wasn't her. She was too feisty for that. She even admitted to herself that she was getting a kick out of pulling the wool over his eyes and she didn't think he'd love *that*. Still, for a second or two she let herself believe that she was being ridiculous and everything was fine. That there was no underhand agenda, just her husband loving her and supporting her back to health. But as the seconds ticked by, the niggle in her chest reminded her that for whatever reason, she did not believe that. She needed more information so she could know the truth – whether that would be the version she feared or the version she couldn't let herself believe.

'Right,' Rob said, breaking the gentle silence between then. 'I'm heading to a few meetings and then taking a client to lunch. Will you be okay until I get back? Do you need anything?'

Beth shook her head.

'No, I'm fine. I'm going to read a book and take a long bubble bath, I think.'

'Perfect. Rest up. We'll get you better in no time.' Rob smiled at her as he picked up his bag and walked out the door.

The moment Beth saw his car drive away, her nerves started jangling. She was going to do this. She was going to work out what the hell was going on here. Was she in serious trouble? Or was her brain still recovering from trauma and was making stuff up? The doctors had said that her memories might be wobbly for a while, new ones included. Would an overactive imagination go alongside that or not? She made a note to ask David at the next appointment. When was that? She couldn't remember.

Checking outside the window for the weather, she flung on an oversized chocolate-brown jumper and went to leave. She put her hand on the door before she realised – she didn't have any keys. She must have them somewhere, surely? Rob didn't expect her to be leaving the house so hadn't told her where they were. She went back into the kitchen to look for a key hook or something. There was nothing by the back door. Nothing on the counters. No bowl or tray that might be used to keep keys in. She opened a few kitchen drawers and finally found some. None were for the front door though. There were a couple that looked like they might fit the back door, which opened into the garden, with a small back gate which she assumed led around to the front of the house. She put the first key in the lock and tried. Nothing. It wouldn't move. She tried the next, and bingo. The lock turned and the door opened. The cool autumnal air hit her face and Beth stood for a moment, closed her eyes and let it invigorate her. She was tired and the chill on her skin woke her up.

Relieved that the garden gate was unlocked, just covered with overgrown bushes, Beth pushed through and into a small passage that she followed until she came to the end of the row of gardens belonging to the houses. She walked back along the front until she came to her next-door neighbour's front door. She would knock and say she was just saying hello. That wasn't weird, was it? At home in Melbourne, her neighbours were practically family. What sort of neighbour had she been here?

Shaking away her nerves, Beth knocked on the door and waited.

The door opened and an elderly man, in a dressing gown over his clothes and slippers over his socks, stood in the doorway.

'Yes?' he said, looking at her with no recognition in his eyes.

'Hi.'

'Can I help you?' he said when she remained silent.

Beth cleared her throat, suddenly lost for words.

'Hi. Yes. It's me. Beth? From next door?'

His brows wrinkled in confusion initially before a wide smile broke onto his face.

'Ah, yes! The young lady from next door! Forgive me, my old brain isn't what it was and I've never had an eye for faces. You've changed your hair too. Confused me for a moment!'

Beth smiled. He seemed nice, if a bit befuddled. She knew how that felt.

'Would you like to come in?' he said, gesturing behind him into the house. 'I've just put the kettle on. Time for a nice cuppa.'

Beth relaxed. Always with the kettle and the tea with this country. She liked it though. Brits were a lot more friendly than they had a reputation for. Sure, they might not invite you over for dinner or to stay like Americans did, but they'd always offer you a cup of tea.

'Sure, that'd be great.'

Beth sat on the sofa in what was a mirror-image living room to hers, the same layout just flipped round. It was confusing and made her realise even further how her own home felt unfamiliar to her.

'Here you are,' he said, settling down into one of the comfy chairs.

'I'm so sorry, but remind me of your name?' Beth said.

'Peter. It's Peter.'

'Thanks.' Beth blushed. 'I... I don't know if you heard but... I was in an accident and, well, my memory is taking a little longer to catch up.'

'Oh no. No, I'm sorry. I hadn't heard.'

Beth was surprised. Had Rob not mentioned it to him? Maybe they weren't close.

'Yes. The crash on the fen road?' she said, wondering if that might spark some recognition, but nothing seemed to come to him.

Peter nodded.

'So,' Beth continued. 'How are we as neighbours?'

'Oh.' Peter seemed caught off guard. He looked confused again and then he smiled. 'You're good. No complaints there!'

'Not too noisy?'

Peter shook his head.

'No. No, I don't hear a thing. Mind you, I'm a little deaf these days. But no. And your boyfriend, Rob, isn't it? Well, he's been most helpful a few times now.'

'Helpful?' Beth said, not wanting to correct Peter about Rob being her husband. She didn't want to draw attention to his mistakes. That would be rude.

'Yes. He's fixed up the fence when it was my job really. It's my side of the garden, see. And he helped me when the garden centre accidentally delivered me a rather too-large Christmas tree. Helped me get it set up. Too much for one pair of hands. Not that I celebrate Christmas much now it's just me. He's a kind one, your man.'

Beth made a sympathetic face. It seemed that Rob was a decent neighbour. No blazing rows were making their way through the walls. Maybe she *was* getting things all mixed up. Maybe the phone had been a surprise, and he'd edited things to try to make everything right. Maybe fixing things for people was what he did.

'Um, might I ask a favour?' Beth asked suddenly.

'Oh. Of course. What is it, my dear?'

'Might I make a quick phone call? We don't have a landline, and my mobile hasn't been replaced, you know, after the crash, with the water...' She trailed off, wondering if the additional detail might make Peter remember the accident. Something he might have heard on the grapevine or read in the papers. But nothing was said.

'Oh, of course, my pet. It's in the hallway, help yourself.' He smiled, indicating the door and taking another biscuit to dip in his tea in the same movement. He was open. Trusting. If they'd been bad neighbours, if he'd heard rows and problems, he'd not be so kind, would he? Or perhaps he'd not mention it. He was English; he'd be too polite to interfere.

'Thanks,' Beth said, getting up on shaky feet. She was going to call home. She willed her family to pick up. Hoping that the sheer strength of *wanting* something would make it true, she picked up the phone, closed her eyes and let some long-embedded memory dial the number for her. ...And she waited. It felt like an age while the number connected and then...

'Your call could not be connected. Please check the number and try again.'

Beth took the phone down from her ear and looked at the digital screen. The number was right. She *knew* it was. She knew that number like her own birthdate.

She tried again.

'Your call could not be connected. Please check the number and try again.'

Beth let the message repeat over and then she disconnected the call.

Disconnected – from her family, from her home. From everything she knew. From everything she could fully count on. Rob had been telling the truth – the number wasn't working. What else was he being truthful about? She had been convinced that by talking with their neighbour, by calling home herself, she'd catch him out in whatever game he was playing? But how? Maybe he wasn't playing a game at all and he was just a kind, lovely husband trying to help her to recover and her own mind was playing tricks on her. Maybe she was internalising her own guilt about the crash and the lives it had ruined and was punishing herself for it by refusing to admit that her life was good. Why was she fighting so hard against that?

'No answer, dear?' Peter said as Beth returned.

'No. Not to worry,' Beth said, pushing brightness into her voice. 'I best get home. I get... I get tired still. After the accident.'

'Well, give Rob my best. I haven't seen him in a while. Nor the kiddies either.'

Beth stopped. She felt cold. The children? The ones from the accident? But he said he'd not heard anything.

'Pardon?'

'The kiddies. Sometimes hear them in the back garden. Playing. It's a nice sound.' He smiled kindly.

Beth relaxed. He didn't mean the accident. Though what he did mean she couldn't say, and now Beth wasn't convinced that Peter had any idea whatsoever who she really was. Or which of his neighbours he thought he was talking to. He'd got Rob's name right but thought he was a boyfriend. Maybe he had meant the family the other side? She hadn't said *which* next door she was coming from. Now she questioned whether anything he said was to be taken at face value. He was as unreliable as she was. Nothing was solid enough to hold on to. Trying not to sigh out loud, Beth smiled at him and went to the door. It would have been faster to go out of his back garden and across to the back gate but then she'd have to explain that she didn't have a front door key, and tiredness was draping itself over her fast and unexpectedly. She just wanted to get out without any more chit chat.

'Thanks for the tea.'

'Anytime. You know where I am,' Peter said as he followed her into the hallway.

She waved at him as she walked away, and if he looked confused at her turning right towards the back alleyway rather than left to her door, she didn't see it. And anyway, he'd got her mixed up, hadn't he? This had been a total waste of time.

Back in her own home, Beth locked the back door again and

replaced the key. She didn't want to have to explain herself to Rob either. She was too tired, and she could see that it did look as though she had been snooping on him, which she had been. Only now she was more confused than ever. Was he a threat to her? Or was he a kind man who helped out his elderly neighbour? Could he be both? Or had Peter got confused and said all those nice things about someone else?

Wanting to relax, Beth ran the bath that she said she was going to have and watched as the hot water and bubble bath mixed together in swirls in the tub, creating a frothy, cloud-like structure on top, rising to the edge of the tub as it filled up. She wanted to sink into it and pause. It was exhausting, this second-guessing all the time. She wanted it to stop. So what that Rob had hidden the phone. So what that he'd tried to edit a timeline to make things look okay. That wasn't criminal, was it? And the arguments she had been remembering... well, everyone rowed. She was being a drama queen. She knew she was like that. She'd have a row with her brother sometimes for the sheer adrenaline of it.

Dipping her toe into the scalding water, she slowly eased herself in and sat down. She was like a lobster, cooking herself until she was pink. She lay back and closed her eyes. She felt held by the water and relieved that it didn't bring back any memories of the accident. This water was warm and relaxing. Just what she needed. She had been lying there for a while, enjoying emptying her mind of everything, when she heard the front door go.

'Okay, thanks!' Rob called to someone.

Beth could hear him walk around the house looking for her, before popping his head around the door of the bathroom and smiling at her. His smile was too wide, too forced.

'Hi, Pooky. How've you been?' he said, coming into the bathroom without asking if it was okay and sitting down on the closed toilet seat. Beth immediately moved to cover up her nakedness. Even with the bubbles, she was exposed, and she was in no way comfortable with him being in the room with her in this state of undress. Why hadn't he asked? There had been little slips like this already, his forgetting that she didn't remember him and so didn't *know* him, nor have the same ease in his presence that she may have had before.

'Fine.'

She hoped he would pick up on her tension and realise his mistake, but his mind was elsewhere. He had something he wanted to say.

'Peter next door said you popped round?'

There was a forced lightness to his voice that made Beth's skin come out in goosebumps. Or was that the cold, above the water line? She felt vulnerable.

'Yes. Yes, I thought it...'

'Thought what? I asked you to wait, didn't I? We don't know how people are going to... going to be. With you. You *know* what I mean.'

He was talking about the children. The accident. That she was a child killer.

'I just thought meeting someone else I knew might help. You know, remind me of who I was.'

'Who you *are*. Well, we know that, Pooks. You're *my* wife and I can help you remember. You know that. I've said that.' He stood up, turned away from her and started tidying the items on the side of the sink, lining up bottles and lotions in a rigid order, wiping away condensation even though the room was still in use and it would return almost immediately. Beth could see the tautness to the line of his jaw as he ground his teeth. She was torn between sitting up further in the bath or staying put. Being so laid back felt wrong for the conversation they were having, but moving would put more of her naked skin out above the water line and she didn't want to do that either. She felt trapped. He was stood between her and her towel so it wasn't as though she could get out and into some sort of coverup in order to balance out the power here. She wondered if that was somehow a deliberate choice. She really hadn't got a handle on Rob and his intentions, and she swung back and forth between benevolent and anything but.

'I know, babe,' she said, seeing his ears lift from the back of his head as a smile crossed his face. 'But I can't rely on you for everything, all the time. It's too much. It's not fair on you.' She had slipped down in the bath and had to quickly remove the hand covering her bust to push herself back up. She did this just as Rob turned, giving him a full flash of her chest. She blushed. She hoped that the hot water had made her skin pink enough to hide it.

He smirked as he looked at her. 'It's not too much. I'll do anything for you. You know that.' He glanced at his feet as he considered his words. 'He said you called someone. Said that he'd hoped you'd get through to them next time as apparently your face had "looked like a child who'd slept too long and missed Christmas" when it didn't connect. Who... who were you calling?'

'I...'

'Are you not happy here?' He suddenly looked devastated. 'I... I know that you don't remember me, remember *us*, but I'm doing my best. I just want what's right for you.'

'I know you do...'

'So who were you calling then?' His voice was almost whiny now.

'I just had...' She had to think fast here. She needed him

calm and she could see he was getting wound up. 'I had a moment of inspiration – I thought I remembered Mum's number and I wanted to call it asap, in case it went again.'

'You... you called your mum?' He sounded wary, or hopeful. She couldn't tell which.

'Yeah but... you were right, the number wasn't working.'

'You called the house number? I *told* you I'd tried that already!'

'But I...'

'But what?' He looked pained. 'You don't believe me? You think I'm keeping you from them? You think *I'm* the one who's causing the rift?'

'No, no, I just...'

'That's so unfair, Pooks! I've done everything. Everything for you!' A pink tinge painted itself across his face as his emotions took hold. He moved towards her and suddenly time moved at double speed.

He lost his footing on the wet bathroom floor, slipped, fell and in holding out his hands to stop himself, pushed Beth down and under the water line. She yelped, taking in water as she went under, and her lungs burned with it. She could feel the sting of the bubbles in her eyes, the pressure of his hands holding her under and the rising panic in her chest as she struggled without oxygen. Then almost as suddenly as she went under, she was released and the same hands that had held her down were desperately pulling her above the surface. Her lungs gasped for air as she broke the water line. The whole thing must only have been seconds but it had felt like an eternity to her.

'God, oh my God. Beth, are you okay?' Rob was stammering over and over. He put his hands either side of her face, then onto her shoulders, and then kneeling over the edge of the bath, he pulled her to him like a wet rag doll. She was in shock and did not resist.

'I'm so sorry, I slipped, I... I'm sorry. Are you alright?'

Beth pushed him off her.

'You nearly drowned me! Give me some space!'

'I... I'm *sorry!* It was an accident, I slipped!' He looked pained, hurt beyond measure that she wasn't accepting his immediate apology.

Beth opened her mouth to argue but then thought better of it.

If it was an accident then she didn't need to make him feel worse about it, and slipping was easy enough as the floor was tiled and she'd made the bath super hot, so the room was steamy. Accidents did happen.

And if it wasn't an accident?

What if it had been a *warning*?

The doubt sneaked up on her and half-whispered into her ear. Had he deliberately held her underwater, knowing her fear of it, knowing how recently she'd nearly drowned, in order to show his displeasure at her *disobeying* him and talking to Peter without his say so? She felt chilled to the bone, despite being in hot water.

'Of course. Course. An accident. Sorry, I was just in shock.'

Rob's face calmed immediately. He hugged her again, then got up and turned to straighten out the towels hanging on the rail, ready for Beth to use.

'An accident. Exactly. I'd never hurt you, Beth, you know that. We're a team.'

'A team,' she repeated quietly.

'You and me against the world. Just us,' Rob said, stepping out of the room abruptly. 'I cancelled my lunch meeting to come home. I'll go make us some food.'

Beth was left, shaking and shivering in the bath. Who was this man? Did he love her or want to *own* her?

Why didn't she *remember*? It was so frustrating. She couldn't trust herself to know if she was being ridiculous or if she was in real trouble here.

Perhaps she could force the issue to see what Rob would do. Push back to see if she could make him lose his cool. How far should she push?

Would that even be wise?

11

Later that evening, after a stilted afternoon and evening together, Beth curled up in bed and closed her eyes. She wanted to squeeze them tightly shut but knew that this would look wrong. She closed them gently instead, as though she was already asleep. Rob usually came to bed after her, taking a bike ride and shower before bed. He said it fought off the effects of sitting a desk all day. Tonight, though, he had not gone out, having spent the evening practically glued to her side, and now moments after she had gone to bed, Rob got in beside her. Beth wished that her bedclothes offered her more armour than they did. She wondered if they were even hers or if he had bought them deliberately, wanting her to wear the strappy silky camisole and French knickers. They didn't feel like her. She was more a pants and oversized tee sort of girl.

As they lay there, side by side, a familiar feeling of dread came over Beth. A 'please go to sleep and don't try to touch me' feeling. She knew she had felt this before. She saw the two of them together in her mind clearly, though the room was different, the bed was different – but the anxiety was the same. If she chose to believe her instincts, to believe her own mind, then this marriage was not a happy one. Not now and not before. She pushed herself down under the covers to try to signal that she was going to sleep. Rob did the same and for a fleeting second, Beth felt relief, until he moved towards her. She turned onto her side away from him, but he shuffled next to her, wrapping his body around hers, his arm over her side as he pulled her back into him.

'Ah, big spoon, little spoon. I've missed this, Pooky.' He sighed into her neck. The warmth of his breath on her skin made it feel clammy and wrong, and she swallowed down her reaction. If he noticed, he didn't show it. Beth tried to force herself to relax. She couldn't show him her real feelings. She felt afraid but had no concrete evidence that her feelings were rational. How reliable were these flashbacks? Her memory was flawed. He'd spent all evening saying over and over how what had happened in the bathroom was an accident. He was mortified that she might think otherwise. What if she was making it all up? What if it was all in her mind? No one else seemed to think there was a problem – not in the hospital, she had no friends coming to check on her, and David the nurse hadn't raised any real concerns. What if she had got this all wrong?

'Me too,' she said, immediately regretting it. She just somehow felt that she needed him not to be angry with her, and the more she spent time with him, she felt that making him angry was an easy thing to do. Otherwise, how could she think what had happened in the bathroom was anything other than an accident?

'Pooks…'

'Hmm,' she managed to utter. He pulled her tighter as he echoed her words, pulling out the sound, making it guttural.

'Hmm…'

It made her skin itch.

He moved closer still, pushing himself into her back. She caught her breath and held it, her mind racing as she tried to work out his full intentions, and how to craft her response. Affection she could act, but she could not fake desire. She wouldn't.

'My baby...' he whispered into her ear as he started peppering her neck with kisses, moving his hands over the satin material that clung to her body. His purpose was clear. 'I missed you, I missed this. You're still mine.' His hands were roaming all over her, with no pause to see if she wanted this too, no moment of considering her feelings, of checking in with her.

He shifted upwards in the bed, moved his arm over her stomach so he could grab her waist. He then flipped her onto her back.

Realising that this was her moment, she cried out.

'Ow!' she shouted, breathing hard, suggesting pain but in reality feeling sheer panic.

At first, he did not register this, pushing her shoulders down to move her further onto the bed so he could move over her.

'Ouch! OW! My neck!' Beth said, clutching at it to further make her point.

He pulled up short. He stopped then sighed.

'Did that hurt? Did I hurt you?' he said, sitting himself up on one arm.

'Yes.'

'Oh. Sorry. I'm sorry, Pooks.'

'That's okay,' she said, rubbing at her neck.

He didn't look sorry. Disappointed. Pissed off.

'I guess I'm not quite ready... for that... yet.' She tried to look demure. Tried to seem disappointed herself.

He nodded and sighed out loud.

'Okay. That's okay, Pooky. We can try again, can't we?' He brushed his hand over her chest again.

She smiled tightly.

'Besides.' A lascivious smile crept onto his lips. 'There's other things we can do.'

'I'm tired,' she whispered, aware of the 'please don't' that her words contained.

He tensed.

'Soon though,' she said appeasingly. 'It's just, it's not been long since the accident and I'm still sore.'

Rob sighed again and lay back flat on the bed.

'Fine. No, that's fine. You need to recover. I understand that. We've all the time in the world, haven't we? You and me. The rest of our lives.' His tone was respectful but clipped. She could feel the tension radiating from him.

'Exactly. The rest of our lives.' Relief was flooding her every fibre and yet she knew she had not escaped but merely delayed things.

Rob got up and went to the bathroom.

Beth was confused. Rob was too hot and cold right now. He was holding something back, she knew that and she needed him to reveal himself to her, without being aware that he was doing so. She also needed to admit there was a possibility that her mind was damaged from the accident, and this was all drama that she was concocting herself for whatever reason. Maybe some sick form of self-protection, of keeping everyone, keeping Rob, at arm's length. But why would she feel the need to do that if he wasn't a threat to her? No. She needed another opinion, more information.

Rob returned to the room, got back into bed, leant over to give Beth a chaste kiss on the forehead and then he turned over heavily and switched the room lights out. They lay there in total darkness until Rob began to snore. Beth smiled briefly at how such a sound could often be an irritant in a marriage, but here it was a sign that she could relax. Her mind tried to run through so many scenarios that could play out but eventually, her own weariness took over and she fell asleep.

When she woke the next morning, the light was already streaming through the now open curtains, and she could hear Rob moving around in the kitchen. A damp-looking towel was hanging over the door to the bathroom, so she assumed she had slept right through his morning preparations. She shuddered – she'd been unconscious and vulnerable, asleep when he was awake, but her body clearly needed the rest. She used the bathroom herself and then, dressing for the day, she moved to the main part of the house. Today she would get as much information as possible and then decide what was best to do with it.

'Morning,' she said as she joined Rob in the kitchen.

'Morning, sleepyhead. I didn't want to wake you but it's getting late.'

Beth glanced up at the clock. It was 8 a.m.

'It's not so late,' she said without thinking.

His eyebrows wrinkled.

'It is if one has to go to *work*.'

'Are you out today?'

He bunched up the tea towel he was holding and dumped it onto the counter.

'For a bit, yes. I'll be back soon though, don't worry, I won't leave you too long.'

'That's fine. I just wondered.'

'What are you going to do? More TV?' He picked up the towel, straightening it out and placing it neatly back on the rail that they hung on.

Beth took the opportunity.

'I thought I might take a bus into town, see if anything jumps out at me. Walk with no plan but just see where my feet take me. In case my toes know more than my brain.' She laughed. Who *was* this inane version of herself? Was this who she was with him?

'Riiiight.' His brow wrinkled. 'Are you sure that's wise?'

'Why not?'

'Because of, you know. People. Wait until this afternoon and I'll come with you at least?' he suggested, holding his palms out in front of him as if he was giving his time as an offering.

'I suppose...'

'That's my girl,' he said, turning back to packing his bag.

'I could go out into the village this morning. Or maybe a local café. Did I use to go anywhere in particular? Maybe someone will know me, and I can have a chat with them.'

He didn't look at her.

'Not really. You didn't tend to talk to many people.'

'Okay. Well... did I go to a gym? What did I spend my days doing?'

'You kept yourself to yourself, you looked after our home. You looked after me. You were... you were shy.'

'Really? Shy? But I travelled the world?' This version of her was not registering.

'Yes. You were shy. And lockdown changed lots of people's outlooks. Look, maybe I should stay home today. You seem... agitated. It's understandable.'

'I'm fine, really,' Beth said, pushing a lightness of tone into her voice. 'It's just a bit strange not to know anything about myself, you know? I'd hoped that something would have come back to me by now.'

Other than our rows, that is.

'*I* know you.'

'Well, then maybe you can tell me.' *Tell me your version of me.*

Rob chewed his lip as though he was weighing something up.

Beth sidled up beside him and slipped her arm conspiratorially through his, resisting her body wanting to push him away, instead pulling him closer. She could feel the warmth of him seeping into her own skin.

'Tell me about *us*.' She smiled up at him. 'Tell me everything.'

The Instagram profile popped up in her mind as though her brain were the phone screen.

He turned to face her, a quizzical expression on his face, before he took her arm and led her to the sofa where he put her down and sat beside her.

'Ah, our origin story. I do love this.'

Beth got ready to take as many mental notes as possible. Her mind was often tired and fuzzy, especially with the painkillers she was still taking for her neck. Rob brought them to her each morning to make sure she didn't forget, saying the doctors had said to keep on them, ready to taper off rather than just to stop. He hadn't brought any to her this morning yet though, so despite the fact that she could feel the tightness in her neck more, it wasn't so painful, and she was more clear-minded in a way that she appreciated.

'So how did we meet?'

Rob's face broke into a genuine grin. Like the cat who'd got the cream. 'I won you.'

Beth blinked. 'What?'

'I won you.'

'I... don't know what you mean.'

Rob smirked. 'So you were working in this bar in London. Flash place. Very classy. I was there with some colleagues after work and one of them was thirsting after you. Hard. He wasn't listening, not taking no for an answer. You know. The classic "persist until you wear them down and they give in" routine.'

Beth understood this one. She may have been missing a lot of her past memories, but she had enough recall to remember countless situations like this in her life. She knew she had worked in bars before and there was always someone who, because you had been polite while taking their order, or smiled when they took their drinks, decided that you had the hots for them when in reality, you were just trying to do your job.

'Yes, I know that one.'

'Exactly. I thought I could kill two birds with one stone and get him off your case but in a way that would save his pride, but also impress you in another cos I wanted you myself.' He bit his bottom lip and tipped his head sideways.

Beth smiled as though this was flattering. He was talking about her like she was a prize rather than a person. Had her younger self been flattered at being considered a trophy, with men fighting over her? She assumed so. Maybe London had made her lonely, grateful for attention.

'So what did you do?'

'Ha! I made a bet.'

'A... bet? You made a bet.'

Rob looked pleased.

'Yes. I bet him that whoever could down ten shots of tequila fastest and not throw up would get to go on a date with you.'

Beth said nothing. She had been expecting some sort of romance story about her finding an English prince who had swept her off her feet, persuaded her to stay in England, forsaking her family and her homeland. She had expected fireworks, romance, tortured longing. Something that if you made a film about it, it would have Hugh Grant in it somewhere. But this? This sounded like something a bogan would do.

'But he was so drunk that he accepted and didn't notice my passing my shots to you to pour into the drip tray.'

'He drank all ten? Surely that would have made him ill?' Beth was concerned. She should never have served that in the first place. She could have got into trouble. Despite this guy being an arsehole, she wouldn't have wanted him to get alcohol poisoning.

'Nah, he was going so fast he spilt a fair amount, and don't worry, he started throwing up soon after he admitted defeat and said I could have you.'

'You could *have* me.'

'No, not like *that*. We're not animals!' Rob looked amused. 'No, just that he'd leave you be, and I could ask you out instead. You could have said no, and I'd have been disappointed but that would have been that. I'm not like that. But you said yes. You thanked me for rescuing you and then agreed to go out with me that weekend.'

'So, did we?' Beth steeled herself for another horrific laddish story. Her past-self seemed to have little self-esteem. How had that happened?

'Well, duh. Of course we did. I took you boating in Hyde Park, then for lunch by the Serpentine. After that we wandered up to Notting Hill for the afternoon and then we grabbed a cab to Hampstead Heath.'

Beth drew in a breath. She realised what he had done.

'Did you know?'

Rob smiled.

'How did you know?' Beth felt flutters in her stomach. Good ones. She was not expecting this. She had been painting Rob as the bad guy and suddenly he was romancing her?

'You said you liked Hugh Grant and asked was I like him. And, well, other than being English with floppy brown hair, I'm not really. I'm more working class than that. But I figured an arm-in-arm walk through some of the film locations just might persuade you otherwise. Worked too. Swept you off your feet.' His chin jutted forward as he beamed.

Beth smiled. She had watched Hugh Grant's films with her mum when she was growing up and he was her epitome of an English gentleman. It was thoughtful of Rob. He had wanted to win her over, rather than just win her. But how had this been enough to keep her here? From all the people she loved.

'Then what? Once I worked out you didn't live in a flat with a blue door near Portobello Road market?'

'No, I didn't, but I did have a flat in Camden and we ended up back there. It was... intense from the start. You were, you *are*, hot. I mean, English girls are reserved, but you? Oof.' He fanned himself.

Beth felt her hackles rise. Was he calling her a slut?

'And we just didn't stop. Seeing each other, I mean. Covid hit and we moved in together, then I got a new job, and we moved here, and we got...'

Trapped?

'...Married. People were *not happy*,' he said, lowering his head while raising his eyebrows.

'My family?'

'Your family. They thought we were rushing things, being impulsive. And hey, they were probably right but you're only young once, right? Why not do stupid things?'

'Was us getting married stupid?' Beth asked, tears trying to form at the back of her eyes, stinging as she fought to keep them there. It seemed stupid to her – that she had found herself here, alone, with Rob, without knowing whether or not he was a good man or far from it. No matter the good things she heard about him, from him, she couldn't shake that feeling of doubt. Now she was alone, and afraid. That sounded to her like a fairly stupid place to be.

'No. No! I said it then and I mean it now. You and I are meant to be. Destined. I want what's best for you. I do. And that's being here. With me. Your parents didn't like that they no longer had *control* over you.' His face darkened with disgust. 'They thought I was stealing their baby from them. But I've proved to them ever since that you're my girl and I'd do anything for you. Romantic, no?' Rob said, running his fingertips over her shoulder and down her arm to take her hand. He squeezed it, running his finger over where her wedding ring had been. A flicker of annoyance darted across his face, turning his eyes a shade of black for just a second.

'You're still not wearing your ring.'

'Oh. I know. I just, they took it off when I was in the coma in case my hands swelled up and I've just not...' *Wanted to put it back on.*

'Let me get it for you now.' Rob jumped up and walked at a pace into the bedroom before coming back moments later with a small zip lock bag. Smirking, Rob took out the ring that was inside and theatrically dropped to one knee, proffering it up to her.

'Not quite as romantic as the first time!' Beth joked and widened her eyes as she realised that she remembered that day.

'My proposal?' Rob said, suddenly tense as he processed what Beth had said. He didn't seem to look pleased, which surprised her.

'It was at a lake. Or rather, from *within* a lake? You... walked into the water, wearing a white billowy shirt and then walked back out of it, holding a ring.'

'You remember? Ha. I, uh, I was working on channelling Hugh Grant via Mr Darcy. Ruined my white shirt – that water is not clean.'

'I remember... Darcy meets Excalibur...' Beth whispered. 'I... there isn't a lot of detail coming to me, but yes... I remember!' She grasped his hand in joy. Real joy at her mind being returned to her, albeit for the briefest of moments. Joy at being given back a happy memory.

'I clearly made an impression!'

Beth nodded. She was too overjoyed at the idea that her memories may be returning to her to notice how, once again, Rob had made it about him.

'So we got married and...'

'Yes.'

'Why did we move here?'

'I told you. I got a better job. And we needed more space.'

Beth looked around at the small house they were in and wondered how much smaller it could have possibly been in London. Ignoring the sliver of irritation in his voice, Beth pressed him for more information.

'Why? Were we not happy in London? Why did we need more space?'

'What do you mean why? London flats are tiny. You were used to space. I wanted you to feel more at home.'

Her throat closed up as she realised that had they stayed in London, they would have never been anywhere near that ditch. Those poor children would still be alive. Had it been her who'd wanted to move? Was this all her fault?

'I had a job in London though. What did I do here?'

'You didn't need a job, I've told you this already, Beth. I looked after you. You looked after me.'

'I was a housewife?' she asked incredulously, her inner feminist surprised at this.

'A homemaker. You kept things nice and tidy. You cooked us both meals, you looked after me and yourself and we were happy. We were.'

'Were we?'

'Yes. Yes! We were. I worked and provided and supported you while you pursued your little photography business dream, taking photos of all these big landscapes out in the fens near here. It was perfect.'

Suddenly his face was set hard, his mouth fixed in a tight line.

Until she'd ruined things. That much was clear, if unsaid by both of them.

'What happened?'

'What do you mean?' Rob's jawline was tense as he clenched and unclenched his teeth. Beth could hear him grinding them together in the silence that grew.

'I mean, did something... did something change?'

'Things change all the time, Beth.'

'You know that's not what I mean.'

'No. No, I don't. Don't be coy with me, Beth. If you want to ask me something, then *ask*.'

She hadn't heard this tone from him before. Or at least, not in recent memory. There was a warning in it, a 'don't mess with me' edge that made the hairs on the back of her neck rise in anticipation. She suddenly felt chilled and felt herself physically shrink from the conversation.

'Okay. I'm sorry, I...'

Immediately, a huge smile spread over his face.

'Oh, don't look so serious, Pooky. We were talking about how happy we were. And we were. We were...' He looked wistful almost.

What on earth was going on with him? He seemed to flick between contrasting emotions so quickly, it left Beth almost breathless as she tried to work out what was going on. She reminded herself that he was grieving. His wife didn't remember him. He had somehow lost the person who was standing right in front of him. That had to be hard to deal with.

'Look, I have to go to work. Will you be okay? I think it's probably wise to stay here, don't you? I'll be back in a couple of hours. We can then go for a walk together, okay? Just... wait for me, will you? Wait for me. Look what happened last time.'

'The bath?'

'No! With Peter – he got himself all muddled up. He's old and he's not really with it a lot of the time, poor man. I don't want you any more confused than you already are.'

He looked at her, eyebrows raised in expectation. She nodded silently.

'Good girl. I'll be back soon. Why don't you watch some TV or something.'

He patted her in the middle of her back, kissed her on the top of her head, picked up his bags and left.

Beth was left standing in the kitchen, bemused. She felt patronised, looked after, threatened, cared for. Her mind was a confusion as to what she and Rob *were*. Were they a happy couple? Had she felt trapped before? How did he feel about where they were now? There were so many things going on here it made her feel dizzy just trying to follow a single train of thought.

One thing was clear though. He was not going to tell her anything without being directly asked and he had made it clear that she should not do that. That edge to his voice when he told her to ask had scared her. It almost felt like a threat. Ask – if you dare.

It was obvious that he wasn't going to help her find out about their life other than his version of it, and something inside her told her that she couldn't wholly trust that. So she was going to have to work out how to find it out herself, and for now, from within the confines of the house. She couldn't get into town and back again in time. If she defied him again and went into the village and got caught – well, she didn't think that was wise either.

She was going to have to look, no matter how scared she might be of what she might find.

12

After Rob had left, Beth waited until her pulse had calmed. She was becoming aware that whenever he was around, she was on hyper alert. He was too hot then cold to manage, too unpredictable. Whatever Beth thought best, Rob had made it clear that she ought not to go out without him. Maybe there was something he knew that she did not. That made more sense. Would she be putting herself in danger by leaving the house? Were people angry with her? Peter next door had not been but then again, she wasn't sure he actually knew who she was. She felt so much guilt about what she had done. Those poor children. Rob was trying to be supportive but surely he felt the same disgust for her that she felt for herself? She did not feel strong enough to face anyone in case they upbraided her about the accident and so she stayed inside. She could find out as much about her previous life as possible while staying within these four walls.

She had the feeling that Rob was hiding things from her. Little oddities that didn't make sense – the clutter of everyday life that just wasn't here. The fact that she never saw any post arrive. Either nothing was sent, or Rob intercepted it before she saw it. A sense of being utterly cut off from everyone else. It wasn't exactly the outback but either she was being melodramatic about being out in the fens, wide fields surrounding them, or something wasn't right.

The living room held very few clues. There were no pictures, no memories, no photo albums, not even books, which would give her a clue as to what things were like before her accident. She'd have thought there might be photos or knicknacks, maybe coffee table books of photos as she had been such a keen photographer. She thought she would look for her camera – surely that would be here in the house – and it might have the last few photos taken on it even if she had lost the rest.

'Where would I keep a camera...' Beth whispered to herself. There wasn't a lot of storage in the house. The rooms were small so once you took into account doors and window space, there wasn't a lot of wall on which to put cupboards or shelves. She went into the bedroom and slid back the mirrored wardrobe doors. There was a side which had a full-length hanging rail and another half-length with drawers underneath. She slid the drawers out but found only clothes, towels and bedding. Pushing the hanging clothes to one side, in case something was stored behind them, she looked into the very back of the wardrobe but there was nothing there. Surely there would be a camera bag somewhere, with lenses and one or two camera bodies perhaps? She'd seen enough professional photographers to know that they usually had a selection of kit. If she was taking it seriously, it's not like she'd just be using her phone camera.

Sighing, Beth turned back to face the room and as she did so, another thought occurred to her. If Rob was trying to protect her, trying to let her mind return her memories in its own time, rather than via an onslaught of imagery that she could not recall herself, perhaps he would have hidden her camera? Tucked it away somewhere safe until she was ready to use it again. Controlling or caring – either way, this idea made sense.

She needed to think where a good hiding place might be. Somewhere she wouldn't necessarily stumble on it by accident. He must know that she didn't spend all her time sat on the sofa watching the TV so it would need to be somewhere inaccessible. She sat down on the bed and viewed the room differently. She looked at the ceiling in case there was an attic hatch somewhere. She bounced a little on the bed as she thought. Then she stopped. And then bounced a little harder, listening to the sound that the bedframe was making. She sprung up and looked *at* the bed she was sitting on. It was a divan. It had drawers.

Beth kneeled on the floor and ran her hands down from the mattress to where it met the bedframe, and then she lifted up the... What were those things called? Valances – the word popped into her head from somewhere. She lifted it and tucked it underneath the doona to keep it out of the way. Yes, there were drawers. She pulled one open. It barely had anything in it. A blanket, folded and put to one side. A box file that on opening held a random selection of paperwork. She could come back to that another time in case it held any information. Other than that, nothing.

The other drawer was prevented from being opened by the bedside cabinet and she tried to move it to get the drawer open. The cabinet was surprisingly heavy and she couldn't shift it. Crouching on the floor, she wondered if she could move the bed instead but that was too heavy as well. Refusing to admit that she wasn't strong enough, Beth went back to the cabinet, stood up and moved the lamp onto the bed to stop it falling off. Then, rocking the bedside cabinet from side to side, she 'walked' it a little way away from the bed. She tried the drawer again but couldn't get it open wide enough. So she 'walked' the cabinet a bit further and tried again. She'd grown up climbing trees; she wasn't about to let a piece of furniture win. If he was trying to hide things from her then Rob had underestimated her. She'd got the drawer half open, wide enough to look inside. No bulky bag or anything that looked like a camera bag was there, but there was another cardboard box, which looked like a delivery from a bike shop, with a logo of a bike tyre wrapped around the rectangular shape. Frustrated, Beth sat back and rested against the bed. What a waste of effort. But...

Why would bike stuff be here? There was a shed. That was where Rob kept all his bike stuff. He didn't like it in the house because he didn't want dirt and mud getting in. She'd not have minded – her brother was often to be found fixing his bike in the kitchen, much to their mother's disapproval.

Beth reached her arm back through the opening and carefully prised open the end of the box. Inside was what looked like a laptop case. Why would there be a laptop here? Her breath quickened. Was it hers? Feeding her arm into the drawer up to her shoulder, she grasped the case and pulled it towards her and brought the laptop out, placing it on the bed.

She opened it up, and nothing. The battery was dead. *Damn.* She was about to put it back and keep looking when she realised Rob was obscenely tidy and organised to the point of obsession. He would hate to separate a laptop and case from its charger. Getting back down onto the floor and painfully feeding her arm back through the barely opened enough drawer, she reached about for the box and put her hand fully inside it. The feeling of success as her hands closed around what was clearly a length of cable, neatly wound and stored, was amazing. She pulled it out and, leaning the bedside cabinet back at an angle to allow her to reach the plug socket, Beth plugged it in at the wall and into the laptop and she waited. Her hands grew hot and she wiped them on the bedcover as she waited for the laptop to charge enough to turn on. *Come on.* The information on this machine just might change her life, and she couldn't find any patience. As she waited, she noticed a piece of paper that had fallen to the floor. It must have been tucked inside the laptop. She opened it. In Rob's handwriting was a list of random words.

~~Pooky123~~
~~NottingHill00~~
~~BethnRob~~
~~Beth&Rob~~
~~RobnBeth~~
~~RobBethUK~~
~~Melbourne88~~
~~Altona88~~
~~Daisy88~~
~~BrewGirl00~~
~~BrewGirl123~~

Had Rob been trying to guess her password? Had he succeeded? Beth laughed at his assumption that her password would be about *him*, or *them* at the very least. At his belief that he was her whole world – when she had seen more of the world than he had. He had at least been grabbing at the straws of what he knew about her life before him – the café, her hometown, even her cat.

Finally, Beth thought enough time had passed, so she pressed the power button and the laptop started up. She was just trying to work out what her password might actually be when suddenly a red light flashed at the top of the screen, the words *Welcome back, Beth* appeared and the home screen loaded. Beth jumped back in shock. How did that work? Did computers have face recognition now? This must be her computer. But how... Whatever. She shook her head. She could marvel at how technology appeared to have learned from various sci-fi movies later. Right now, she had information to find. She needed to track down someone – a friend, her brother – someone, anyone who she trusted enough to tell her the truth before she lost her mind in all this uncertainty.

Her hands grew clammy as she hovered over each icon. This computer possibly held her memories, her past life, the life she had ruined, all the information she might need but that her brain would not give her. But... *why* was her brain withholding it? What was it trying to protect her from? Suddenly terrified, she moved her hands away as though the laptop was hot.

Rob had *hidden* this laptop, hadn't he? What was he trying to hide from her? Details of the crash? Information about the children? Was that it?

She opened a web browser and found herself looking at a Facebook profile. She'd not used Facebook in years but the profile picture was her: same name, same information, birthday etc. Beth's mind swirled. What on earth? Was this real? The Instagram account that she'd found on the phone had no contacts, no nothing. She clicked on the friends tab on the screen and a huge list of people came up, some she instantly recognised from home. These were her actual friends. Faces that, for the first time since the accident, she recognised. People from her life *before*.

Suddenly Beth's eyes filled with tears. She was instantly utterly homesick. For a place, for a time and for people that she knew. Here, she was alone. So alone. She had not known a single person she had met since waking up. It was like walking around in a world packed full of strangers. Every conversation was hard work. She was terrified of the man who was her husband. She did not know his intentions, his thoughts. If she was safe or not. She had no one she could reach out to, and this was all her own doing. How had she got things so completely wrong? What had happened to her? What poor choices and bad decisions had led her here, sitting, with tears falling freely down her face, looking at pictures of people on the other side of the world who apparently no longer cared about her? Did they even know about her now?

Beth searched for Rob's profile but they were not connected. Hers didn't reference him nor vice versa and his was locked down. She looked through the profiles on the feed – it was mostly old stuff from when she was younger, before people had moved onto different platforms. It was like a time machine back to the life she remembered, but now it seemed everyone had moved on. Their lives continuing offline in a world she did not recall or know. She threw the laptop onto the carpet beside her and rested her head upon the bed. She wished again that she had someone to talk to, someone who could either confirm or deny what Rob had told her. What she herself had found out. If she could... She stopped.

She picked up the laptop again and looked at the profile. Clicking on the message function, she opened it, half expecting it to be empty, like the other one, only to find string after string of messages! Mostly old ones, but her heart leapt into her throat as she opened the top one from someone called Dee. Beth checked the date. It was recent – really recent! A matter of weeks ago!

BETH

This is SO hard!

DEE

I know, babe, I know. I know it's gonna be hard but I'm here for you. You can do this. I'm here

BETH

I know, it's just…

DEE

What? You have to hide things from him. That's not normal, is it? You know that

BETH

It's just, he's their dad. And he's not all bad

DEE

Not yet, no, but you know how this goes. How it always goes. He's already stopped us from seeing each other

BETH

He hasn't stopped us directly. He doesn't know you

DEE

No? Just made it so difficult that we don't get to see each other?

BETH

Don't be mad at me

DEE

I'm not, babe. I'm not mad, I'm worried. I'm scared for you. You know how this time can be the most dangerous. When you're leaving someone

BETH

I know. I'm being as careful as I can

DEE

I know you are, babe. Just. Please. Don't push anyone trying to help you away. Okay? We just want you safe

DEE

Beth? You still there?

DEE

Hey. What's up? You've gone quiet. What's going on?

DEE

Beth? Where are you? You're not answering your phone. Not seeing messages. Are you okay?

DEE

Beth, I'm really worried now. Can you just message me and let me know you're okay. Please. I've got your voice note. You're not picking up. Call me. Please

DEE

What has he done? Are you all right? Call me!

Beth's hands were shaking too hard for her to scroll any more. There was someone else. Who knew. Who *knew* that something wasn't right. Beth checked the date – this was barely three weeks ago. Just before the accident. Beth checked Dee's profile-and the location was Cambridge. She was here, in the same place as her. Beth put down the computer again and closed her eyes as the room swam around her, her heart beating so fast and so hard that she could feel it in her chest. There was someone she could talk to! She wasn't alone.

Wiping her hands on her jeans, she picked up the laptop and set it down on the bed. Her hands hovered over the keyboard; she wasn't sure what she wanted to say, what she ought to say. Who was Dee? What did she know? And what did *she* mean about a dad? They had been friends, good friends, clearly, and yet Beth had no recollection of her. Would Dee understand? Beth considered closing the laptop and taking her time to think about it, but then wondered if she would have this chance again. Would she have the time, the courage, the opportunity? Realising that she may not and if she was correct in this it was even more important to take this chance, Beth lowered her fingers to the keyboard and typed.

BETH

Dee?

Then she waited. How long might it take Dee to reply? Beth thought she ought to give some information to her, but what? What could she say? She had no idea where to start. Beth formed sentence after sentence in her head but they all sounded insane. *Help. I think my husband is trying to keep me captive.* Come on! She sounded a number of sarnies short of a picnic even to herself.

Then there was a ping and a new message landed on the screen.

DEE

Beth? Beth, is that you?

Beth drew in a breath and let it out slowly, trying to calm herself.

BETH

Yes, this is me

DEE

Where the hell are you? How are you? Are you okay? Are you safe?

A sob escaped from Beth's mouth.

BETH

I'm safe. Yes

Was she?

DEE

But where are you? Jesus, Beth, you disappeared and then I saw the news about the crash, but the hospital wouldn't talk to me cos I'm not next of kin. I only just managed to persuade someone to tell me you'd been discharged by pleading with them.

BETH

I'm sorry

DEE

Don't be. Just where are you?

Beth's chest tightened. What a weird question. Who was this woman?

BETH

I'm at home

DEE

No you're not. I know you're not. I've been there

BETH

What? I'm at the house. Rob and mine's house in... it's in a village

She felt ridiculous as she realised that she'd never asked the village's name. Dee was going to think she was a nutter.

DEE

Beth, you don't live in a village. You live in town. With the kids

What? Beth's heart sank. What did she mean? What kids? Maybe Dee didn't know her at all.

BETH

The kids?

DEE

Yes! The twins. Why are you being so weird? What's going on?

Beth felt the world going fuzzy, her eyesight starting to fade. Twins?

DEE

They were there but you weren't. They were with—

What? Beth willed Dee to keep going. She could see that Dee was typing but nothing was coming through.

BETH

I'm sorry. You said twins?

DEE

Seriously, what is wrong, Beth? Yes, your twins

Beth felt she was going to pass out. She didn't have twins. She didn't have any children. The other woman involved in the accident had twins, ones that she had unwittingly caused the death of and she... Beth threw up a little into her mouth and reached for a tissue from the bedside table to spit it into. What if... What if... No. No. That was *insane*. She was not the mother of twins in the newspaper article, that was the other car, the other woman. Because, well, Rob would have... He wouldn't... He couldn't have... Would he? So was she the other woman and not his wife at all? No – that didn't fit! What in God's name was going on? What had Rob *done*?

DEE

Describe the house you're in to me. Now

Beth forced herself to focus on this one task. Everything else threatened to overwhelm her entirely. Her breathing was shallow and rapid, and she had to blink hard to make herself concentrate.

BETH

Number 12. It's end of a terrace. Something Row... It's new

She thought harder.

BETH

The village has a duck pond that's about five minutes' walk away

Was that weird?

DEE

I'm google mapping, hang on

There was a long wait. Beth was trying her best not to think about anything other than working out where she was. Of telling Dee where she could find her. Someone other than Rob to know her whereabouts, someone else who knew her before the accident. The wait was interminable. How many villages had duck ponds? She didn't know; in her head she'd never even visited England, let alone lived here.

The message screen pinged again and there was a photo. Of the pond.

DEE

This one?

BETH

That's it! Yes. You're a genius!

Then the thread pinged again with an image of a house. This house.

DEE

Is this it?

BETH

Yes!

Someone in the world besides Rob now knew that she was here. That alone made Beth feel… something. Something good. She couldn't find the word for it.

DEE

God damn him. You're at her house. Is he there? Is he there with you now?

BETH

Whose house? Who is 'her'? And no, no, he's gone to work, he'll be gone a couple of hours

DEE

I'll tell you when I get there. I'm on my way. Be there in 20 mins, max. Stay there. If he comes back before I get there let me know? Like, open the front window or something?

BETH

Okay

The little icon at the top that said 'Active Now' changed and the conversation stopped. Dee had gone.

Beth slumped back and leant against the bedside table. Her mind couldn't keep up with all she'd just learned. She was *not* at her house but at someone else's? Why? How did she even know Dee? Why did Dee seem to think that Beth had twins? That was ridiculous! That was just beyond crazy. Beth wasn't sure that Dee wasn't about to make things more confused than ever. Good God, she *needed* her family!

Going back to the laptop again, she opened the messenger function and searched for Ben, her brother. He was there but they'd last messaged years ago on here, but it was worth a shot. She quickly typed.

BETH

Hey. It's me. Can you message me please? I need your help. It's urgent. Please. I don't know what's gone on or what's going on but please, message me

She paused then added:

BETH

I have no phone. Don't call Rob. Just message here. Love you

With adrenaline coursing through her body, Beth then opened another window and selected her email, the one she knew from before. It needed a password this time but luckily, it was the same one she'd had for years and years, back from the time she hadn't forgotten. Easy to remember, easy to crack – but thank goodness she'd ignored Ben when he'd told her to make it more secure! She opened up a new message to her mum. Her work and personal emails to cover all bases. She paused as she considered what to write. So much to say but she didn't feel that she could pour all of it into a first email. It was too complicated, too emotional. She decided to keep it minimal for now.

Dear Mum,

I miss you. Things here have got complicated. I can't call you – I've lost my phone and don't know your new house number. Can you email me? I need to talk to you.

Sorry – for everything.

Love you.

Bethany x

Beth closed her eyes and imagined her message winging its way to her mum. She had to hope that her mum didn't think it was a scam. She felt a lightness that she hadn't felt since she had woken up to this nightmare. She had reached out to her mum and her brother and everything was going to be okay. There would be an actual grownup in the scenario. She knew *she* was a grownup, but she doubted she would feel that way even if she did get her missing five years of experiences back.

She opened her eyes just in time to see the new message arrive. From her mum. Her breath stuttered as her heart soared with relief. Her mum hadn't abandoned her. Her relief was short lived. It was an out of office. Her mum was away from work – for ten days. A hot ball of frustration exploded in her stomach. For fuck's sake! Why couldn't she catch a break? She knew her mum was religious about not checking work or emails on holiday. She would be out of reach for anyone who didn't know where she had gone. She used to leave a printout of the hotel contact details stuck to the fridge. This vital piece of paper would be stuck to a fridge in a house she didn't know, across the other side of the world.

Beth swallowed hard despite her arid mouth, and she closed her eyes. Everything was spinning; her whole body was flooded with a buzzing that she could not control. Her head pulsed with a band of pressure just above her eyes. The overwhelming urge to go home hit her as she pictured herself closing the door behind her in her childhood bedroom, throwing herself onto her single bed, with the blanket at the end that her gran had made for her when she was a baby and curling up under it. She loved that blanket – it was her only connection to her gran now that she was gone.

The sky outside the screened window was a different shade of blue to the one outside her window now. A swimming pool blue to this slate grey. She could smell the warmth on the air, and she wished that she had never left Australia. All the experiences she might have gained had been lost to her and all she had left was... this... mess.

And the house in her mind was now being lived in by someone else. All the connections she had to the life she actually remembered were scattered to the wind. She felt as untethered as one of those balloons that had been released into the sky – directionless and with no idea where she would land.

13

The twenty minutes waiting for Dee to arrive felt like an eternity. Beth had nothing to hold her thoughts on to. They didn't make any sense. What Rob had told her did not make sense. What Dee seemed to be suggesting did not make sense. No one version of the truth seemed to feel solid as she ran through them in her mind. There had been children involved in the crash – that much had been reported and confirmed by the witnesses. But whose? And what had happened to them?

And who was this Dee? How did she know her and why did she seem so concerned for Beth's welfare? Yet Beth felt that her arrival would start to fill in all the blanks that Beth knew she was missing. This constant guessing, constant wondering, this inability to ask Rob anything without it making him angry was driving her to distraction. Was that his plan? Why? What was he trying to gain?

When the front door buzzed, Beth could barely breathe. She pulled herself from the floor where she had slumped to stop herself from relentlessly pacing. Beth's hands shook as she held them on the cool metal of the doorknob. She glanced at her watch. Rob had been gone an hour already. That meant she had less than sixty minutes to meet Dee, work out if she could trust her, find out everything she needed to know and then decide what to do about it before he got back. She laughed emptily at the sheer ridiculousness of it all.

The door echoed as Dee knocked gently on the other side and Beth turned the handle to let her in. As she did so, Dee swept into the room and quickly closed the door behind her. She was tall, taller than Beth, with long dark hair, and there were tears in her green eyes. She stepped towards Beth with her arms outstretched but stopped when she saw that Beth was looking at her warily. She took a half step backwards and brought her arms back towards herself, her palms facing outwards.

'Beth,' she said, smiling at her. The light that shone in her eyes spoke of affection. It had a warmth. It made her realise how Rob did not have warmth in his eyes when he looked at her but something else. What, she couldn't say.

'Dee?' Beth felt shy, nervous of this person who she knew but did not know.

Dee nodded. She pressed her lips together as she tried to hold her composure. A couple of tears fell as she blinked, slowly working their way down her cheek as she smiled and shook her head at Beth.

'You don't know me? What?' she said, her voice a whisper, trembling with concern.

Beth couldn't push her sense of shame away as she fixed her eyes on her feet and shook her head. 'No. The accident, I...' She lifted her head to face Dee and gestured to the scar on her forehead. 'The airbag didn't deploy properly. I hit my head hard and... it's not abnormal apparently. To lose... I haven't lost all my memory, just about five years, give or take. I... I don't remember leaving Australia.'

Dee's eyes deepened with pity as she looked at Beth.

'Shiiiiit. Oh my God. Babe, I'm so sorry.' Dee reached out to Beth. 'That... that's unbelievably hard. How are you doing?'

Beth felt her own tears prick at the back of her eyes as she saw the genuine care on Dee's face. Since leaving the hospital, she had felt totally and utterly alone and somehow, suddenly, with Dee here, she no longer felt that way. Even though she had not a clue how this woman and she knew each other.

Beth was so overwhelmed she couldn't speak at first. She let Dee hold her for a while. The two women stood there, in silence while Beth let someone else take the strain for a moment. She then pulled back to look at Dee again. She felt that she could trust her – or maybe she just wanted to.

'I'm okay? I'm shit. Bit of both?' She laughed, and Dee laughed with her.

Dee's face then clouded over. 'I still can't believe he's done this. Or rather, part of me can believe it, even if I don't want to.' Her jaw clenched. 'He's *such* a bastard.'

'I need you to tell me everything,' Beth said, looking intently at Dee, trying to read what she wasn't saying out loud. 'But can we do it bit by bit? Everything is... too much right now and I keep getting overwhelmed and then my brain shuts down. Is that... is that okay?'

'Of course, babe. Look, let's sit down and I can tell you about me, about you. Whatever. Okay? Just ask. I will tell you anything you want to know. Then when you know me, know us, then we can go from there, eh? How does that sound?'

'Thank you.' Beth reached out her hand to Dee, who took it in hers and gave it a friendly squeeze. Beth knew that she wasn't wholly ready to hear the answers to all she was about to ask, but there was something about the way Dee was with her, friendly in a way that felt she'd known her a long time, without expectation or pressure, that felt natural. Like a sister might be. It felt like the best fit of anything since she'd woken up in the hospital, and she was beyond grateful that the universe or whatever had made Beth open up that message thread. Though there was a ball in the pit of her stomach from the last messages that Dee had written before she replied today. She had been genuinely frightened for her and she seemed relieved to find her unharmed, amnesia notwithstanding. What did she know about Beth's life that she didn't?

'Let's go through,' Beth said, ushering Dee into the living room. Something made her reach behind her and put the chain on the door, her instinct telling her that Rob would not be pleased to find Dee here if he returned sooner than expected.

They sat down, Dee on the chair, Beth on the sofa at right angles to it, the coffee table between them. Beth closed her eyes for a moment. Everything was exhausting. Nothing felt quite *right* and hadn't done since she'd woken up. Though somehow, this silence did not feel like all the others. There was no tension. The atmosphere was heavy but not between them, merely in expectation of all they were about to discuss.

'So I guess... I don't know how I know you.' Beth smiled at Dee. 'And I'm really confused and... lost and... I don't know what's going on or anything right now. But... I know something isn't right here. Rob... I don't know how to feel around him. He scares me sometimes. Which is why I messaged you. Cos I feel like you know why he might? I'm hoping that perhaps you might be able to help me. This feels weird as I feel like I'm asking a stranger to help in a really messy situation, but we're... we're friends?'

'We are that. You're my sister from another mister, babe. I

can't even begin to tell you how scared I've been looking for you. No one would tell me anything, and I knew something wasn't right. But you really don't remember anything?'

'Nope. My last memory was of being at home, in Australia, with my parents. My head thinks I never left.'

'Wow. Okay.' Dee looked shocked as she let this information settle. 'Let me start at the beginning then, shall I? Shall I tell you how we met? Would that help? I can't quite imagine how weird it's got to be to know no one and nothing about the life you're living in. That's got to be seriously stressful.'

Beth's eyes welled up as she nodded her agreement. 'It's been difficult. That's an understatement. It's like standing on sand dunes on a windy day. Nothing under my feet is solid.'

'Typical Aussie, making it about the beach!' Dee laughed, deep and throaty, which immediately made Beth feel relaxed. She recognised that laugh.

'I guess so!'

'Right. Well, I'll start at the beginning. We met at a playgroup. I work as a nanny and I was there with the kids I was looking after at the time. They were happily getting on with some craft, enjoying getting properly messy, and you crashed through the door with your two in a double buggy looking as though you'd had the morning from hell, so I went over and said hi and got you a cup of tea.'

Immediately, Beth felt a rock in her stomach. What on earth was Dee talking about?

'With my two...' Beth stared at Dee, wide-eyed and panicked.

Dee looked at her, puzzled and concerned. 'Babe, I know you said you don't remember, but does that mean... that you don't remember... having the twins?'

Beth looked up at Dee, covertly, to see what her game was,

what she was trying to achieve here. A heat was creeping over Beth's skin as a wave of nausea crashed over her. What in the ever-loving fuck was going on? *Twins?*

'I... I don't *have* twins. I'm not a mum. I... I don't remember, no, but I *would* remember that! Of course I would. I'm not a monster! But I'm not a mother either. So... I think we're done here. I don't know what you're playing at or what you're trying to do...'

'Rob hasn't mentioned anything about them? Why they're not here?'

'No, why would he...'

'He's their *dad?*' Dee said incredulously.

It's just... he's their dad. And he's not all bad. The message Beth had sent echoed back at her. What was going on?

Dee was open-mouthed in shock. She said nothing for a moment.

'So, Rob seriously hasn't said anything about them at all? Henry and Amelia? Your twins.'

'Stop it! STOP it!'

Dee held up her hands. 'Look. Sorry, sorry. This is just... low, even for him. Look...' she said, getting out her phone. 'I've got photos. Let me show you?' She started swiping through her photos until she found one. 'Do you... do you want to see?' she said, proffering it to Beth.

'Fine,' Beth said. She'd look, know this was all a mistake and clear everything up. Maybe she'd worked as a nanny too. Maybe she'd been babysitting. Maybe...

She took the phone from Dee and looked. There was a photo of her, looking pretty much as she did now, with two children sat on her lap. One boy and one girl, about two or three if she had to guess. At first, Beth barely glanced at them, but then she looked again and she saw it. How the boy was the spitting image of her brother when he was little. How he had the same little pixie ears and cheeky grin. How the girl was like looking at a photo of herself from her childhood. Her whole body went rigid. Her windpipe felt as though it suddenly had a hand around it squeezing it tight, and as much as she gasped, she couldn't get her body to take in any air. Then suddenly, as though a switch had been flipped, Beth was hyperventilating, her breath coming in short sharp bursts as she tried so hard not to dissolve into hysteria. Everything was wrong, so wrong. She whimpered, trying to keep it all together.

She was a mother. She had been a mother. Those children had been hers.

Dee leapt from the chair and squished herself alongside Beth on the sofa, flinging her arms around Beth and holding her tightly as she cried.

'It's okay. It's going to be okay. We will fix this,' she whispered into her hair as she tucked her head underneath her own chin and held her as though she was a child. She did not let go until Beth's tension eased and her breath settled. 'It is going to be okay, love. I promise.'

'How? *How?*'

'Because, babe, I won't let it not be.'

Dee was so forceful, so determined, that Beth believed her, no matter that she couldn't see how. She nodded and sniffed.

'Rob said... Rob said the children in the accident. The ones in the newspaper. They died. He said...'

'No.' Dee shook her head vehemently. 'No one died. Everyone was okay. The person most injured was you, babe. The kids are fine. They are absolutely fine. I've seen them. I promise you this, babe. I promise.'

What? How? Beth's mind couldn't keep up.

'So... the police don't want to...'

'No. No police. What on earth has Rob told you?'

'That I… that the children, not *our* children, but *the* children, died. And it was my fault.'

'He said *what*? I'll kill him, I'll bloody kill him,' Dee yelled in frustration.

She was as angry as Beth was numb. So much was happening that her body felt like it was shutting down. This information wasn't going in even if the truth of it had settled on her.

'Okay. Tell me more. I need to know more.'

Dee sat back from her a little but kept her hand on Beth's knee. A reassuring presence.

'Are you sure?'

'I am.'

I need to know everything. Whether I like it or not.

'Okay.' Dee cleared her throat. 'You have a set of non-identical twins. Amelia, or Ammy, and Henry. They're three. I know where they are right now and I have laid eyes on them. They are safe, I promise. I will get to the details in a moment but for now I want you to know this. They are okay. Right?'

'Amelia and Henry. Those were my grandparents' names.' Beth smiled. A connection, something from past to present. It felt strange. It felt *good*.

'And that's how I met you? Because I have children?' Beth said, trying the words out on her tongue, as disorientating as they felt.

'Right. We met at playgroup. You were a first-time mum of twins with a hands-off husband and no family support. You didn't know anyone else with children. To be honest, you didn't know many people at all, as you'd moved here from London when you were pregnant. You picked the playgroup both brilliantly and poorly.'

'How do you mean?' Beth looked at her, confused.

'Well, in a nutshell, the other mums there were bitches. All insta blah, image-obsessed, activewear-clad, tribal bullshit people. You know, the sort of so-called friend who judges your every decision and resents you if you make different choices to them. There was a real mum/nanny divide too, which is just rude. Like, I'm not *less* than you just cos these kids aren't mine. You're young, like me, younger than them, and they didn't like that either. Anyway, poor choice for making mum friends, but brilliant choice cos you met me.'

Beth smiled. She clearly had liked Dee then and she could see why now. She was honest and funny, took no prisoners but was kind with it.

'It seems so.'

'We got chatting that first day and your two and my two seemed to enjoy hanging out together, so we met up the next week and the next and we sort of went from there. We sometimes ditched the playgroup and its awful tea altogether and would just hang out in parks. Away from all the judgy mums, I'd like to think I helped you see how important you were. You are.'

Beth felt a familiar sensation, unworthiness, wash over her.

'Did I not feel important?'

Dee shook her head sadly.

'Babe, Rob took you for granted. As far as it seemed to me, he'd met you in London when you were having this amazing life experience travelling away from home, snared you, charmed you, moved you in when Covid hit, got you pregnant, then shipped you up here away from everyone and everything you knew and married you against your family's wishes. You were utterly isolated. You were lonely, homesick and overwhelmed. And who wouldn't be? Children are hard work. Twins are harder still. Two babies, one pair of hands, it doesn't take a genius to work that out, but it seemed Rob thought it more important to be at work, forging his career "for the family", but leaving all the caring for that family and for him to you. Like, expecting you to cook dinner for him when he got home when you'd had two hours' sleep. Complaining that the house was messy. Asking when you were going to drop the baby weight. Drop the dead weight of him, more like.'

'So we... weren't happy?'

Dee laughed a cold laugh that said it all. 'Sorry, babe. Sorry, that wasn't kind of me.'

Beth shook her head. She wanted to know. 'It's okay. I just need to know, you know?'

'I do, babe. But you've gone through a lot and I don't want to just load things on you like this. Like, you don't even remember giving birth to them...'

Beth scrunched her eyes closed, wiling herself to remember something, anything, then a realisation hit her. Her mind might not remember, but her *body* would. You couldn't carry and birth twins and there to be no sign of that. Even as a relatively young mother, there was only so far she could 'bounce back'. She leapt up from the sofa and ran up the stairs to the bathroom.

'Beth? Beth, are you okay?' Dee called as she followed her.

In a frenzy, Beth stripped off her clothes, barely noticing the chill in the all-white bathroom as she did so. She stood in front of the mirror over the sink and looked at her reflection. She was twenty-nine. She knew that. Her body would look twenty-nine, not twenty-four. She was prepared for that. She had barely even noticed what she looked like before now, barely glimpsed in the mirror or looked down in the shower. Her face had been changed with age and by what would no doubt be a character-adding scar on her forehead. She simply hadn't wanted to see.

Now her body was the mirror to the truth. And there it was, staring back at her.

Her stomach, soft and slightly doughy and covered in stretch marks. All across her hips, which could be from puberty but also right across, around her belly button. A stomach that had been inflated and then deflated, skin that had stretched taut across a body carrying twins. Her breasts, stretch-marked also, and with a slight sag to them that she knew from magazine articles about post-natal bodies was a tell-tale sign of breastfeeding. The upper, rounded part reduced, flattened. The nipples, darkened and not returned to their original colour. Beth looked at herself and she knew.

She had been a mother.

She could see it. She knew it. But she didn't *feel* it. What was wrong with her?

'Beth?' Dee called from outside the door. 'Can I come in?'

Beth grabbed her T-shirt and pulled it back over her head. She slumped onto the cold floor. This was insane. This was literally insane.

'Sure.'

Dee popped her head round and looked at Beth, her face a picture of empathy and sorrow on behalf of her friend. 'You okay? I mean, you're not, I get that, but—'

'Where are they? How are they?'

Her children.

Beth felt bad for not asking this first, but when you needed to know *everything*, where did you start? Beth needed more than ever now to know that she could trust Dee, but even with this smallest of conversations, her instincts were telling her that she could. She had to. What other choice did she have?

Dee nodded. 'Like I said, they're okay. Well, as okay as you can be when you're two and your mother disappears.'

Beth winced. Even without a memory of who the children were, she could feel their pain as though it were her own. 'Where are they?'

'At home. In your house,' Dee said plainly.

'My house? Home? But this...?' Beth looked around her, as if to remind herself how little this place had ever felt like home to her. She had assumed that this was just part of her healing, just one of many things that she had lost from her memory. But then... 'I... I don't live here, do I? I've never lived here?'

Dee shook her head. 'It's her house.'

Beth wrinkled her nose in confusion. 'Whose?'

Dee took a deep breath. She pursed her lips, clearly considering what to say and how to say it. She looked at the floor.

'*Whose*?' Beth urged.

'Natasha. The woman who currently has your children. The woman Rob was cheating on you with.'

'What? He wha—'

Suddenly, a wave of heat rose up the back of Beth's neck as it flushed her face. She stood up quickly, getting to the sink before she was violently sick, then she slumped back down into a pile on the cold, tiled floor, pushing her thumbs into her eye sockets until it hurt. She needed to feel something other than her emotions, and pain was the fastest replacement.

Every new piece of information Beth discovered felt like it broke everything else apart. She had started off discovering that she was married, then a mother, and now? A discarded woman?

Just what the bloody hell was Rob playing at?

14

Beth was resting her forehead on the cool side of the bath, trying to quell the sickness that kept coming, wave after wave. Her stomach was empty, she knew that by the way it hurt, like it was being pulled in too many directions at once as she had dry-heaved over the sink again and again. There was nothing but bile left, which burned her throat as it rose into her mouth. It was bitter and clung to her tongue.

Every time she tried to get up, another wave hit her and she had to hold onto the side to stop herself from retching. Her throat felt raw, and she just wanted everything to stop. Leave her alone. Not for the first time, she wished she had not woken up from the coma. Life since then had been all different kinds of intolerable. A half-life, a half-mind, she a half-person with much of herself missing. The more she learned of what she had lost, the more she wondered if knowing the truth was going to be worth it. Maybe she should simply slink away. Maybe she should have stayed in the ditch.

But now that was no longer a possibility. She had a responsibility.

She knew now that she had children. Children who were alive. Alive and well and being looked after by her husband's *mistress*. A stranger to them. Unless? Peter had said he'd heard children playing in the garden. Had Rob taken his children with him while he betrayed his wife? This time, her sickness was overridden by anger. How *dare* he. What in the holy hell did he think he was playing at? Both then and now? What on earth was he doing? Beth forced herself to stand up, legs wobbly, head pounding. She steadied herself with a hand on the wall before moving back to the sink and running the cold tap until the water was freezing. She splashed it on her face, ran her palms across the back of her neck, feeling the icy temperature cool her skin, making her feel immediately more awake. She cupped her hands together and then drank from them, rinsing the acid taste from her mouth.

As she stood up, she looked at her reflection in the mirror over the sink. She was pale, and dark circles ringed her eyes. She did not look well. She did not look happy. She did not look like *her*. The person that she knew she was, that she had been. Beth knew she had been strong, excited by life, adventurous even if she had been shy at times; she had always been one to grasp life with both hands. How did she end up here, trapped by her cheating husband, being kept away from her own children, in a house belonging to someone who clearly had no sense of sisterhood whatsoever?

From somewhere, Beth heard her mother, in her mind again.

This will not do, lovey. This will not do at all. Stand up and be counted.

Beth sniffed away her tears and nodded in silent agreement with her mother who, according to Rob, no longer cared. She did not believe him. She no longer believed a single word he said. He had lost his power over her. She would not take this.

'You okay?' Dee said. She had been sat, silently, in solidarity and support with Beth in the bathroom. No expectation, just friendship. Beth needed that now more than ever.

'I'm okay.'

'I'm so sorry,' Dee said, looking pained. 'I shouldn't have been so blunt. You're still recovering. This must all be overwhelming,' she said as they walked back downstairs. 'I'm just' – she glanced back at the front door – 'aware we don't have much time.'

'Before Rob is back?'

'Exactly. I don't want to freak you out, but you do need to know the truth. You deserve it, even if the truth is painful.'

Beth let out a long, slow breath. She looked at her hands, white and shaking, and suddenly a realisation came to her. This feeling of betrayal, of the grief and rage that accompanied it – this was not new to her. She recognised it. Then, oddly, a smell of burnt toast came to mind. And suddenly a scene flashed into her head.

Beth was standing at the kitchen counter, a child on each hip, both bawling, hungry, over-tired, cranky. She looked at the clock. Six p.m. The absolute worst hour of the day. She could see herself – greasy hair pulled back into a bun, smears of God knows what on her top placed there by little toddler fingers. Her face was taut, drained, free of make-up but coated in stress. Her heart rate rocketing as she tried to think straight.

'It's okay, poppets. Dinner will be ready soon. Nice and easy. Toasty toast fingers. Then bath and bed for everyone. It's all okay,' she said to herself. 'Daddy will be home soon,' she said as she glanced at the door, willing Rob to come through it so at least she had a spare hand somewhere to do something, *anything* properly. He'd been coming home later and later recently, often getting back after the children were asleep. He'd weave through the door, sometimes having been for drinks with colleagues, and immediately try to drape himself over her. Often she would find herself gritting her teeth with resentment as he'd offload the stresses of his day onto her, trying to use her body as a relief without so much as asking about her own day, without so much as seeing the tension on her own face. She'd never in a million years imagined that she'd be a lie-back-and-think-of-England wife, but sometimes she didn't have the energy either to engage or to refuse. Sometimes it was simpler all round to just relent.

Waiting for the toast to be ready, her mind had wandered, too tired for proper focus, until the smell of burning came to her. She turned to see smoke billowing from the toaster.

'Shit.'

Beth tried to reach for it to turn it off but whichever way she tried, the little hands reached for it too.

'No, darling. It's hot. Hot,' she said, trying to twist them away from it but still reach for it herself. Two or three times she tried before admitting defeat and walking quickly away from the toaster to put the children down somewhere safe. How long had she programmed the toaster for? Smoke was filling the room now, and the alarm went off, a painful, high-pitched beeping which made both children burst into tears. With one eye on the kitchen counter, Beth moved to put one then the other into the highchairs at the kitchen diner table and was just strapping them in when the front door opened, and Rob came striding into the house.

'What the hell?' he shouted as he ran into the kitchen, taking in the scene in front of him. Two yelling children, a room filled with smoke, an alarm ringing insistently and his wife, a wreck of a woman, tears streaming down her face, trying to fasten a highchair strap with trembling hands. Beth caught the look of disgust on his face as he then ran to the toaster, unplugged it, nudging it from underneath the kitchen cupboard to avoid any more heat damage, before grabbing tongs, removing the blackened charred bread and dumping it in the sink. He opened the window and wafted a tea towel under the alarm sensor before pressing the reset button to stop the screeching noise.

The sudden halting of the alarm shocked the children into silence and the room pulsed with it. Beth stood, breathing hard, trying against all odds to control the frustration and anger, the guilt and the total exhaustion flooding out of her. She was trying hard to calm herself down. Rob was not trying anything of the sort.

'What in God's name, Beth? Are you trying to burn down the goddamn house? With fucking toast? *Toast?* Hardly going to win mother of the year with that, are you? What is wrong with you? Why can't you keep it together? I work so hard and I come home to absolute fucking chaos!'

Beth thought she would cry but when she opened her mouth to trot out the apology that she knew he was expecting, that she had uttered so many times before when she had failed to live up to his expectations, a torrent of rage spilled from her instead.

'Why can't I? *Why can't I?* Because I'm basically a single mother to two toddlers. Who are both going through separation anxiety and want to be held *all day long*. And I've one pair of arms and one pair of hands and you are *never* fucking here! You swan out the door in the morning having only got yourself ready and drop back in whenever the hell you feel like it, having had all day to yourself. You *eat* when you want to, *drink* when you want to, you get to *go to the loo* when you want to and *by your damn self!* You do *nothing* around the house, *nothing* for the children. The kids that you said *you* wanted when I wasn't so sure.' She glanced back at the children, who were staring, open-mouthed, at her. They'd never seen her shout before. 'I *need* your help!'

Rob's face had contorted itself into a sneer, as though the acrid stench of the burnt toast was still offending him.

'I *work*.'

'I *want* to work!'

'Heh, your income couldn't pay for all this,' he said, sweeping his arm proudly over the room.

'We could have got a smaller house. We'd have been fine, but *you* wanted somewhere to show off. But to who? We never see anyone!'

'*You* never see anyone.' He smirked at her.

'What did you say?' Beth's blood ran cold.

'Nothing, nothing,' he said dismissively.

'No. What did you say? Who do *you* see?'

He was silent.

'Tell me!' Beth could hear the desperation that had crept into her voice, and she knew she had lost.

'*Never* raise your voice at me! Do you hear me?' Rob said, slamming his hands down on the table with a force so hard it made the table jump up and crack down on to the tiled floor, making a *bang* that frightened the children back into tears. 'I won't have it!' he said, stepping forward, picking up his jacket, keys and phone, before pausing, looking right at her before reaching past her to the bowl on the kitchen counter where her own key was kept. He picked it up, dangled it dramatically in front of her, then left the room, slamming the front door behind him. Beth heard him turn the deadlock and she knew she was trapped. He only allowed her a front door key to come and go. All the other lockable doors to the house were controlled by him.

He had bought her a four-bedroom detached prison.

'Beth?' Dee said gently, stepping towards her and placing a hand ever so lightly on her arm. 'Beth? Are you okay?'

Beth looked up at Dee, shocked to find her standing beside her.

'I remembered something. I... a fight. Him taking my keys. My key – the only one I was allowed.' She sobbed, tears rolling down her face. 'Allowed.' She let that word, and its implications, settle as she fought to control herself.

Once she had regained her composure, Beth looked at Dee. She didn't want to see pity or even sympathy on her face. She felt stupid. Weak. Like she'd fallen for the oldest trick in the book. Fallen for a good-looking, charming man who had promised to treat her like his English rose, his princess, had promised her a life she'd known only from the movies she'd watched growing up, only to find herself like Cinderella before her prince, not after. Trapped, alone, powerless and right now, being lied to on such a scale it made her breathless. As Beth sat with this a moment, she felt a shift. Her humiliation transmuted into something more palpable. Something she could work with.

Rage.

'How did I let it happen?' she said, her jaw clenched so hard her teeth hurt.

'Truthfully?'

Beth nodded.

'You know how you can't eat a whole cake in one sitting because you'd feel sick? But if you took a small bite every time you walked past it over the course of a day, you'd eat the whole thing and feel mostly okay?'

Beth tipped her head to one side. 'What do you mean?'

Dee put her palms up in front of her, a sort of surrender gesture.

'This is just my perspective, okay? Things always look different from inside a relationship than from outside it. We all see different things and interpret them differently. Okay? I'm not judging you here cos this is not your *fault*. The only one I'm judging is that dick of a husband of yours.'

Beth laughed, though she wasn't sure where the humour had come from. 'Okay. Tell me everything,' she agreed, urging Dee to continue. She was hoping that if Dee gave her more information, then more memories might come back to her. It would be overwhelming if they all came back at once, but at least she'd be herself again.

'Right. So when we met, you'd already moved from London, away from all your friends. You'd stopped working as a freelance photographer to look after the babies, so you had no colleagues. Your family are on the other side of the world and time differences are hard when you've got to sleep whenever you can because, well, twin babies. So you're basically alone.'

Beth felt the weight of this sorrow immediately. Her family missing out on the early years of her babies, their first grandchildren, while she struggled without them. Even without her memories of this time, she knew that was how she would have felt.

'We met and you had no one to talk to. He controlled the money and said you needed to economise now you were down to one salary and so your smart phone had to go. He needed *his* for work, of course, but you had a pay-as-you-go dumb brick. You hated it, not only because the camera was awful! You had all this skill, beautiful babies, and your photos of them were grainy and shit.'

'He said all my photos were lost. A backup error or something. You don't think he... he's deleted them? Their childhoods – gone?' She felt sick. She might never recover those memories. The twins might never have baby photos of themselves to be embarrassed by when little or to treasure as adults.

'I don't know. I'd hope not, but, well, I wouldn't put it past him. I remember once suggesting we go for coffee after playgroup, a decent one, and you said you didn't have any cash. You told me that you had a bank account but once there was no money coming into it, he said it made sense to close it down. So your money only came from him, in cash. He wanted to see receipts of what you spent it on so that he could "budget properly". You were utterly dependent on him financially for yourself and for the children.'

'Wow. That's... Why would I agree to that?'

'What alternative did you have? He had all the important paperwork locked up "safely"' – she made quotation marks with her fingers – 'but that meant you no longer had access to your passport. No ID. You couldn't open your own account if you wanted to.'

'I had my driver's licence though...'

'We'd just managed to get that back. He'd hidden it. He insisted on knowing your passwords for social media accounts and emails and he used to check them. The ones he knew about, that is.'

'Is that why I've got the old Facebook account? The one I messaged you from?'

'Exactly.'

'You saw all this happening? Did I see it?'

'Not at first. You had this image in your head that he'd saved you. That he was your saviour.'

'Saved me? From what?'

'You'd left Australia in a flourish about making your own way in England and it wasn't going so well when you first met him. You'd been earning minimum wage in a shit job and trying to break into photography any time you weren't working. You met him and then, not long after, Covid hit and everything fell apart. He let you move in with him, and he supported you when your job disappeared. You felt that he was being chivalrous in looking after you, that he had your best interests at heart and that you... well, you *owed* him.'

'But I'm not like that – I've never fallen for any scams. I'm too cynical!'

Dee raised her eyebrows and nodded in agreement. 'Yeah. That's why it's so effective, isn't it? We don't want to believe that *we'd* fall for that trap. That we'd be too clever, too wise, too *smart*. But it doesn't work like that, babe. He used your insecurities against you, to make his own feel less overwhelming. If he controlled you, then he was in control of something. Your weakness made him feel strong.'

Beth looked pained. She knew something wasn't right, but was it this? Truly? What if Dee was making all this up? Beth knew that she wasn't the type of person to give up her agency like that, pandemic or not.

As if Dee could read her mind, she continued. 'Look, like I said, I know this is a lot to take in. You don't know me as much as you don't know him. But... I'm worried.' She wrinkled her brow. 'No, it's more than that. I'm *scared* for you, Beth.'

Beth inhaled sharply. 'Scared?'

'Yeah. Look at what we *know*. At what *you* know. You are married to Rob. You have two children who were in the car with you when you had the accident. They're okay thankfully – the combination of a good crumple zone, rear-facing car seats, and the fact that the car behind you wasn't speeding. They had nothing more than shock and a bruise or two. They kept them in overnight and that's all. So why is Rob keeping them from you? Why is he lying to you about them? To whose benefit? Theirs? Yours? Or his?'

'I... I don't know. I...' She had almost forgotten about the children in this; it was still alien to her that they even existed. Guilt flooded her.

'And more than that, the accident itself. I was so worried because you tried calling me, but I didn't see the phone. You sent a voice note but it didn't make sense. You were all over the place, talking about leaving now, you had to go now, that you'd fill me in later but that there wasn't time. I tried calling you back, but I guess you were driving by then. Other than that, I don't know much more than you.'

Beth nodded. 'Oh, one thing was that the car garage was meant to have sent a letter about the airbag. Apparently it needed replacing.'

'Exactly. Why didn't they? Or perhaps, if they *had* sent it, then who would they have sent it to?'

'Well, to Rob, cos the car is registered—'

'To him. Yes.' Dee's face was stony, her eyebrow raised as she waited for Beth to fill in the blanks.

'You're saying... he *knew* but didn't say anything?'

Dee said nothing.

'He didn't mention it because... he didn't care?'

Dee crossed her arms in front of her. 'That's what I think. He is an insecure, nasty, selfish piece of work. And while I don't necessarily think he wanted you to get hurt like you did, he did let you drive you and your kids around in a car that wasn't safe. Because it suited him to feel like he was getting one over you.'

Beth let out a long, slow exhale through pursed lips. This was just beyond... Wasn't it?

'So, say this is all true. What... what does he want now? Why is he doing this?'

'I don't know for sure, babe. His thinking doesn't make sense to me. But I'm scared of him, for you. I'm scared for you. If he will let you drive around in a knackered car, if he will *lie* to you about the fact your children even *exist* and keep them from you, and lie to you about what your life actually looks like, pretending to start afresh with you, then I don't know what he will do. And that terrifies me because from what you told me before, he has a whole lot of temper on him too. He doesn't like losing – what he sees as losing anyway – and he has no problem with playing dirty.'

'And the kids? Are they safe? Amelia and Henry? Are they safe with...' It still felt so odd to be saying their names, but there was a flicker, a spark of something inside Beth that was beginning to recognise that this was real. A maternal care for them.

'With Natasha? I think so. I went to your house looking for you and they were there with *her*. Natasha may be the other woman but from the little I saw, she was being kind with them. Everything changes so fast when you're small, and children often just accept what they've been told. I don't know what her game in this is yet, but it seems she's looking after them well.'

'That's something, I guess? What have they told them? About me?'

'I don't know. I'm sorry. But they didn't look distressed; they were clean, relaxed. They seemed okay. Happy enough around her.'

Beth took this in. Did they think she'd abandoned them? Did they think she was dead? Would they even have a concept of what that was? Probably not. Suddenly, her rage was back. Who the hell did he think he was?

'What's to stop me just walking out of here now with you,

turning up at my actual home and demanding he give me the kids? I can just do that! I should do that! I can go and get them right now! Make you take me to them!' she yelled as she turned around, deciding what she needed to take with her, before realising she had no keys, no wallet, no phone; nothing. Her energy dropping again, she turned to look at Dee, whose face was pinched.

'On one hand, nothing. If that's what you want to do right now, I will take you there, but...'

'But?'

'He has a plan, even if we don't know what it is yet. He's mean, babe. He's calculating, he's controlling. There's no way he doesn't have a plan. You? You are just out of hospital, you're recovering. You have ongoing medical appointments and...' Dee bit her tongue.

'And? Be blunt with me, Dee, we don't have time for anything else.'

'You have nothing. No money, no family, no home. No memory. He and you are equal parents, legally. And right now, if a judge had to pick who to give the care of the children to, well, I don't think it would be you. He would win. And then you'd have an even bigger battle on your hands. But also, think of them. They need you back, yes, but not like this. Not in a storm of rage and half-recalled memories.'

Beth sank to the sofa, all of her fight draining from her in an instant. Dee was right. What was she thinking? That she could just rock up, demand and be given the children she didn't remember having, after causing an accident in which, thank God, they were unharmed? Or that she could insist her husband, who on the surface had been nothing but dedicated to her care and recovery, get out of the family home and leave her in sole charge of them? Even she could see how ridiculous that was.

'And while I don't want to piss on your parade, you and I both know that leaving a partner is a dangerous time. We have to... be careful.'

'So I... do what?' Beth whispered, her hopeless situation seeming even more so now.

Dee smiled at her, warm and supportive. 'You get smart.'

'How do you mean?'

'I mean, you know now something that he doesn't. You've remembered something from your past. You *know* about the twins. You *know* he's lying to you about your kids. You *know* about Natasha. You *know* he has a plan in mind. So your job now is to do three things.'

'Three things?'

'One: keep yourself safe. Two: find out what he wants. What he's planning. Three...'

'Three?'

'Stop him.'

It all sounded so simple. Beth wanted to believe that it was; she wanted to believe that Dee wasn't lying, like she had come to believe that Rob was lying. Everything felt so smoke and mirrors, like nothing might be true. She ached again for her family, at the knowledge that her mum wouldn't get her message for another ten days. *Ten days.*

How much could go wrong in ten days?

15

Beth and Dee were just working out the next step for them both when the landline rang. Beth jumped – it was a sound she had not experienced in all the time she had been back from the hospital. She had had no visitors other than David, the nurse, no phone calls, no contact with anyone but Rob and her brief chat with Peter next door. Who on earth would be calling? Her nerves jangled as she tried to decide what to do.

'Are you going to answer it?' Dee said, looking surprised at Beth's delay.

'Um... do you think I should?'

'See what I mean? He's got you questioning whether you should answer your own phone.'

'Ouch,' Beth said as she marched over to the handset, picking it up just as it seemed to stop ringing.

'Beth? What took you so long? What were you doing?'

'It's Rob,' she mouthed at Dee. Dee's eyebrows lifted.

'I... didn't know where the phone was. Took me a while to find it.'

Rob laughed. 'Oh, Pooks, you are a ditz sometimes, honestly.

Look, I just wanted to check in with you, make sure you're okay. I'm stuck at work, an impromptu meeting. I'll be back later.'

Beth tried to keep the relief from her voice. 'Oh. Okay.'

'You could pop my dinner in the oven if you wanted.'

'Oh. Sure. Righto.'

'Are you okay? You sound... different.'

'No, no, I'm fine. Just some birds squawking outside, that's all. Distracted me.'

'Fine. Okay. I'll be back as soon as I can. Love you. Bye.'

'Bye.'

Knowing what she now knew, what Dee had told her, Beth couldn't echo Rob's sentiments. He'd hear the venom in them if she did.

'All okay?' Dee asked.

'Yeah. Rob's going to be back late.'

'Oh good. That gives us a bit more time.'

But to do what? Beth thought. She couldn't work out where to go from here. It felt like she was in a pool with high sides, no steps, no way of getting out, and all she could do was tread water and try not to drown.

'I was thinking,' Dee said, 'I could get you a phone so that we can keep in touch. It won't be fancy but it should be enough. I can look into legal support and how to get you separate finance. For now, you've got to convince Rob you're on board and get him to let his guard down. He's after something, he has to be. But I'm here for you, I'm on your side. I won't let him do this, I won't let him destroy you.'

Beth reached forward and pulled Dee to her, holding her tightly, desperately. She was all she had between her and God knows what Rob had planned. She felt overwhelmed, scared, grateful for Dee.

'Take me to them?'

'What?'

'The children. I need to see them. It... it still doesn't feel real and I feel awful that I can't remember them even being here. Rob won't be back until after dinner and he always expects dinner at seven sharp. That gives us' – she looked up at the clock on the wall – 'at least three hours. We have time.'

Dee looked concerned. 'I'm not sure. What if...'

'Please. *Please.* For me. For them.'

'You can't just ambush them, Beth.'

'No, I know. I don't mean to *meet* them as such. I know I can't rush that. I don't know what they've been told, what they know or anything, and having them see me might cause issues right now. Even without any maternal instinct I can see that much. But I need to *see* them, to know they're real.'

Beth knew she was likely being beyond paranoid, but it had occurred to her that photos could be manipulated, couldn't they? Was the photo that Dee had shown her even real? Was Dee to be trusted? She wanted to see actual, real-life children, children with a face like hers, to know that it was *true.*

'Okay. If you promise not to rush at them or whatever. I can take you to her house. To your house. To where I think they'll be, and we can keep our distance. But we have to be careful. Okay?'

'Promise.'

'Fine. Though... Do you have a key? For here?'

'A back door one, yes. We can get out round the back.'

'Okay. Let's go. We'll have to be quick.'

Beth couldn't stop her feet from tapping as Dee drove them out of the village and out towards town. She was nervous being somewhere other than the house, where it was possible that Rob would return and find her gone.

Would that be so bad? Maybe she should just run, hole up

in a hotel somewhere and wait for her mum to reply. Though she had no way of paying for a hotel. And once there, no way of accessing her emails having put the laptop back as she had found it. She was nervous because she knew from what Rob had said that the fastest route out of here took the same road that the accident had happened on, and she would be going past the site where her life had been turned upside down.

Most of all, she was nervous because she was going to set eyes on her children. It didn't escape Beth how strange this was. Normally, you have time. Time to get used to a pregnancy, time to meet your children as they enter the world and get to know them. These would be ready made, rambunctious kids. She hoped that she would recognise them as her own blood, that some bond would pull her to them, memory or not. She was terrified that she would look at them and feel nothing, beyond a basic humanity. Was that why Rob was keeping them apart? To avoid the psychological damage that could do to a young child, or to delay her own recovery? Was he actually doing the right thing, mistress or not?

The journey passed in a blur, and if they passed the site of the accident, Dee didn't say and Beth didn't notice, and soon enough they pulled up in a cul-de-sac of what looked like 1960s houses with gardens at the front.

'Here we are,' Dee said.

Beth surveyed the street, hoping that *her* house, *her* home, would immediately be clear to her, but they all looked the same. A large window at the front at ground level, with two smaller windows above. Some gardens had roses in them, lovingly cared for, others had grass that could do with cutting. And in the corner garden, where the road curved, there was a woman, tall with dark hair, and two small children playing with a mini trampoline.

'Is that them?'

'Yes. That's them, and that's... *Natasha* with them.'

Beth was surprised by the disdain in Dee's voice, but then she felt good, like it showed how much she was on Beth's side in this. She was furious on her behalf like a good friend would be.

'Did I ever mention any friends from home?'

'Eh? That's a pivot. You want to talk about this now?'

'Sorry, it just came into my head and sometimes if I don't say it, it doesn't stick and the chance is gone.'

'Ah, yeah, I see. Well, no, not really. You said most of your friends were still working and partying and didn't really have much in common with you any more. None had kids like you. Like you had these.' She pointed back at the children, apparently trying to make Beth focus on the task in hand.

'Can we get any closer?'

Dee crinkled her nose. 'I can try but we ought not to get too close, in case Natasha sees the car.'

'She doesn't know me, or you, though?'

Dee nodded. 'She doesn't know me well but... Okay, I'll nudge a little closer, but two grown women sat in the car just looking and not getting out might look weird, so not for long, okay?'

'Sure.'

Dee moved them a couple of houses closer and then pulled over and turned the engine off. The children and Natasha hadn't seemed to notice them so Beth could just sit and watch.

It was surreal. It was like watching one of her dad's fuzzy home movies from the nineties of her and her brother playing outside in the yard. Sure, the sky wasn't a blazing blue and she and Ben weren't twins, but the genetic link was clear to see. These *were* her children. So why didn't she *feel* anything? She was ashamed of herself. She was looking at her babies and she was numb. She had expected, hoped, feared that she would have a surge of maternal love and that Dee would have to physically restrain her from leaping out of the car and going to them. But she felt nothing.

'Beth?'

'Take me back.'

'What do you mean?'

'I can't be here.'

'You don't want to see them more? Look, Ammy is running around after Henry. They're giggling like little idiots.'

'They don't miss me. They don't need me.'

'You're their *mother.*'

'Am I?'

'Beth. What's wrong?'

'I don't remember them. I... I feel nothing. No connection at all. They're just... kids.' Her voice was ice.

'Really?'

'What do you mean?'

'I don't want to overstep.'

Beth turned abruptly to face Dee. What was she talking about now? What else did Beth not know? *How* could there be more?

'Do overstep. Step away,' she spat.

'Babe.' Dee took Beth's hand in hers as she turned towards her so that they were facing each other. She glanced nervously across the street to where the children were playing, but they had been undetected. 'You had post-natal depression when you had the babies. It's quite common in mothers of twins. Partly because it's *harder*. You told me that when they were born, you felt nothing. Numb. That you felt that they weren't really yours.'

Beth gasped.

'Might you be remembering *that*? Rather than actually

feeling that now? Like an echo or something? I don't know how memories coming back works but, might that be it? You've found out so much today, I'd not be surprised if you're exhausted, low, terrified. Much like you were when you gave birth.'

Maybe that was it. Maybe she wasn't a horrible, unfeeling mother. Maybe she had just reached all she could emotionally cope with today. Maybe she needed time to let this all really sink in.

'What's Natasha like?'

'Um... I don't know. I barely know her.'

Something in Dee's tone made Beth uneasy. What was she withholding? She was getting used to what people sounded like when they lied to her. Did anyone ever just tell the damn truth?

'Are my children truly safe with her?'

'Yes, I've said this already,' Dee said emphatically. 'I know she's a decent person.'

'Other than sleeping with my husband.'

'Well, other than that.'

'Take me home. Rob and I need to talk.'

'What? What do you mean?'

'I mean I need to talk with my husband about why he hasn't told me about our kids. I can't live with him, in the same house, in the same *bed*, knowing this and say nothing. I can't.'

'Are you sure? Wouldn't keeping your cards to your chest be safer for now? Please be careful. Please, babe. He is a dangerous man.'

'I will be careful. There's something we don't know here. I can tell. I don't know how I can tell but I know.'

Dee looked pained.

'I won't tell him about you or about our coming here. I won't tell him everything I know. I will keep some secrets like he's kept his.'

Dee didn't look convinced. 'Okay, you're a grown woman. I can't force you. But please. Be cautious.'

'No, you can't, and he can't play me like this either. I am about to make that clear to him. I will not take this. I won't.'

They sat in mostly silence as Dee returned them both to the little house in the village that Beth now knew belonged to the woman currently living in her house, with her children, and she assumed that this was where Rob went every night, rather than for his bike ride as he'd told her. God, she'd been so stupid. She felt like she'd been asleep since the accident and it was only now that her eyes were really starting to open and see the truth.

'I'll bring a phone, as soon as I can,' Dee assured Beth as she pulled the car up to the kerb. 'I'll keep an eye on my messages. If anything happens, if he does anything, then *please* get in touch. I will be here in a heartbeat. Okay?'

'Okay. Thank you. Really, thank you.'

Beth hugged Dee and then quietly stepped back into the house, ready to sit and wait for Rob to return.

She'd have thought she'd feel horrible, scared, powerless, in an awful situation that she really only knew half of, and yet she didn't. Something had shifted. Knowledge is power, and Beth felt that. What Rob would not know was that Beth now had the knowledge of her own situation. That made her a strong adversary. But she had something more powerful than even knowledge, something that gave humans all the power, the power to raise mountains, the power to move tides.

In her children and the life she had been stepping towards before the accident. Beth had this. She had something to fight for.

16

Knowing that she had someone else on her side gave Beth a sense of bravery as she awaited Rob's return. She looked at the house now through different eyes, eyes that had been opened. It wasn't wrong that she felt no connection to where she was. This was not her home, which was why she had no memory of it. This simple truth told her that her mind wasn't broken, it was just biding its time. Only time was what Beth didn't have.

Rob would be back likely within the hour, and Beth was going to confront him. To *make* him tell her the truth and explain himself. She would put them back on an equal footing, if they'd ever been on one, and work out from there how best to extract herself from this, whether that meant leaving Rob or not. How could she stay with someone who lied to her, who was cheating on her? Who scared her? She wanted to get out.

Dee was right. Beth *could* just walk out of here. But she had nothing more than the clothes she was wearing, and she knew from so many horrific news stories that leaving a volatile man was a fraught time. Someone with a fragile ego might do awful things to retain some upper hand. She had to tread very carefully if her fear of Rob was right. When Dee had been talking about Rob, Beth had sensed that there was more to her hatred of him, but there was little time to go into that then. Beth hadn't wanted to ask for fear of the answer, and Dee hadn't wanted to overstep, it seemed. And now, it wasn't just about her anyway, was it? There were the twins to consider. It was more complicated now.

What did Rob *want* with her in this messed-up scenario? What was his goal with all of this? Why was he keeping their former life at such a distance? Had she found out about Natasha? Was that why she was so fraught driving that day? Did he want to keep the children and be rid of her but couldn't do it now while she was still recovering? Surely this would be the perfect time to make a break from her if that was what he wanted? Beth couldn't work it out. But she knew that he had a temper, and it reminded her of a guy at Beans and Brew. Beth and her work friend had liked to work out how best to wind him up and watch him blow his top. Silly, childish behaviour but now, at least, useful experience. Beth was furious with Rob and yet she needed to not show him that, not directly, not until she knew what his game was. Why on earth he had this ridiculous set up running. But she also wanted to get her own back for what he was doing to her, even if in a little way. Petty, maybe, but when she had no control at all, she wanted to take it back wherever she could. He couldn't treat her like this.

Beth walked into the kitchen. It was immaculate as it always was. She filled the kettle and switched it on, opening the cupboard above it. There was a single set of four matching mugs on one shelf, and a single set of four matching glasses up above. Knowing now that a single person, the other woman, lived here, the sparseness started to make sense. Reaching into the cupboard, she took a mug down. Then, pausing, she put one mug on the shelf with the glasses and gently closed the door. A smirk flickered across her lips which then broadened into a smile. That small detail would annoy him. Good. The whistle of the kettle brought her back to the task in hand. She heaped coffee grounds into the coffee plunger, which he insisted they call a French Press, making sure to scatter a very small amount onto the worktop. A little splashed water added to it would dry into an insignificant stain. Once she had made her coffee, she left the milk out on the counter and folded the tea towel neatly, placing it next to the kettle with a flourish rather than hanging it back up. There. Beth marvelled at how much pleasure she was getting from these microaggressions and wondered if this had become her life with Rob before the accident. Had she fought back without knowing how else to do so? He was stronger physically and seemed to hold all the cards. Sometimes you put your foot down the only way you could.

She was back in the living room, idly flicking through the TV channels, drinking coffee, when she heard the key in the lock of the front door. Thankful for the advance warning of his return, Beth jumped, then settled, reminding herself that she *had* to be calm and measured despite her anger flaring up as she looked at him. If she went full on at him, he would lose his cool for sure.

'Hey, Pooky. How are you doing? Sorry for taking so long. Work. Is dinner ready?' he said, looking into the kitchen, taking off his jacket. He wasn't looking at her.

'Hey... babe. No, I waited to see what you might like...' She struggled for the right word. Was there a name she called him like he did her? She had to stop herself from flinching every time he called her Pooky. It made her shudder. 'How was work?'

'Ah... so so. You know, fine.' He ran his hands through his hair, pulling his forehead taut. 'They said, um, they said' – his words were heavy – 'that I could take it easy while we get back onto our feet. I could come in less.' He looked at the floor. 'So I can be *here* more.' His face soured and his eye flickered just a touch when he said this.

So, not fine at all then, Beth thought. *Not great timing, but I have to talk to him now. This can't wait. His whole life just might implode in one day.* Well, then he'd know how she felt, wouldn't he?

'Sounds good. Did you want a coffee maybe? Sounds like you could do with one, and there's a fresh pot made. Why don't you grab a cup and we can talk. I need to talk with you.'

His head flicked up again, a nervous smile on it this time. 'What's that about then?'

'Go get a drink and then come join me.'

'You can't tell me now? What is it?'

'Humour me...' she said, keeping her face neutral. She had pushed all her rage, confusion and fear down into her stomach where it sat, bubbling. She would be rational about this. Despite there being nothing rational about it.

His jawline relaxed as he fake-rolled his eyes at her, a smile dawning on his face. Honestly, his mood switched so fast it was like dealing with a toddler.

Beth listened for a reaction as he walked into the kitchen. There were the sounds of Rob walking into the room, and at first, nothing. Then a loud sigh of irritation, and back to silence. Soon aggressive noises of someone cleaning up and moving things in a cupboard filtered out of the kitchen. Good. He'd noticed. Would he say anything?

She was curled up on the sofa as he came back into the room holding a cup of coffee. He looked tired. Like he needed to sleep for a week. He sat down next to her, not too close, and took a coaster from the set in the centre, before placing the cup down on it. He then moved the cup so that the handle was at the same angle as the top of the table; if he was aware of this meticulousness, he did not show it, but as Beth watched him, she knew that she'd seen him do it before, over and over. It was a thing he did. Neat lines, no clashing angles.

'So…' he said, a tone of admonition in his voice, turning to her and holding his hands together in a prayer position.

'Yes?' Beth replied, making sure to keep it light and breezy, like she did not know what was coming. If he was going to humiliate her, she was going to wind him up.

'The kitchen. I'm glad you're up and making drinks, but you know I like a neat home, don't you? There was… *mess* and… detritus all over by the kettle. Don't do that again. Clean up.' He smiled. A Tom Cruise sort of smile that was all teeth and no eye sparkle.

Widening her eyes innocently, she said, 'Oh. I'm sorry. I guess I did know that before…'

His smile fixed into a line. 'And now you know it again. See? Progress!' He laughed wildly and artificially.

He must be under such stress. Well, let's relieve him of some of his lies. 'I'm sorry, I guess I didn't think it mattered so much.'

'I just don't like it. I like coming home to a nice place. Okay?' His voice was tight, with a threat behind it.

Beth nodded. There was a knot in the pit of her stomach. Why had she thought deliberately winding him up was a good idea? She was grateful she had just chosen such a small thing. She needed to be smarter than this; she had to remember that she didn't know everything she needed to. She wanted to go off at him, but she held back.

'Okay.'

'There we go. Not so hard, was it?' He took her chin in his hand, his thumb pressing down on her jawline as he touched it. Just a fraction too hard so it hurt. 'There was one other thing.'

'Yes?'

'The cups and glasses don't live on the same shelf. Glasses on top. Cups on the bottom.'

Beth said nothing. He kept hold of her. His touch felt oppressive. There was no affection here. Was that why he had strayed?

Rob's expression glitched, just the tiniest impression of rage in between a fixed neutrality. He held his tongue between his teeth to one side of his mouth, like he was biting away his first reaction.

'See, that's how we do it, Pooky,' he said, his face suddenly all sunshine, with the dark clouds forced away. 'Now. What did you want to tell me?' He let go of her face.

Beth blinked hard as she could feel tears forming and she didn't want to let him see them. She could see an anger still simmering as he forced himself to look nonchalant while still prickling with resentment at the mess he had been forced to deal with.

She twisted her body towards him and she hoped he could not feel her trembling. She took a deep breath. *Here we go.* 'I know.'

He looked confused. 'Know what?'

She paused, seeing if he would give himself away, but his face was a picture of innocence. How dare he?

'I know. About...' Her lips were trembling. 'I know about Natasha. And the twins.' She swallowed hard as she watched the colour drain from his face. He looked horrified. *Good.*

'I...' he stuttered as he scrambled for words.

Beth felt stronger than she had done since she had woken up into this absolute chaos. She had him on the run.

'Would you care to explain why Natasha is living in my house with my children? Children you failed to tell me even bloody *existed*? What the hell are you doing? How could you?'

So much for calm.

But the rage Beth felt actually felt good. She was a mama bear protecting her cubs. She *felt* something, a spark, an ache to be with them, to have them with her so that she could love them, care for them. *Mother* them.

Rob reached for her. She flinched away.

'Don't even think about touching me,' she growled at him.

'Pooks, it's not what you think.'

'*Don't* call me Pooks. Or Pooky! I hate it. *Hate* it!' she snapped.

He looked as though she had slapped him. 'Beth...'

'What?'

He looked annoyed. 'Can you let me speak? I can explain.'

'Oh, I bet you can...'

'Beth, please.' He held his hands towards her, in an almost apologetic manner. 'Let me talk. I can explain all of this.'

'Fine.' She crossed her arms and bit her lip to stop her from commenting further. Let him dig himself into a hole. Then she could bury him in it and be done with him.

'It's true. That we have twins. Our twins.' He cleared his throat. 'How... how did you find out? No, wait. That doesn't matter for now. It's the truth. We have two beautiful children. A boy and a girl.'

'Ammy and Henry.'

'How did...'

'Go on...' she said, eyebrows raised.

'They were in the car with you when the accident happened. I swear, when the police called me, it was like the world fell apart. My whole world.' He looked so terrified. 'You were all taken to hospital, and I promise, I don't even remember the drive there, I just had to get there, you know?'

'Are you comparing my amnesia to a difficult drive?' she said pointedly.

'No. No! Just, it was awful. Horrific. You were in a coma when I arrived, but they were fine. Asking after you but fine. They were kept in overnight, and then what could I do? I needed to be in three places at once – at work, with them, and by your bedside. No one knew if you'd pull through or not. It was the worst time of my life.'

He looked genuinely distraught. Surely it would have solved all his problems if she'd died, got her out of the picture?

'It had been just us, Pooks, no grandparents, no nursery. Nothing. I couldn't do it all, I needed help.'

'So you asked your floozy? Your bit on the side?'

'My what?' he stuttered.

'Natasha – your young hot ass, to replace your tired, exhausted frumpster of a wife. You took our kids to *her*?'

His face turned red. 'What in the world are you talking about?'

Beth felt sick. Was he really going to deny this? Classic gaslighting? Really? After everything else? She pulled her shoulders back and tilted her chin upwards, looking at him defiantly.

'I am talking about your cheating on me with Natasha. I am talking about you going there *every night* when you think I'm asleep. I am talking about *giving our children to her* while I am stuck here!'

Rob looked at her, his mouth curving upwards in a smile before laughter escaped his lips.

'What?' he said incredulously.

'Do. Not. Laugh. At. Me.'

'Beth, I'm sorry. I'm just... this is ridiculous. Natasha is a *nanny*. I hired her to take care of the twins while I was with you. And when you woke up and it was clear that your recovery was going to take time, I asked if she would stay on.'

'Rob...'

'It's true! When you were in hospital, the doctors and I discussed what to tell you, what not to overload you with, and the fact that you did not remember having the children... Well, we felt it best not to freak you out. It wouldn't be fair on you but also, what about *them*? Having been involved in a terrifying accident and then to have their mother look at them like they were strangers to her? We didn't think that was good for them.'

He had a point.

'So where do they think I am?'

'We've told them that you're poorly after the accident and being looked after and you'll be home as soon as you can. They're little. They don't think days ahead.'

'But I'm not home, am I? I'm in *her* house!'

'That was Natasha's suggestion. You needed somewhere to recuperate. We didn't want to move the children out of their family home. They're recovering too, you know. And we felt it best to keep everything as normal as possible for them. She moved in and that left here empty. She said we could use it. Like a house swap, especially as I didn't have time to try to house hunt for another place with everything else going on.'

'And you don't think she's getting her feet under the table then?' Was he really that naive?

'What, by having sole care of two children? Like that's an easy ride?'

'No, I mean...'

'What, Beth? What do you mean?' His face was going redder as his surprise turned into anger. 'You think that instead of my busting my guts to look after everyone, to take care of everyone – you, the twins, my job, the house, *everything* – that I've been swanning about having an affair? That my going there every night is not so that I can see my kids, help them feel safe and secure, but so I can get my end away with the nanny? After all, it's not like I'm getting any affection here, am I?'

'I...'

'Don't think I can't see it, Beth. The way you look at me – like you're disgusted by me, you're scared of me. Do you think that's easy to deal with? We were happily married, and now suddenly I'm a stranger to you, and one you can't even hide that you don't like. All while I'm taking care of you and the family you don't remember, and trying to keep everything going? I...' He ran his hands through his hair, his eyes brimming with tears. 'You can't even let me touch you. In any way, not just in *that* way. And it *hurts*, Beth. I've lost you but you're still here.'

Beth reached out to him but couldn't do it. He was right.

'See? And now you're accusing me of cheating? Of deliberately keeping the twins from you? Like I'm some sick bastard. Who do you think I am, Beth?' He exhaled heavily as he turned his face away from her.

'You told me that the children *died*. Not ours, maybe, but you told me I was a child killer, that the police were after me. You made me think that *everyone* was looking at me in disgust. That I was a horrible, awful person. Why would you do that?'

Rob bit his lip. 'Yeah... I'm not proud of that. I... I didn't know what to say, what to tell you. I wanted to keep you here, inside, where we could look after you, where someone wouldn't ask after the kids, or you, and... honestly? I panicked. As soon as I'd said it, I realised it was a stupid thing to say, but then how could I unsay it? But yeah. I'm sorry, that was wrong, really wrong. Can you forgive me?'

He looked ashamed as he looked at her. *Could* she forgive him? She had hated herself, had wished she was the one who'd died.

'I was struggling, we both were. You know that. But it doesn't mean I'm lying now. I promise, this is the truth. You must believe me.'

She felt sick. She had taken everything that Dee had told her at face value. Why? Why had she done that? Who even was Dee? A friend – that was all Beth knew or thought she did. At least she knew *for sure* that Rob was her husband, from the photographs and all that he knew about her and what the authorities had said. But Dee? Beth had been so desperate not to feel alone that she had grasped onto Dee like she was a life float in this ridiculous storm. Had she stopped to question Dee's motives?

Beth was more confused than ever now. She hadn't even considered that Rob might not be the villain here. He had a point – what was he supposed to do? He had been trying to protect everyone and she had accused him of awful things. Were her supposed memories an extension of that? How could you trust your judgement when your memories were so mixed up and missing? Who would you know who you could trust, and who you ought not to?

Rob turned back to her. His face was calming but the hurt and affront was still clear to see.

'How did you find all this out anyway? I'd *told* you to stay home. This is why – I wanted to help you find all this out in good time, in the right way, in a healthy way.'

'I... Dee. Dee told me.'

Beth omitted the detail of finding the laptop. She still didn't wholly trust Rob, his temper. She needed to keep some things to herself.

'Oh, for fu— Her?'

'What?'

'She is a crazy, feminist nut bag that you met at some baby group. She befriended you but brought all kinds of drama to our lives. She hates men and took against me and was always convincing you of some stupid conspiracy. I can't stand her. And now this? I assume she turned up at our house, saw Natasha and made one of her usual inane assumptions? Honestly – you thought her scenario made more sense than mine?' He almost laughed, sheer disbelief in his voice.

Beth said nothing. One: she didn't want to give up the laptop, or the possibility of reaching out to her family using it; and two: she didn't know what to believe right now. Was she being lied to now by Rob or by Dee? She had remembered some awful things about Rob but she had no memories of Dee. Why couldn't people just tell the truth? Why wasn't there anyone she knew to help her navigate this hell? How on earth was she meant to focus on getting better when people who claimed to care about her kept pulling the rug out from under her feet and letting her fall?

17

'I want to meet her.'

Rob raised his eyebrows. 'I don't think that's wise right now, do you?'

'Why? What are you trying to hide?' Beth said with disdain in her voice. She was done with people withholding information for her 'own good'. She'd decide what was good for her on her own, and if she was going to work out if it was Rob or Dee who was lying to her, then she had to meet this Natasha and see for herself.

Rob sighed. 'I'm not trying to hide anything, Beth, I've told you all there is to know. You are not well. You're not *yourself*. You don't remember having the children. You seem convinced I'm some villain, and honestly, I think meeting Natasha just might send you over the edge.'

'What edge?'

'You know what I mean, Beth. The doctors said we need to take things at your own pace, not to force anything.'

'You can't keep me from them. The children.'

'I'm not trying to, Beth. But you have to think about them, not just yourself.'

Ouch.

'Are you saying I'm a bad mother? Not putting them first?'

'Now you're just putting words in my mouth. You're still fragile, unstable. Unpredictable. If you can decide to concoct a whole scenario where you're a victim of this awful betrayal, based on the words of some random woman you don't remember, then I don't necessarily think that unfettered access to our two young and vulnerable children is for the best, is it?'

Beth took a moment. He had a point about the children. Now that she knew they existed, knew they were hers, had seen them and accepted the truth of this, small details had been coming to her. She had remembered an evening, after bathtime, both of them wrapped up in those little towels with hoods, snuggled up on a big bed with her, reading stories. She couldn't hear what was said, but she could remember their smell. Warm, sweet. Almost like baby powder. Maybe it was the laundry detergent, whatever, but it made her heart lift at the memory of it. It felt like love. She wanted to protect them, from all of this.

'No, I appreciate that. I know I'm not quite ready to meet the twins again yet. Soon, I know, but not now. But Natasha? The woman looking after them? Surely I've a right to meet with her? What harm could that do? One evening once the kids are asleep? Tonight, even?'

Beth had to hope that meeting Natasha, in her own home, would give her enough of a guide as to whether Dee had concocted some elaborate fantasy for whatever reason, or if it was Rob who was lying through his teeth. Perhaps Beth had no recall to work with, but she could see what was in front of her face, couldn't she?

'Tonight?' Rob asked, looking pained.

'Yes.'

He scanned her face, the discomfort on his clear to see. 'Fine. If you promise to leave the kids alone and if it will convince you that what Dee has told you is preposterous, then fine. I'll go and call her now.'

He got up and walked out of the room, taking his phone out of his pocket and dialling as he walked.

Why didn't he call in front of her? What was he saying that he didn't want her to hear?

Beth began to follow him but heard his voice as he started coming back towards her. She tripped over her own feet and fell, banging her shin on the coffee table as she did so.

'Shit! Fuck. Ow!'

She'd have to get that language under control once she got the twins back. She'd always had the mouth of a sailor. Her gran had always disapproved.

Rob walked back into the room, putting his phone away as he did so. 'Are you okay?' he asked. 'What happened?'

'Tripped over the...' She gestured to the table as she rubbed her shin.

'Need an ice pack?' His tone was clipped. He was annoyed still, obviously, but wanting to care for her at the same time. Had she made a horrible mistake in accusing him? Was he really just trying to keep it all together, keep everything going and everyone happy in the most difficult of circumstances? Had the anger she'd seen simmering underneath been about the whole scenario he now found himself in, at his loss? He was clearly a bit of a control freak, and this situation was out of control. No wonder he was mad.

She shook her head.

'No. Thanks. I think it's fine. What's one more bruise?' she said, trying to lift the atmosphere with a joke.

'How are you doing? I... I figured you didn't want my help with your...'

She knew he meant the injuries to her body. She had made it clear, albeit unwittingly, that she didn't want him anywhere near her. How hard must that have been? God, had she got this all wrong? Was he actually a decent man, trying not to take her rejection of him personally?

'Fine. I'm fine. Thank you. Everything is healing well. I'm... remembering things too,' she said, almost an offering to him, a reassurance that they just might be okay.

'Really? That's great.'

He smiled, but somehow his face did not lift. She had hurt him. Or was he being petulant? After all, not all her recovered memories were good ones. She knew he had a temper on him.

'Yes – I've remembered bits and pieces, about the children. About us.'

'Great. Well, hopefully seeing Natasha will clear things up too. She's going to call when the twins are in bed. I'm going to get changed and freshen up. It's been a long day.'

He looked tired as he walked upstairs and Beth felt sorry for him, despite still not really trusting him.

While he was upstairs, Beth decided to look about the house, to try to get a sense of who Natasha was. Who this woman she was about to meet might be like. This woman who was either being a substitute mother, or wife, or both. She was suddenly nervous, like she was about to audition for her own role in her life, unsure that she hadn't already been replaced by the understudy. Maybe as a young woman, Natasha didn't have much in the way of belongings yet, because there was nothing in the house that gave Beth an inkling of her. Much like Beth had failed to find out about her own self when she had thought that this was her own home, there seemed to be nothing here to indicate what Natasha was like. Maybe she'd taken things from here to where she was now, in Beth's house. Having so little of an idea about who she was about to meet was making Beth beyond nervous. She found herself wanting to sneak to the laptop to message Dee, but it was too likely that Rob would find her, and she wanted to meet Natasha and form her own opinion without Dee's input. She needed to work out her own mind on things.

When Rob returned a few minutes later, he was washed and changed and looking smart, almost smarter than when he had gone to work.

'Shall we?' he said, barely looking at her.

'Now?'

'Yes,' he said, looking at his shoes and bending down to adjust his laces. 'Tash has just called to say the kids are down for the night.'

Tash?

'I... I should get changed.' Beth looked down at her rumpled T-shirt and jeans.

'Why?' Rob said, passing his eyes over her. 'You look fine. You said you wanted to do this so, let's,' he said, picking up his jacket and heading for the door.

Beth felt ambushed despite it being her idea, her insistence, but he was right, so she pulled on her trainers and followed him out the door.

They were silent on the journey, Beth too nervous to speak but also not wanting to accidentally admit that she had already been to their house, already seen Natasha and wasn't as clueless as Rob was assuming she would be. Whatever he was thinking, he kept it to himself, and as they parked the car and walked up to the front door, Beth felt it could almost be as though they were returning home to a babysitter. Which, she supposed, was sort of what they were doing.

Rob knocked on the door and then used his key to let themselves in.

'Natasha?' he called out. 'We're here.'

Back to Natasha now, is it?

Beth stepped inside the hallway and was immediately hit with a funny feeling, like her skin was tingling but in a good way. She knew that she and her mum had loved watching property shows together, and she was a believer in the eight-second rule. That you know almost straightaway if you like a property, and Beth instantly felt that she *knew* this place, and yet it also made her uneasy. The house, or the situation she was going into? Or was it that her babies were so close, sleeping upstairs, and if she wanted to, she could just go to them despite her promises not to? She didn't know, but her body was reacting to being here in a way that it had not done at the other house, at Natasha's house.

The woman that Beth had seen in the garden earlier walked into the living room to meet them. Now in closer proximity, Beth could see that Natasha could only be described as a younger version of herself. She was how Beth had looked before time, stress and trauma had stripped her of her sparkle.

Natasha had the same hair as her: brown, tousled, cut above the shoulders. Same eye colour, same face shape. She was a little shorter, something she knew Rob would like, being paranoid himself that he was under six foot, as if somehow that was a flaw. She wore the same sort of clothes as her; in fact, Beth was not sure that she wasn't wearing *her* clothes, which she assumed were still here. There was something about the jacket that looked... familiar. She looked very much at home in the house, in the role of carer to the children. This was not doing anything to dispel the idea in Beth's head that Rob and Natasha were together.

'Hi. Beth?' Natasha said as she stepped forward to greet her. It felt like Natasha was the hostess here, despite it being Beth's home. She had a bold confidence about her.

Beth nodded, momentarily dumbstruck with all she was trying to process. She looked at Natasha, trying to gauge what she might be thinking. Was she innocent in all this? A young nanny, like Dee, helping out a family at a terrible time? Or a woman with no morals, using this situation to move in on a family while Beth was incapacitated? Beth couldn't tell.

'Shall we sit down?' Rob said. He was being authoritarian somehow, in control without being controlling. Was this because Natasha was his employee, and this was his home? It suited him; he was more relaxed here than at the house with Beth. Was it her who made him so tense as he did her? Or was he relaxed with Natasha because she was his girlfriend?

'Yes, I've just made some tea,' Natasha said, smiling as she walked back through the hallway into a large kitchen diner, which had been extended with a modern, airy room, all whites and windows. If there had been any childish clutter strewn about the place as Beth had expected then Natasha had tidied it all up. It seemed that Natasha was like her, only better. Beth swallowed her pride and sat down.

'So, Beth wanted to meet you, to, um, understand what's going on here and get to know the woman who is so *kindly* taking care of our children,' Rob said as his arm moved towards Natasha before he pulled it back.

'Yes, thank you,' Beth said awkwardly.

Who is this woman? I can't decide if I want to hug her or slap her. I should know, be able to tell, but I can't.

'Why don't you tell her?' Rob said, nodding his head towards Beth, indicating that Natasha should speak.

Did Beth imagine it or were they having a silent conversation between themselves? Were they patronising her or caring for her wellbeing?

'Okay, well, I work as a nanny, part time usually, as I'm trying to get gallery assistant work. I'm an artist.'

Like Beth had been. *Was*, she corrected herself. She would go back to her camera when she was better.

'And I was contacted by someone I know from a nursery who said she'd been contacted by a family in a difficult situation and might I be able to help. Well, once I'd spoken to Rob and understood what you were all going through, I couldn't say no. Honestly' – she reached out to squeeze Beth's hand, and Beth, too shocked to do anything, let her – 'I can't imagine how hard this is for you all. You're being so brave.'

Beth looked at her face, young and earnest. She glanced at Rob, who was looking at Natasha with, what, respect? Admiration? Lust? She was a good-looking woman, and she could see how Rob might be pulled in by someone sympathetic to his situation. But Dee had suggested that their relationship had pre-dated her accident. So Rob would have just been straight-up cheating on Beth, rather than being guided by circumstance.

'Thank you. I... it's been hard. Really hard,' Beth said as relief crept over her. She felt that Natasha was telling the truth, something about her felt open. Honest. The idea that this was some elaborate scam to pull the wool over her eyes was ridiculous. Dee had got the wrong end of the stick or had some agenda that Beth did not know about.

'It was Dee who told Beth that something funny, something inappropriate, was going on.'

Rob had obviously told Natasha all about it when they'd spoken on the phone.

'Oh goodness. I'm so sorry. I'm *so* sorry.' Natasha looked appalled.

'What? What is it?' Beth said. Clearly both knew something she didn't.

'Dee is my ex-partner,' Natasha said. 'And she didn't take our break-up well. She gets jealous. If she thought I was anything near happy, she'd do her best to wreck it. I'm only sorry you've been pulled into this. You've enough to be dealing with without my crazy ex-girlfriend.' Natasha looked at Beth apologetically.

Dee is Natasha's ex? What? Why had Dee not mentioned this?

'Tash has been so kind. She even leant me her car when...' Rob stopped.

Natasha's face turned pink. Was she embarrassed by the praise?

'The least I could do,' she said, turning her face to Rob, a question on her face that she did not ask.

'Are we done here?' Rob said brusquely, turning to Beth with raised eyebrows. She would have to apologise on the way home, but she didn't want to have to do it in front of Natasha. It was like being told off in front of Mary Poppins.

'Yes,' Beth agreed in a soft tone. 'Thank you, Natasha. For everything.'

Natasha waved the thanks away.

'But... before we go...'

'Yes?' Natasha asked.

'Can I see the children?'

'Beth, you promised...'

'No, I don't want to wake them up, I just want to look at

them. Please. I miss them.' And as she said it, Beth realised it was true. She did. She *ached* to know that they were so close to her and yet she couldn't go to them. It felt wrong. But she was overjoyed too – her feelings were coming back to her. She wasn't a cold, distant mother. She was loving, and warm. She was just dealing with a lot.

'I don't see why she couldn't?' Natasha said, asking permission of Rob, as though Beth wasn't right in front of them both.

Rob softened. 'Okay. Fine. But Natasha, go with her please? If they wake up, I want them to see you and know things are as normal.'

Except this isn't normal – this is the exception while I heal. I am their normal.

'Okay. Sure. Come with me, Beth,' Natasha said as she led her out of the room and towards the stairs.

Too nervous to question how she was again being treated as a guest in her own home, Beth followed Natasha to a bedroom door. Natasha turned to her, held a finger up to her lips in a ssshhh motion and then gently opened the door.

The room was dark, with a nightlight to one side, providing just enough illumination to see two little beds, both with the outline of a small child, with shoulders rising and falling gently as they slept. Beth felt a pull towards them. She wanted to scoop them up in her arms and cover them with kisses and promises that she'd never leave again. It shocked her how strong this pull was. She was their mother, and now she felt like she wanted to be that again. Wanted it now.

'Okay,' Natasha said, guiding Beth back out into the bright light of the hallway again.

Beth stood, dumbstruck, on the landing of her house. She had been so silly, so trusting of Dee. She had allowed her to use all the doubts that she had been having to build up an image of

Rob as a terrible person, a liar and a cheat. The memories of his temper, surely they could be a figment of her imagination rather than actual memories, couldn't they? Now she could see that if she just worked with him then she could have all this, she could have her old life back, her old family back, and she would be happy and loved. She could fix whatever had happened with her family and all would be well.

She could have it all back.

18

Beth awoke in the bed back at Natasha's house. It felt strange knowing that she was sleeping in Natasha's bed, and she was sleeping in hers. *Is Rob sleeping in both?* Beth thought before pushing it away. She had to stop inventing stuff. Rob was awake and looking at her from his side of the bed. He had a look on his face that was warm, affectionate.

'Did you sleep okay?' he asked.

'Yeah. Probably the best night in a while.'

'I agree, you're usually unsettled. You sometimes murmur in your sleep.'

Did she? What did she say? 'Oh.'

'Sounds like a chat with your mum sometimes.'

Beth smiled a bitter smile. It was still too many days from when her mum would see her email. She was exhausted with missing her. How long had it been since she had spoken with her?

'Sorry, Pooks. I didn't mean to upset you. I know you miss her. Maybe we can track her down. We can try again, can't we?'

He looked at her like it was an olive branch, like he was forgiving her for thinking such awful things about him.

Beth opened her mouth to tell him about the email that she'd sent, the laptop that she'd found, but again, something stopped her. She had decided that she needed to try again, to work with Rob to rebuild their life together, but there was still a flicker of something that made her hold back, just a bit. She still felt that she was defending herself, from some unknown enemy, and it was hard to fully let her guard down, Beth still had her armour on, and it would take time to shed it.

'What do you want to do today? I'm not... needed at work so I can stay here with you.' He scooted across the bed towards her. She felt herself tense but then forced herself to let it go. She needed to open up to him. She took his hand.

'Why don't I bake? I could make some Anzac cookies. I used to love those.' She smiled at him. Wasn't the way to a man's heart through his stomach? She was surprised that she wanted to make him happy. Maybe this was progress. 'Maybe we could take some for the twins? As they are half Aussie!'

He wrinkled his nose. 'Lots of sugar?'

She tipped her head to the side in a cutesy, *please* sort of way and a huge smile flooded his face.

'Oh okay, for you, Pooks. I suppose once won't hurt. Natasha can give them to them for you.'

That's not quite what I meant. 'Do we have the ingredients?'

'I don't know – maybe not? I don't know what you need or what's here. Maybe back at our house.'

It felt good to have things all out in the open. After weeks of feeling off kilter, like Rob was withholding information from her, like she knew that there was something that she didn't know, things felt like they could now move on. Perhaps the distance she had felt from Rob had been caused by all the half-truths he was having to concoct. That had to be hard on a person. Beth thought that she understood why the doctors and Rob had decided not to tell her about the children. It perhaps would have been too much all at once. But now, once a few things had settled, it felt better.

'Could you go get some?' She smiled winningly at him. 'If I give you a list? For me?'

While she felt more relaxed around Rob, she still wanted him out of the house, just for a bit. She wanted to check the laptop in case her mum or her brother had replied. It was almost like she still wanted another opinion on things. Sure, Rob's explanation and Natasha's corroboration of it made sense, but all the horrible times that Beth had remembered – were they real? Or had her confused and stressed brain made up what she *thought* was her past based on the difficulty that she was experiencing in the here and now?

'For you, okay. I'll have to hop in the car. Let me make your breakfast first,' he said, kissing her on the cheek before hopping out of bed.

'Maybe...' Her heart fluttered. 'Maybe I could take some to Ammy and Henry myself...' She felt she was ready to meet them again. Even if not to move back in yet, but that didn't feel as far away as it once had. She felt that she had opened a door to getting everyone home.

'Maybe,' Rob said as he left the room.

Beth stayed in bed for a while, trying to let this new way of being settle within her. She wanted to trust Rob. She wanted the life that he seemed to be suggesting they'd had. But... there was always a but. Why had Dee said what she had said? Why was she so *scared* for her? Why did that message thread between them seem to suggest that Beth had been about to leave him? Why could she hear her mum in her mind, telling her to come home? There was still... *something* that wasn't quite right. She just needed to figure it out.

'Here,' Rob said when he returned a while later, handing her a cup of coffee and kissing her briefly on the cheek. 'I've left the breakfast things out. I'll pop to the shops now.'

'Thanks.'

Beth got up and wrapped herself in a robe and wandered downstairs. It felt like a weekend morning – coffee and chill time. She felt relaxed in her own company. Not in danger. It felt good. She'd missed this.

Just as she flopped back onto the sofa, the doorbell rang, and she immediately tensed. Who would that be?

She opened the door just a small amount and peered out.

'Hello?' she said nervously.

'Beth, it's me. Dee. Let me in.'

Beth paused. Did she want to let her in? After all the lies she had spread, all the damage they could have caused.

'Beth! I've got your phone, let me in! I know Rob's out, I just saw him leave. Open the door!'

Rob still hadn't done anything about getting Beth a new phone; perhaps it was too much on top of everything else he was dealing with, and the lure of having her own access to the world, to her family, was too strong. She opened the door and let Dee inside.

'What was all that about?' she said as she bundled into the living room and put her bag down. 'Why didn't you want to let me in? What's happened? Are you okay?' She came to her, holding Beth by her arms, looking at her face as though she would find something there. 'Are you all right? Did he hurt you?'

Beth shook her arms free from Dee's hold and rolled her

eyes. This woman was ridiculous. How had she ever believed her?

'You're being crazy, Dee, let go of me.'

Dee looked confused. 'I'm being what? What do you mean?'

'After you were here last, I confronted Rob. Like I said I would.'

Dee looked surprised. 'Are you okay? What did he do? What did he tell you?'

'I'm fine. He told me the *truth*.'

Did he? A small voice asked Beth a question she was trying not to ask herself.

Dee's face clouded over. She didn't respond. She took a step back from Beth, crossing her arms defensively. She looked angry.

'What?' Beth said, surprised at this change in Dee. She had expected Dee to explain herself, to fluster, to be... something. But not this. This silence, this *disappointment*.

Dee looked close to tears, hugging herself. She let out a breath. 'Right,' she said.

'What?' Beth asked, softer than before. Dee's behaviour had thrown her.

'He's got to you, like he always does.' She sighed. 'Every time.'

'What do you mean by that?' Beth was on the defensive. Who did Dee think she was?

'I mean, Beth, that he has pulled you back under his control by feeding you some crock of shit lies, and you have fallen for it, again. Before the accident, this happened over and over. You tried to leave him, you tried to change the dynamic, and every time he would spin some sob story, and you would fall for it. And then, knowing he'd got you, he got worse. I thought this time, like just before the accident, that you had finally seen through his bullshit veneer to the bully that he is. I thought this time you'd be smarter.'

'There's been lies all right, *Dee.*' Beth's eyes flared. She was tired of being told she was wrong, stupid, illogical. She was just trying to get her life back on track. 'Natasha – how do you know her?'

Dee's mouth settled into a line, but she said nothing.

'She's your ex-girlfriend. Isn't she? And so, all this is for what? For my own good? For the twins? Or to make Natasha look bad? To make her life difficult because she left you. Is that it? You've got a vendetta against her maybe and you're using my accident as an excuse to get back at her. Is that right? Were we even friends before?'

'Wow. Just...' Dee looked floored. 'Okay,' she said quietly. 'Okay, yes, Tash and I had a thing for a while, and I should have told you that. But there was so much else to tell you. And yes, knowing her is how I found out about her and Rob. But this is not about me or me and her. How would it be trouble for her if she and Rob are telling the truth? It would only cause trouble if they're lying, if they're cheating. And I am certainly not using you. We were friends. I thought we still were.'

Beth could see the hurt on Dee's face, and she felt bad. But if she was messing with her, then that wasn't fair. This was her life. Not some drama to be moulded.

'Maybe you want to ruin her reputation as a nanny?'

'She isn't a nanny. She's an artist,' Dee said, with no emotion in her voice. 'Google her if you want. Here,' Dee said, holding out a mobile phone. 'It's not the most up to date model but it's the best I could get at short notice on my budget. It's a pay as you go thing, and I've put some money on it already. You can keep trying to get hold of your family, research whatever you need to. You can get hold of me, if you want to. Here,' she said again, holding it out as Beth hadn't taken it the first time. Her face was stony; she looked as though she was about to cry. This was not the crazy ex-girlfriend that Beth had been expecting. She looked like a sad and worried friend.

Beth reached out to take the phone. The lure of being able to reach her family was too strong and Rob hadn't made any moves yet to try to help her, despite saying that he would. She couldn't give up the chance, even if it meant taking this offer from Dee.

'Thanks,' she said quietly as she took it. As their fingers brushed, Dee caught hold of Beth's hand suddenly, looking at her with a quiet desperation in her eyes.

'Beth, I can understand why you want all this not to be true. I can. I get it. I understand why you want to believe what he's told you. You've been through a lot, you just want to rest. But... Okay, so Natasha is my ex. That's how I was able to work out so quickly where you were when you said about a village. But I don't want her back, nor to cause trouble. I don't want her in Rob's clutches as much as I don't want you in them. He is bad news.'

'Dee, let it go. Please. He's the father of my children, he's my husband and he's helping me get better so we can go back to how we were.'

'How you were? What about what you've remembered, Beth? You *know* if you really listen to yourself. You've been manipulated and sad and lonely and scared for so long that you no longer trust yourself when you should. You can.'

Can I?

'I'll be here when, if, you need me,' Dee continued as she picked up her bag to leave. 'But just, babe, ask yourself this – has he tried to reach your family yet? Has he got you any way of contacting them? A new phone? A laptop that isn't hidden? Is he trying to help you remember anything other than a Hollywood happy life together? No. Has he kept your children from you, not admitting they exist? Told you that your accident *killed two other children*, for crying out loud? Have you heard anything from anyone since the accident? Friends, the medical team, anyone? Or has it been just you and him "against the world"?'

'You're just stirring for the sake of it.'

'I'm *scared* for you, Beth. Ask these questions and ask yourself why. If he is so innocent and I am the crazy one, then why can't you answer these questions? Take a look through our message chats, see what you told me about how "perfect" life was before the accident. Ask yourself why you were leaving him then, that day. The day of the accident. And why he was happy enough to let you drive about in a potential death trap of a car.'

Beth opened her mouth to speak but had no words.

'No? Exactly,' Dee said, walking to the door and opening it. 'I will be here for you, Beth, like I've always been here for you. When you're ready. Because we're friends. No transactions, no demands. Just friendship. You let me know what you need, okay?'

She walked through the doorway. As she turned to close the door behind her, she added, 'But please, Beth, think on what I've said and please be careful. Don't underestimate the depths to which he will sink to get his own way. He is not a good man. You need to keep yourself safe. For you and for the twins.'

And with that, she left.

19

Beth was in the shower when Rob returned. She heard him calling from downstairs as she rinsed the shampoo out of her hair. After Dee had left, Beth had been in turmoil. Dee was so convinced that Rob was bad, that something was very wrong here and that both she and Natasha were in some sort of danger, the twins too. Beth had been shaken and immediately taken the phone that Dee had got her and logged onto her Facebook account. She checked if her brother had seen her message, but it was still unread. She then read the thread of her and Dee's messages, but there was so much missing, things unsaid online because they had been said in person. References to 'what happened last week' and what Rob had said, but no detail as to what that *was*. It was clear though that Beth had been leaving him. But no definite indication of *why*. Had it something to do with the rift with her family? Had he left her too much with all the domestic and childcare tasks and Beth had had enough? Had she wanted to go home, and he didn't want to come with her? Or was there more, like Dee insisted and Beth's memories had suggested? Who was she really married to? She needed to think, and she always thought best in the shower. Something about the water and the peace made her mind settle. It gave her clarity.

By the time she was done, she realised she wanted to talk with Rob. Just be open and honest and ask what she wanted to ask. Grown up to grown up. Even if he did have a temper, it didn't mean that Beth couldn't deal with it. She couldn't believe that she would be with one of those men who gaslight and trample their wives. It wasn't her. She wasn't like that. That was what she told herself.

She dried off, dressed and sorted her hair before coming downstairs. Rob was in the kitchen unpacking the ingredients that she had asked him to get. Would a controlling man do that for her? Wouldn't he make her do it herself?

'Hi,' she said as she walked, barefoot, into the kitchen.

'Hey, Pooks. I think I got everything. It's just the little local shop so there wasn't much selection.'

Beth viewed what he had bought. 'No, you've got it all. Cheers.'

'Heh, yes I have,' he said flirtatiously, pulling her towards him with his arm around her waist. He planted a kiss on her neck as he moved to stand behind her, pushing her up against the counter as he did so. She tried not to tense but he caught it. He immediately let go but Beth felt his disappointment. She had spoiled the moment. Again. She was going to have get over this. What more did he have to do?

'Let me bake for you?' she said, smiling, as she put her hand on his arm.

'Music to my ears,' he said, smiling weakly.

They were both trying; it would be okay.

Beth moved about the kitchen to find the things she needed, and before long, a batch of cookies was in the oven and the house started to fill with the smell of warm oats and coconut. It smelt like her childhood and Beth relaxed into the comfort of that. She walked into the living room where Rob was sat, flicking through his phone. Maybe this was a good chance to talk. Get everything out in the open. She sat down next to him.

'Hey,' she said.

He glanced at her. 'Hi, Pooks.'

She bit her lip. How could she start this conversation? He wasn't being wholly truthful with her, she knew that. They had been in a bad place the day of the accident and she needed to know more. She didn't want to talk to Dee; she couldn't be sure of the truth from her and only one other person knew the reality of it. Rob.

'What is it? You look serious. You'll give yourself wrinkles frowning like that.' He smiled.

She lifted her fingers to her forehead, between her eyebrows and then to the side, over the healing scar where her skin had split on impact in the accident.

'I've been having some... worrying memories.'

He shifted towards her, immediately, full of concern.

'What? What do you remember?'

'I... Rows. You and me. Arguments, fighting. Yelling at the twins. You being...'

His face hardened. 'Being what, Beth? What are you accusing me of now?'

'No, no, I'm not. I... I just... We can't have always been happy, can we? No couple always is. And with two babies, it can't have been easy. I just want to know...'

'Know what, Beth? How much of a monster I am? Why are we here again? Sure, we probably bickered, you're right, people do. But fights? No. We were a team. Together. Always.'

Then why was I leaving?

They sat in silence. Rob simmering, Beth trying to work out which way to take this conversation. She just wanted Rob to admit that things weren't always great. To give some context to the snippets she had recalled. Suddenly, she realised. What if the problem had been *her*? Had her eye been turned by someone? Was *she* pushing to move back home against his wishes? Was she the one ruining things?

Changing tack, Beth tried again. 'What was I like? As a wife? Was I... a good wife?'

Rob stalled.

What was he not saying? Oh God, was she the problem?

'You were great. *Are* great,' he said, moving towards her on the sofa until their thighs were touching. 'You're the best.'

Beth felt *something* in her stomach at his words. Relief? Affection? She leaned over for a chaste kiss to Rob's cheek, but he met her midway, pressing his lips gently to hers. It felt... nice. Beth leaned to kiss him again. Maybe they could get back some of how they were; maybe they just needed more intimacy, more closeness. Beth knew that she had been keeping Rob at arm's length; maybe she needed to let him in. He moved closer to her still and grasped her face either side with his hands. He pressed his lips forcefully to hers. It hurt. She could tell he was trying to prise her mouth open with his tongue, but this was so much so soon that she couldn't react.

She went to pull away, but he would not release her. He kissed her neck.

'Rob, I...' she said as she tried to twist herself away from him. His grip on her was too strong as his hands moved to hold her by her shoulders, pushing her back against the couch as his mouth moved down her neck.

'Rob!' she said again, more urgently. She didn't want to upset him, but also she wanted him, *needed* him, to stop. This was ridiculous. Whatever he had in mind, she was not going to do this. It was too much. She was only just starting to trust him.

He wasn't listening; he couldn't hear her. He wasn't really here. He was kissing her neck and pulling on her hair and pressing himself into her. She shifted to try to escape but the weight of him only pushed her further back down against the yielding cushions, trapping her between him and the hard frame of the sofa.

Rob moved fully onto her and Beth knew she was trapped. The tang of his sour breath wafted across her face as he whispered to her. His words made no sense; his brain wasn't functioning. Somehow, he was out of control and yet she was under his control. She could only stop this by convincing him to stop. She forced herself to touch him, to put her hand on his shoulder, and she pushed back, forcing him away from her, gently but with intention. She had to make him listen but not make him angry.

'Rob. Rob... not like this. Not like this.' She meant not at all, but she had to break the moment, to make him return to his senses. For everything they had gone through together, she did not think that he would want to force her against her will. She hoped he would not. She just had to reach him.

'Rob. Babe. Please. Stop. Stop!' she said, more firmly now, moving underneath him to try to slide herself out from under his body, to drop off the edge of the sofa, letting gravity put space between them, to let her escape from this. He misinterpreted her movement as consent.

'Yeah. Yes,' he whispered breathlessly into her ear. 'I know you've missed this too. Us. Really us.'

'No. No,' Beth contrasted as she managed to pull an arm free from under him, using it to drag herself upwards along the sofa, freeing some of her body. Rob reached up and pinned her arm to the sofa with his own, pushing it down at an angle that hurt.

'Ow!' Beth managed to pull her arm back from Rob and push him away. It broke whatever spell he had been under and he stopped, shocked, and moved away from her. He looked wired; his pupils were blown, and his hair was all over the place. What had just happened? Beth looked at him in horror.

'Don't look at me like that, Beth.'

'Like what?' She was still trying to catch her breath, and she rubbed at her shoulder where he had hurt her.

'Like this was *my* fault.'

'What do you mean?'

'You come in here, asking me if we used to fight, accusing me of yelling at the kids. Then you kiss me, pull me into you and then push me off? Like, what am I meant do to with that? You're giving mixed messages all over the place. I don't *know* you any more, Beth! You're not who you were, you're... I dunno.' He ran his hands over his chin.

Had this been her fault? She didn't think she'd meant to initiate anything. It had just been a kiss. A kiss didn't mean anything else, did it? Consent before didn't mean consent now. And things were clearly different between them since the accident so why would he assume that it would be okay? Beth was furious at him and furious at herself for fumbling this.

The kitchen timer went off, breaking the tension that hung in the air, both Rob and Beth angry at the other. They leapt up to go to the oven.

'I'll get them,' Rob said, striding ahead of Beth towards the beeping timer.

'No, let me, they're my cookies.' Beth could hear the ridiculous whine in her voice, but she needed to feel that she had accomplished something today other than making things worse, and Rob was taking over.

'It's fine,' he said as he picked up the oven gloves and opened the oven. A waft of hot sugary steam drifted into the room as he did so.

'Give them here, I'll sort them. Thanks.'

'Look, let me just—'

'I've got them, it's fine, it's—'

'Beth, you're in my way, look, let me do this for you.'

'Rob, no, I want to… ow! OW!'

Rob pushed the hot tray away from him, in a moody 'here then' gesture, lifting it up just under Beth's arms, where the metal made contact with her skin. She heard the sizzle as her flesh took on the heat. In pure reaction, she flung her arms sideways, away from the tray, knocking it out of Rob's hands, sending the warm, soft biscuits flying, landing all over the floor in sad little clumps.

'Now look what you did! Look what you made me do!' Rob yelled at her, pulling the gloves off and throwing them onto the countertop with a flourish. 'You won't let me do anything nice for you, will you?' He stormed out of the room. From where she stood, rooted to the spot in bewilderment at what had just happened, Beth heard the front door slam.

As the numb of shock started to wear off, the burning sensation on her skin began to overwhelm Beth and suddenly pain flooded over her. Snapping out of her disbelief, Beth rushed to the sink and turned on the cold water, putting her forearms under the stream, hoping to minimise the damage. It stung like a hundred wasp stings, and she winced as she forced herself to keep her arms under the icy flow. As the cold water gradually took all feeling from her arms and spread up to her fingers, Beth's mind started to find clarity. She ran through what had just happened, from the talk to the kiss, to the row and her ending up with burns on both her arms. Rob hadn't stopped to check if she was okay, if she needed any first aid, if she needed medical attention. He hadn't said sorry. And, as she played the scene in her head, over and over, she homed in on the expression on Rob's face as he had pushed the tray of cookies towards her. He had been angry, petulant. His face a sneer. He had done it on purpose. He had burnt her deliberately and then told her it was her fault.

Oh God, Beth thought as the realisation sunk in.

Dee was right. Beth wasn't safe with him. The twins, Natasha? None of them were safe.

20

Once Beth had kept her arms under the cooling water for as long as she could bear, for as long as her first aid training from the café had taught her, she scrambled about in the cupboards, found a first aid kit and bandaged up her forearms. She probably should have got it checked out by a doctor but that was not her priority. Right now, she had to get to the twins and make sure Rob was nowhere near them. If he could lose his temper like that with her, then he could lose his temper like that with them.

With hands that wouldn't stop shaking, Beth pulled out Dee's mobile phone from where she had hidden it inside a sofa cushion and dialled. It rang and rang then went to voicemail. Was Dee screening her? Had Beth burnt all her bridges?

The phone jumped in Beth's hands as it rang out. It was Dee calling back. Beth answered immediately.

'Beth?' Dee sounded flustered.

'Dee... I... I'm sorry. You... I think you're right.'

'Where is he? Are you okay?' There was not a second of a

pause, no moment where Dee had to think about anything other than Beth's safety. That told Beth a lot.

'He... he went out. I...'

'I'm coming over. Leave if you need to but I'm on my way.'

Dee hung up.

Needing to do something to distract her while Dee arrived, Beth got out the laptop and checked her emails. Nothing. Her mum still hadn't replied, not that Beth had expected her to. Beth bit her lip so hard in frustration that it bled, and she tasted the metallic tang on her tongue. Her adrenaline was running so high after the burn, and her realisation that she was most likely in danger meant that she barely felt it. She felt invincible, which, seeing as she was probably more vulnerable than she had ever been, was unwise. She tried to remind herself of this. She searched for Natasha online. What was her full name? Did she know? Did anyone ever tell her? She searched Natasha, Cambridgeshire, Nanny. Nothing. Not really surprising. She searched Natasha, Cambridgeshire, Gallery Assistant – and there she was. A little biography and a headshot from a gallery that had closed during the pandemic but still had its dormant web page up. Though, Beth supposed she could still be working as a nanny while looking for something new. Now armed with her surname, Beth tried again to look for a record of her as a nanny. There was nothing. If she ever had worked in that field, she had done so without it ever leaving a digital footprint.

Beth's stomach fell. She had begun to realise that she had got this so very wrong. She had believed the wrong person. She had wanted to believe Rob. Perhaps that was how he had got her, and how he had kept her at first – by making her *want* to believe what he said, rather than to *see* what he actually did.

The buzz of the phone in her hand nudged Beth from her spiral. There were too many things to consider and her brain was glitching with the effort of trying. Realising she didn't know when or if Rob would be back and what mood he would be in when he did, she quickly switched the laptop off and returned it to its hiding place. Then, she thought that she didn't know if he would move it, or get rid of it now that he had slipped up and shown her his true temper and so she returned the empty box to the drawer and ran to the kitchen. She got down on her knees, wincing as the side of the cabinet pushed against her burns. She pulled the kickboard off its clip, posted the laptop into the space underneath the cabinet and closed it again. If Rob went to find the laptop and saw it was missing, he would take a while at least to find it there, she hoped.

The phone buzzed in her hand again and Beth took it up to see.

DEE

I'm here.

DEE

Babe? Where are you? Answer the door. Are you okay?

Beth went to the front door and opened it and Dee burst in, as though she was walking onto a battlefield.

'Is he here?' she said, looking around, frantic. 'Is that why you didn't answer? Are you okay?'

'Dee.'

Dee turned to face Beth, clocked the bandages on her arms, the split lip, and she grabbed Beth to her and held her. Beth choked out the tears she had been keeping in check since Rob had pinned her to the sofa what was probably only forty-five minutes ago but somehow felt like an absolute lifetime.

'Babe. Where is he?'

'I don't know. He left.'

Dee gently pushed Beth away.

'What happened? What did he do?'

Beth explained to her about the chat, the sofa, the cookies and her arms.

'The lip was me. I bit it, accidentally.' She felt so stupid. 'You were right. Natasha isn't a nanny – not anywhere I can find, anyway. Rob is angry, unpredictable. He scares me. I've been pretending to myself that he doesn't. I... Not long after I was back from hospital, I was taking a bath and he slipped in the bathroom and held me under the water.'

'He did *what*?'

'He said it was an accident; he was apologetic, so sorry, so gentle afterwards. I believed him. But now? Now I think I've been a total chump. A fool. So stupid.'

'No. No, babe, not stupid. This is not on *you*, do you hear me? This is him. This is how he operates. And we need to get you, the twins and Tash out of his reach. And now.'

Beth nodded and moved to sit down. Her legs suddenly felt weak, as though they were no longer capable of holding her up. How had she got this so wrong?

The more she remembered and the more she now accepted as the truth, Beth could see that Rob had been slowly chipping away at her life for years, almost since the first time they'd met, to put him in a position of absolute power over her. The accident had reset that in some ways, but not all. Emotionally, he no longer had the hold on her that he once had. Logistically, legally and practically was another matter altogether.

'He's got me in a chokehold, hasn't he? I can't leave without the kids. I can't leave with them. I've got no money, no job, no passport. Nothing. I've still not been able to reach my family, who might be able to help me. I'm stuck.'

'No, not stuck, we can fix this. We can. He's been breaking you all over again. The first time, I could see it and it made me so angry. I see it all the time as a nanny.' Dee's face clouded over. 'Either in the families I work with or the ones I work close to. The women going into motherhood wide-eyed and innocent and having their dreams crushed by the inequality that was hiding in plain sight. The stacked odds of maternity vs paternity leave and it just spirals from there, with the woman's input being devalued as "not work". But Rob? He was worse. He didn't just dismiss the value of what you did, he dismissed the value of who you *are*. And he wanted to control you, bend you into whatever he needed you to be at any one point. What he wanted to see in himself. He wanted a mother and a mirror, a hooker and a maid.'

Beth's eyes widened. 'Wow,' she whispered. 'You really hate him.'

'He's trying to do it to you again and I can see he's doing the same thing to Tash. Just a cycle of reel 'em in, break 'em down and then control them. I said as much to her, and the recognition in her face as I described how he was with you was powerful. I think she was aware of it at one level, but it's insidious, isn't it? It creeps. Little by little. Like replacing the handle and brush of a broom so often that nothing of the original is there. It's the same but it's not the same.'

'I guess. You've spoken with Natasha then?'

'Yes, I went to her as soon as I saw that he'd got to you, made you question your own mind again. I made her let me in and listen while I told her what was going on. I think I got through to her. We spoke for a long time. And actually... Well, I'm not sure if you're ready for this or not?'

Uncertainty flickered across Dee's usually certain face.

'What?' Beth's stomach dropped.

'She sent me a video. For you. Of the kids. I... I just don't know if you're ready to see it or not?'

Desperation flooded Beth. 'There's a video? Now? You've got it?'

Dee nodded as she got out her phone, opened the video and held it out to Beth, who grabbed at it.

'Sorry...' she said, noting her rudeness but focusing entirely on the screen.

'What do you want to say to Mummy?' Natasha asked from behind the screen. Beth noted with happiness how kind she sounded, how gentle. Both children looked at each other at first, confused at this situation.

'Where did Mummy go?' Ammy asked, moving towards the camera almost as though she could be found inside it.

'Mumma is here?' Henry added, looking at his sister for confirmation.

'Not yet, lovelies, but soon. We'll get Mummy back soon. How about you blow her a kiss until then, eh? So she knows you love her like she loves you?'

'Mwah!' they shouted in unison before almost immediately being distracted by something off camera, and then they wandered out of sight.

Beth's heart flooded with joy at seeing them, then almost immediately broke with the want of them. She *needed* them back. Ever since she had discovered they existed, this need for them had been growing, with every memory she recalled and with everything new that she learned about them. She knew she was a mother but now, she felt like it too. Rob wasn't just being selfish in keeping them from each other, he was being *cruel.* They seemed fine and well cared for in the video. But she knew from other people that how children could be in the daytime was different to when they were tired or hungry or just in the sort of mood when all you want is your mummy. She still had that now, the need to call her mother.

'So what's our plan?'

Dee smiled. It was clear that she was going to right some wrongs and she was going to take Rob down, and she was going to enjoy doing it. Beth smiled too. She felt the same. He had messed with the wrong women, and he would pay for it. Rob had it coming. He thought he'd play both her and Natasha, but he'd underestimated them both. He would learn to regret that.

'We've got a long list of things we need to do in order to get you out of here, safe and with your twins. We have to get you documents, money, a place to go, a way to support yourself. Oh, which reminds me – did he mention anything about his work?'

Beth nodded. 'Yeah. Something about being given more, what do you call it, compassionate leave? As he's been needing more time away to be here.'

'And there. I'm surprised he's had time to be at work at all. Which is probably why they've let him go,' Dee said, crossing her arms. 'Natasha said they fired him last week. He was raging about it apparently. He's worried about money – being that he's now paying for two households and paying Natasha too.'

'I can't decide if it's better or worse that he paid his girlfriend. I guess he was paying her to nanny rather than paying her to be with him.' Beth took a breath. 'He really was cheating on me then. He was with us both?'

'I'm afraid so, babe. Of course he told Natasha that it "wasn't like that with you, he was just there to get you better for the kids". She feels awful. She's made some bad decisions for sure.'

Beth was hurt at first but then realised that by being so greedy, by wanting his cake and eating it, Rob had unwittingly shot himself in the foot. Because *one* woman scorned was enemy enough, but *two*? They would destroy him.

'But because he's out of work we need to move fast as he has no income, but he has access to yours. And your joint assets with him.'

'To my what? I don't have any?'

'We could probably get you half the house, the car, and then there's your fuck-off fund.'

'My what now?' Beth said, her face open in shock.

'Sorry. I forget sometimes about the amnesia and that you remember nothing from your time here. It still seems wild to me. Anyway, you had no access to money at all, no account of your own, like I said. But you and I came up with a plan before this all happened. You set up a photography business at play-groups that we went to, taking really gorgeous photos of people's kids. You were doing really well.' She smiled at this. 'We set you up a PayPal account to take the money and we were going to work out from there how to get it to you in actual cash. But then, the accident happened. But it's there, waiting for you.'

'I have my own money?'

'Not a huge amount, but yes. But we'd got you a phone to use it from and if Rob has that now then he might see it as a recently used app.'

'No.' Beth shook her head. 'My phone was destroyed in the accident. Water damage.'

'Who told you that?'

Beth closed her eyes in disbelief at her naivety. She tipped her head back to the ceiling. When would she stop being so *stupid*?

'Rob.'

'Right. Maybe be meant your brick phone. Maybe the new

one was lost as no one was looking for it. Maybe he's telling the truth, maybe he isn't, but either way we need to get that money safe and then go from there. Natasha promised me that she will look for your passport, to see if it's at your house. She wants to help.'

'Does she? Or does she just want me out of the picture? If she's sleeping with Rob, how can we trust that she's not saying one thing to us and another to him?'

'I know her, Beth, she's not like that. She got suckered by him just like you did. She was many things, but a cheater she was not. She did not know about you and the children.'

'But she did though, didn't she? She took them in and carried on with him after knowing about me. It's not like she's some angel we're dealing with.'

Dee bit her lip. 'I know. You're right. But none of us are, are we? Are you going to hold that against her? When she's offering to help now?'

'If we're sure we can trust her. I can't even imagine what Rob would do if he knew we were planning something.'

'Which is why we need to make sure he doesn't find out. Once we have some ID, you can open another bank account. One of your own that he knows nothing about. You can use my address for it until we get you set up somewhere. Or get you back home.'

'The police said that they retrieved my driver's licence at the accident. Maybe we have that back. Though Rob won't have been happy I had it. That might be here. I'll look for it.'

Beth's heart lightened. It wasn't about money as such but the freedom that it could afford her. It was a start. In the face of this overwhelming mess of a situation, it was the first step to unlocking an *after*, a time when she could begin to put all the mess behind her. She started to believe that there was a future, one that she actually wanted to be in, one that might just be in her reach.

'I want him away from the twins though. He can't be trusted with them.'

'Tash has them. They're safe with her. She won't let him take them anywhere and she won't leave them with him. So next, we get what is still *yours* safe away from him, finance wise. Then we work on what we need to do to get the kids back with you, legally, above board and away from him. We can get some legal advice. We will get your life back from that goddam monster.'

Beth looked at Dee, this absolute powerhouse of a woman who was not going to let her friend be destroyed by her husband, and felt a flood of gratitude. What on earth would she have done without her? Where would she be now if she had not found their messages? If she had not reached out? She would be stuck, without hope, without friendship. Taking a moment, Beth thanked the universe in all its depth for friends. True, ride or die friends who showed up time and again, with no expectations but just support and love. She made sure to promise to herself that she would do whatever it took to repay Dee her kindness, to be the sort of friend that Dee was being now.

'You okay?' Dee said, looking quizzically at Beth.

Beth smiled a wide smile. 'Yeah. Just thanking God for you, that's all.'

Dee returned the smile. 'You "nana".' She paused. 'Love you.'

'Love you too.'

Beth smiled as she realised that it had been Dee who had encouraged her to trust her instincts, to trust herself. Rob had only encouraged her to trust *him*. Putting this alongside everything Beth *knew* and everything that she *felt*, she was sure now that trusting Dee was the right thing to do.

'There's something I wanted to ask actually,' Dee said. 'Have you seen any doctors since you've been out? Like, has anyone checked up on you?'

Beth thought about it. How long had she been out of hospital for? She found that she couldn't pinpoint it. Her days and nights all blended into one, memories merging as she tried to unpick all the messiness that her mind contained.

'There was one appointment.'

'Just one?'

'I *think* so. I don't recall any others but, honestly, my mind has not been at its best and right after I came out of hospital, I found it hard to trust my memory, short or long term. I... was dealing with not knowing Rob, or this house or... I was on a lot of painkillers too, and they made me woozy. The hospital gave all the information to Rob.' She screwed up her face in anguish. 'I don't think I asked.' She felt sick. She'd handed everything over to Rob: her freedom, her money, her health. Her children.

Dee sighed. 'Do you think he'd keep you away from appointments? In case the doctors asked about... things he's not told you? About the kids?'

'I don't... I don't know any more. I'm so tired.' Her emotions bubbled up, threatening to overwhelm her. She trembled as her lip started to shake, her tears fighting against her need to keep herself in control. 'I... I just needed someone to look after me. The accident, it... I could have died. I just needed someone who was supposed to love me to take care of me while I recovered and... my mum' – she gasped – 'doesn't even know it happened. I've emailed her but she's away and I don't know if we're talking or if she still cares or...'

Dee stepped forward and held her. She stroked her hair and

whispered to her. 'Oh, babe. We can fix this. I will help you fix this. We will find her, I promise. You said about your argument and how you wanted to fix things after Rob.'

Beth broke away, wiping her face and looking desperately at Dee. 'I did? What did I say?'

'Just that she wasn't happy about you staying in the UK with him. She didn't like him. You said she was angry that you went ahead and got married without her. Hadn't told her about being pregnant at the time. She told you it felt like you were deliberately cutting her out of your life.'

'But I wasn't! I... I don't think I was. I think I got swept up and was young and stupid and... Do you think she'd forgive me?'

'Babe, I don't think there's anything to forgive. She's your mum. She loves you.'

'What if I said terrible things, hurtful things? What if we had a huge row...'

'Okay. We're spiralling here. None of that happened. You'd have told me. Let's take a moment, shall we?' Dee took Beth's hands and looked at her with raised eyebrows until Beth focused on her face. 'Now breathe. Deep breath in, deep breath out. Again. Okay. Right. So we need to find out who your medical team are. They will no doubt be able to help.'

'With what? My memory is coming back, little by little, and I'm not in pain any more. There's nothing more they can do.'

Dee looked at her, confused. 'They can help with the coercive control.'

'The what?'

'What Rob is doing, what Rob has done to you. Controlling you, isolating you, separating you from your children and not even telling you that they exist. That!'

'Don't talk to me like I'm an idiot.'

Dee held out her hands. 'I'm not! I'm not. I just mean that there are organisations, support. And the doctors may be a good way to access help.'

'I'm not so sure. If they've been trying to set up further appointments with me, they're not trying too hard. God knows what Rob has told them if they have been in touch with him. They *could* just turn up here if they wanted to. If anyone had any issues, they could send the police round, couldn't they? And no one has come. No one. Apart from you. No one is coming. I know that.'

'I'm here, I will help you.'

'Thank you.' Beth reached out and squeezed Dee's hand. She was so thankful for her but in this moment, she also knew a truth that changed everything. 'I am grateful for you, I am. But I need to rescue myself. Me and the twins.'

Dee nodded, understanding what Beth meant. 'We will do what you want to do, what you need to do, and I will be here to do whatever I can to help.'

'Thank you. First, I need to meet her again. Natasha.'

'Again?' Dee looked confused.

Beth blushed. 'When I got it wrong, when I didn't believe you, I made Rob take me to her. To my house.'

Dee gasped.

'I'm sorry, I should have told you. I met her. She lied to me. Lied to my face about being a nanny. Lied to me about being with Rob, and I don't trust that she's not still doing that now. She's got my kids; she's got access to everything I need to get my life back. Hell. She's currently got my *life*! My family, my home, everything. Why would she give it back now?'

Dee started to speak but then stopped.

'Will you take me to her? To the twins too?'

'I don't think that's wise. Not now, not yet. For them but also *because* of them.'

'What do you mean? I'm their mum.'

'Yes, but think of it from their point of view, babe. You have an accident. They go to hospital. They come out. You're not there. No one says where you are or when you're coming back. A strange woman moves into their home and looks after them. Then one day, Mummy turns up. But she can't stay or tell you when she will be back and then she's gone again.'

Beth gasped at the cruelty of the truth of what Dee was saying. She kept forgetting that they'd experienced loss too. She couldn't make it worse for them. She would have to wait until she could be back, fully, for them. And she would be. She promised herself that.

'Okay.'

Dee looked pained. Beth could tell she felt awful too.

'And also kids aren't exactly known for keeping schtum either. "Ooh, Daddy, Mummy came to visit us today." You know?'

Beth sighed. There had to be some solution. She just knew she couldn't stay with Rob, not a moment longer than absolutely necessary.

'I know. It's...'

'Maybe...' Dee said.

'Maybe?' Beth's heart jumped a little. A spark of hope flickered.

'Maybe I can persuade her to come here. If she can take the twins somewhere safe. That just might work? Then you could see just how much she is on our side, on *your* side, and we could get a plan together?'

'Do you think you could persuade her? And... does this' – she waved her own phone about in front of her – 'receive videos? Might she send me another one of the twins? I... I have to remind myself what I'm fighting for. I know that sounds insane, but my memory is still so patchy and it really helps to have something *solid* to look at.'

'You'd have to be absolutely sure that Rob doesn't know about this phone. Absolutely one hundred per cent sure. It's too risky otherwise.'

Beth smiled. 'I've been hiding it in the sofa, but maybe I can put it in with my sanitary products. He'll never look there.'

Dee threw her head back in laughter. 'Okay. I'll speak with her. About a meeting, about a video. She's looking for anything at your house that will help. You see what you can find out about your doctor's appointments and if you can find your driver's licence. Stay strong. And as far away from him as possible. Keep him docile, keep him sweet, but keep you safe first. And if he... does anything, or you feel in real danger, then go straight to plan B.'

'What's plan B?'

'Run. Call me, grab the kids and run. But if we can take them and what you're owed, legally, safely, properly – well, that's better, isn't it?'

Beth took Dee's hands in hers and held them to her chest.

'Thank you. I'm... sorry that you've got caught up in all my mess. This is my fault. I will get us all out of it.'

Dee shook her head. 'This is not *your* fault. Don't think that. And we're friends, you would do the same for me.'

'I would.' Beth was floored by the sudden flood of protectiveness she felt for Dee. 'If anyone so much as *tried* to... well, I would be there with a shotgun and a shovel!'

'Absolutely,' Dee said, pulling Beth into a hug. 'I will message you when I've arranged a meeting with Natasha. I don't think it's wise for you two to be in direct contact – just in case. Rob isn't smart, but he's also not a total idiot.'

'He's disgusting, that's what he is.' Beth sneered.

'You'll get your revenge but let's get you safe first, eh?'

'I want to make him feel like the smallest man alive,' Beth said. He had done so much damage to her, she wanted to do some in return and he would have to sit there and take it. She would not be cowed by him. Not any more.

21

It was gone midnight by the time a heavily drunk Rob returned. Beth's bravado had shrunk hour by hour as she tried to second guess what mood he would be in when he returned. Would he still be angry and lash out? Would he be full of remorse, apologetic, begging her to forgive him, or would he claim it was an accident, or worse still, her own fault? She had played each scenario out in her mind and was shocked how in every single one, all she wanted to do was *hurt* him back. She thought she was better than that, but she was so angry at him. For everything. Rage slithered through her veins until she was entirely swamped by it. She was both furious and afraid.

She sat on the sofa, wringing her hands over and over. The room was half dark, half bathed in moonlight as she awaited the return of someone who said that he loved her but was intent on destroying her. She wanted to be nowhere near him, and yet she had to be. For the plan to work, she had to survive just a bit longer while she got her escape route laid out.

'You're... schtill awake...' he slurred at her as he stumbled into the dark room. He didn't turn on the light and the sight of his silhouetted form made her come out in goosebumps. He was so tall, so broad, so much stronger than she was. How would she ever win against him? She swallowed and reminded herself that she was sober, she had knowledge that he did not and that most of all, she was still *her*. The strong, feisty woman who had followed her dream across the world, and who had survived everything thrown at her so far. She pushed her shoulders back and lifted her chin defiantly to look at him. He would not win. Not now, not ever.

Beth decided to play the exasperated wife, not mentioning the burns, not letting any hint slip as to how things had changed in the time he had been away. While he had been drinking to hide his true nature from himself, she had allowed hers to take centre stage. He might be disgusted with himself, but Beth was proud of who she was. She would make her children proud of her and for what she would do for them.

'What time do you call this?' she said lightly, standing and crossing her arms. She noted to herself that she was shaking. She hoped it was too dark for him to see.

'You cantellme whadda do.'

He sounded more petulant than angry, Beth was relieved to note. He tripped over his own feet, trying to kick his shoes off, and buckled into a heap on the floor. He was incapable of controlling his own body and Beth felt her muscles relax as she realised that fact. He couldn't hurt her. It would be best for him to be unconscious, sleeping it off. He'd have the monster of all hangovers after this bender and would be in an absolute state tomorrow, but for now, she had the upper hand.

'No, that I can't. But what I would suggest is a large glass of water, some painkillers and a banana.'

She sounded like her mum when Beth had first started stumbling home after one too many cocktails as a young woman. A tone of exasperation in her voice. What Beth wouldn't give to hear her voice now, gently telling her what do to after she'd got herself into this right royal mess.

'I don... I... okay,' he said, picking himself up and stumbling towards the kitchen.

Beth followed him, keeping herself at a distance, more than his arm's length away from him. She didn't want to let her guard down fully, not yet. He was drunk, yes, but so long as he was conscious, he remained a potential threat to her. Albeit right now, a very inebriated one.

He slumped at the kitchen table and put his arms out in front of him to rest his head on. He closed his eyes. Beth could smell the mixture of beer and spirits on him. His head was going to be splitting in the morning.

'You're going to need some epic pain relief, mate.'

She realised she'd said this before – her bar work. She was used to dealing with drunkards in a firm but gentle manner. She could just channel that, and that would keep her nerves at bay.

Beth poured Rob a large glass of tepid water from the tap and placed it in front of him. 'Drink that.'

Rob lifted his head from the table, grabbed the glass and gulped the water down as though he'd just crawled out of the outback and hadn't seen water in days. He slammed the empty glass down and went back to semi-sleeping half propped up.

Beth reached into the cupboard to get him some aspirin when she saw her medication. The super-strong painkillers that knocked her out, made her sleep, made her forgetful and dizzy. Without stopping to think further, she grabbed two, then a handful more and, picking up a banana from the fruit bowl, placed them in front of Rob along with another glass of water.

'There you go. Those'll help.'

Her heart hammered against her chest, and she hoped that

he was too drunk to notice the number of pills or to hear how laboured her breathing had become. She needed him incapacitated. Knocked out. He couldn't hurt her if he wasn't awake.

Without looking at her, he lifted his head, grabbed the pills, downed them with the water, pushed the banana away and then sat up on the chair, his head lolling back behind him. She could see the whites of his eyes in the gloom, and he looked wild.

He cracked his knuckles and looked right at her.

'I could kill you, you know? You and the kids. If I decided to,' he said chillingly, his words suddenly crisp and clear. Then he laughed – threw his head back and laughed.

Beth's blood ran cold.

Finally, he was showing her the real him, just the two of them, eye to eye in the darkness. Alcohol had loosened his tongue, stripped him of his mask, and Beth knew that she was looking at Rob as he really was. A cold, cruel waste of a man. He thought he was better than her.

He thought wrong.

'Not if I kill you first,' she whispered back at him, but he was already closing his eyes, the alcohol pulling him down towards sleep.

Beth left him slumped in the kitchen, picked up her things and walked out of the door.

22

The night was overcast, and the moon kept hiding behind clouds, cutting out the light that Beth needed to see where she was going. Where *was* she going? She had been entirely acting on instinct and now that she was away from Rob and out of that house, her adrenaline was dropping and she realised how tired she was. She wanted to curl up somewhere and sleep. But she couldn't. By drugging Rob, she had put in motion something that she needed to see through to the very end, and something that she had to take advantage of *now*. She had fed him enough drugs to make him sleep for a good time but when he woke up, he would be so, so angry, and his threat to kill her kept repeating in her mind. He would never let her just leave. Especially not with the twins. His ego wouldn't let that happen. So it was now or never if she was going to get away from him, and the thought of never scared her into action.

Beth put her hand in her pocket and was beyond relieved to find that she had picked up the car keys. She hadn't been thinking, more reacting when she had left Rob, and the idea that she'd need to go back inside to retrieve the car keys made her feel sick. She closed her hands around them gratefully and pushed the door lock button. She needed to get to the twins, and fast. It was cold, the wind was whipping across the open fields that surrounded the village, and she pulled her coat around her. The landscape here was eerie at night. She could well believe all the folklore stories of ghosts and ghouls and things out to get you in the dark. She reminded herself of what she needed to be scared of, that who she needed to be running away from was Rob, and that focused her mind.

She got into the car, got out her phone and called Dee.

'Beth?'

'I need you to meet me at mine. My old house, where Natasha and the twins are. Now. Like, right now.'

'Where are you?'

'I left. I had to. I'll explain when I'm there. I'm leaving now.'

'Beth, what happened? No, wait. Okay. Tell me everything when you're at yours.'

'Thanks, babe.' Beth's teeth where chattering; she could barely get the words out. What was she doing? What was her plan?

'Always. Do you need anything?'

Beth hesitated. 'Um, money.' She rubbed the back of her neck in embarrassment. 'I'll pay you back, for everything. Just, I need money now.'

There was a pause.

'I understand. I'll stop at a cash point and get everything I can.'

'Thank you.'

'Love you, babe.'

'You too.'

Beth hung up, took a deep breath, looked back at the house, started the engine and drove away. The car pulled up to her old house just as Beth's feet had started to thaw in the blasting heat of the footwell. As she sat in the car listening to the sounds of the engine starting to cool now that she had switched it off, Beth realised that she hadn't asked Dee not to let Natasha know that she was coming. Beth wanted to ambush her, catch her off guard to test how on board with her she was, rather than still being on Rob's side. Beth hoped that by some miracle, Dee had worked that much out herself. She looked around for Dee's car, but she had not yet made it there. Perfect. She wanted some one-on-one time with Natasha first. She needed to *know* that she was headed for freedom. Headed towards a life with her children without spending it locked up, terrified and small. Without spending it with him.

Beth took a moment as she knocked on the door. She rolled her tense shoulders and something in her neck popped as the tension crackled. What would Natasha be like? Could Beth really trust her? Was she truly as innocent in all this as she claimed to be? What if she was really on Rob's side, and frankly how would Beth tell? No one came so Beth knocked again.

'Beth?' Natasha said as she finally opened the door, dressed in a robe and PJs. Beth had woken her. She looked nervously behind Beth to the dark outside. 'Is everything okay? Is Rob not with you?'

'No,' Beth said as she walked forcibly past Natasha and into *her* home. She pulled her shoulders back, ready for a fight. Ready to test Natasha.

'Beth, are you okay? What's wrong?'

'He's at home. Sleeping.' A truth of sorts.

She took her coat off, revealing her bandaged arms.

'Beth, what happened? Are you hurt?' Natasha looked genuinely concerned.

She said nothing. She was taking in Natasha's behaviour.

Trying to see if there were any cracks in a façade or if this was really her.

'Beth, say something. You're scaring me.' She glanced at the stairs, to where the children were sleeping, and the flicker of fear in her eyes felt like she had reached out and struck Beth on the face. Beth was acting as though Natasha was the enemy, when Dee had told her that she was not. Was she angry at the wrong person?

'I need to ask you some questions.'

Natasha shook her head in confusion. 'Um, sure, okay.'

'Did you know about me and the kids when you started seeing Rob?'

Natasha blushed and looked at the floor.

'I want the truth now. I don't have time for anything else. There isn't *time*, do you understand?' Beth's voice was strained as she tried to keep her voice down but get the urgency across. There was no time for bullshit. Those pills wouldn't work forever, and Rob would probably figure out that she was here and come for her. For them all.

'No. Not at first, but yes, he did tell me he was married with children but that it wasn't working.'

'Aw. Did I not understand him?' Beth asked in a faux-sweet voice.

'Yeah. Something like that. I fell for it and before you ask, yes, I feel stupid. Is that what you want to hear?'

'Maybe. But I'm not here for that. I need to know where you stand.'

'What do you mean?'

'I mean, are you the Natasha I met with Rob – the one who lied to my face about being a nanny, about not being his lover, about the whole set up? Or are you the one Dee has told me about – the one who is on our side, who sees Rob for who he really is and can help me? Because right now, I need help.' Beth had meant to sound fierce, demanding of answers, but even she could hear the tremble in her voice.

'Beth... I...'

'Just tell me!'

'I'm on your side. And... and I'm sorry. I did lie to you. I did let myself get caught up in all this and I didn't mean to. He was just so... charming and kind and always telling me how wonderful I was and how much he loved me and how amazing our life together was going to be and I...'

'Wanted to believe him?'

Natasha nodded with tears in her eyes. 'I'm so sorry,' she whispered.

'He is a *bad* man,' Beth said, her lips tight with tension.

'I know that now. Dee has told me about... what he is, what he does. To you.'

'Can I trust you?' Beth asked. A simple question but one that just might be the difference between her surviving this and not. And for her kids, she had to survive this.

'You can. I swear. Look...' Natasha turned away from Beth and walked to the desk at the edge of the room, where she lifted up a large heavy book and opened it. She held up a small blue book with gold lettering. Beth's passport. 'It took me forever to find it but I did eventually. There's a box with all the paperwork in it. Your passport, the twins' birth certificates, their passports.'

'They have passports?'

'Yes, see?' She turned back to the book and then held up two maroon passports.

We can go home.

'Where were they?'

'You'd barely believe it. It was behind the bath panel.'

'What?'

'You know, the plastic that covers the bath? And the funny thing is—'

'Funny?' Nothing was funny here.

'No, I mean, I only found it because he left in a temper yesterday and he slammed the door so hard that the air banged the bathroom door shut, and it popped the panel off. It was only when I was putting it back together that I saw it.'

'He had a temper? Here?'

'No one can hide themselves forever, right?' Natasha looked ashamed. She paled as she kept talking. 'And... actually, well, I think... I'm pretty sure that he...' She was shaking now.

'What? What is it?'

Just as Natasha opened her mouth to answer, Dee came rushing in through the front door that, in her hurry to get in, Beth had not properly closed.

'Beth. Natasha. You're okay. Is he here? What's happening?' Dee looked frantic.

'We're fine. No, he's not here.'

'What's going on?' Dee said, looking between Beth and Natasha.

'I think the accident was Rob's fault,' Natasha said, blurting it out as though keeping it in any longer was burning her.

'What?' Dee and Beth said together.

'Not all of it, I mean. Obviously. But I think he was involved.'

Beth sat down heavily. She wasn't sure that she was ready to hear this.

'On the day of the accident, he called me, in a state. Asked me to come over immediately. Stupidly, I thought he'd finally chosen me over you, but when I got there, he was rambling about you leaving; you'd taken the kids, and he needed to talk with you. He needed to explain and stop you from "over-reacting".'

'About what?'

'He didn't say. I didn't ask. I should have asked. It could have changed everything. He was furious. He said he... wanted to follow you, to explain, to stop you. And he said he needed my car.'

'How does that make him involved in the accident?' Dee asked.

'The third car.'

'What about it?' Dee asked again.

'Can you just let her talk? Please?' Beth said, exasperated. She had to know what Natasha meant.

'Sorry. Go on.'

'When Dee came to me, told me what Rob was really like, I didn't want to believe her. I didn't want to believe that I'd been so stupid, but it all made sense. All the small things that didn't add up. The times when Rob contradicted himself and then got angry when I asked him to clarify. From the day of the accident onwards he was always wired, and I thought it was because he felt guilty, because you'd left him in such a state and then got into an accident. I thought that he felt that it was his fault. He didn't bring my car back for a few days, and then suddenly it arrived, all cleaned and shiny. Looking like new. I thought he'd been busy at the hospital and then had it valeted as a thank you. But. I don't know, there was something *off*.'

'What do you mean?'

'I don't know. Just something wasn't right, but by then the twins had arrived here, and life got manic and there was just never time to think about it. But then Dee came round and asked me to look at the situation with a different set of eyes and it got me thinking. I looked up the accident. There was a line at the end of the article I read about the third car leaving the scene before the emergency services had arrived and that the police were looking for the driver of what they suspect was a red car due to paint flakes left on yours.'

'What?' Beth said. 'I looked up the accident, I didn't see that. What do they mean, left the scene?'

'Just that, I suppose,' Natasha said, 'that whoever was driving the car that pushed you into the ditch then drove off before the police arrived.'

'And you think that was *Rob*?' Beth said.

'Yes, I do. My car is a bit of a wreck, always has been. And he used to tell me about this garage who did stuff, cash in hand, cheaper, under the radar, you know? Yesterday, after I found the box of your documents hidden away, I couldn't get that out of my head. So I called them. Asked about Rob, asked about my car, if they did valeting as well, and the man on the phone just *blew up* at me. Told me to stop asking so many questions, who did I think I was, told me to tell Rob to control his Mrs, and then he hung up.'

Beth screwed her eyes closed as she took all this in. 'You think Rob is the one who drove me off the road? That he *deliberately* drove me and our children into a ditch?'

Natasha looked as though she wanted to be sick. 'Yes. I do. And I think he took my car to this dodgy garage to get it fixed up afterwards. Before bringing it back to me. He could be implicating me. The police will track it down eventually, surely? And as the *other woman*, how do I prove it wasn't me driving?'

'Show me your car. Now,' Beth said.

'Now?' Natasha asked.

'Right now. I need to see it,' Beth demanded.

As they went outside, Beth looked to the skies, begging for some sort of sign to show her the way out of all this. She both wanted to look at the car and have her memory of the accident return and was also terrified that it would confirm her worst fears. That Rob really would do what he'd said; that he really would rather she and the twins die than leave him behind.

'Here. It's a bit dark but... it's ten years old. And...'

'Red.'

Dee walked around it. She put her hands on the panels at the back of the car and then again at the front, looking close up at the edges in the weak light.

'The front looks newer?'

'Exactly,' Natasha said. 'See? I just hadn't put two and two together until now. I'm not going mad, am I?'

'No. That's what he wants you to think. He can argue with you that the sky is orange and that rain isn't wet until you question your own mind. That's what he does,' Dee said bitterly.

Beth looked at Natasha, first feeling a flash of anger towards her for standing beside Rob while he did all this, while he endangered Beth over and over again, but then reminding herself that she was as much a victim in this as she was. Though, Beth realised, she hoped less than her. She hoped against hope that he'd never been violent towards Natasha as he had been with her. This woman had been caught in this mess and had voluntarily stayed in it, with Rob, in order to care for her children, even once Natasha's own doubts and fears had materialised. Beth could not have been more grateful.

She silently walked around the perimeter of the car and pulled Natasha to her in a hug. 'I don't think you're imagining it. And I'm so sorry.'

'For what?'

Beth broke away. 'For dragging you into this awful mess. For Rob. For the version of him that I helped unleash on you. For all the lies he's told. For anything... Has he... Does he...' Beth looked down at her bandaged arms. She felt Natasha's eyes on her as she followed Beth's gaze and then the smallest of pauses while Natasha processed what she was seeing and what Beth was asking of her with her silence.

'He's never laid a hand on me. At least, not yet,' Natasha said, looking at Beth intently.

'Good,' she whispered. It felt awful to be alone in this, but it would have felt worse to know that he had destroyed someone else in the way that he had destroyed her. Perhaps they could rescue each other before that happened.

The three of them returned to the house in silence, the warmth of the light inviting them back in from the cold darkness. It felt like a sign. They all sat down to try to work out exactly what they had just learned and the implications of it.

'Rob scares me,' Beth said. 'He's unpredictable but I still don't really know what he's trying to achieve here. With both of us. Does he want two separate lives forever? Or does he want to... get *rid* of some of us? Of me? Of the children? Or you, Natasha? And when I say get rid of, I honestly don't know exactly what I mean, only that I can't rule out that he might do something really horrific again. Did he drive us off the road as a warning, or was he actually trying to kill us?'

She didn't mention what he had said to her that evening, before he passed out. She wanted to see if her instincts were right, without leading Dee or Natasha to agree with her.

'Am I wrong?' She paused to look at the other women, to see if they thought she was overreacting. If they did, then they didn't show it. 'Am I being melodramatic?' The room was silent. 'Am I?' Beth begged, wishing for one of them, anyone, to tell her she was taking things out of proportion, that she was being a drama queen and that they weren't really dealing with someone who might be a real danger to them all. That they didn't have a much bigger problem here. She had poked the bear.

No one spoke.

Natasha finally broke the silence.

'No. No, I don't think you are.'

Dee exhaled loudly. 'Shit,' she said.

'Yup,' Beth said. It was both a relief to know she wasn't blowing things out of proportion and terrifying to have her worst fears confirmed. Rob was bad news. And there was no straightforward way to get her and the children safely away from him other than to grab what they had and run, hoping he would not follow them. Should she run?

'He scares me too. Like you say, he's hot and cold. He's either flooding me with affection, with gifts, with compliments, or he's silent, moody. Something seething inside him. It's big gestures or big moods and I never know which it is.'

'And the twins?' Beth needed to know if he would truly hurt them in order to get to her. Were his words just words or was there a danger behind them? The idea that he had driven right at their car still hadn't sunk in yet.

'Nothing. He acts almost as though they're not his. Detached. No affection, no love. Nothing. It's like he tries to care for them but he just... can't.'

Natasha's words shifted something in Beth. Her breath felt like it was stuck in her throat – nothing going in or out. She was frozen, gasping for air. The room shifted around her until she was back in a flat she didn't recognise, a different city outside the window. She blinked but the scene remained, and she watched as a version of herself came into her view. She looked terrified.

'How do you know it's mine?' Rob had shouted, his face ravaged by fury. He slammed his fist down on the table beside him.

'I... who... whose else would it be?' a confused and vulnerable Beth responded. She had not been expecting this. No, the pregnancy had not been planned, but he was always talking about the day they would get married, the children they would have. He'd even told her what names he wanted to give them. Over and over during their time together he'd played out their perfect futures in whispered nothings as he held her in his arms. She had thought that he would be as surprised as she was, but still... happy.

'Well, I don't know. You met an awful lot of people in your *job*.'

'What? You mean my bar job – the one where I'm rushed off my feet for eight hours at a time serving drinks to loaded drunks in the city? That one?'

Rob's mouth curved into a nasty grin. 'Are you saying I'm not enough for you?'

Beth screwed her eyes up in frustration. 'This again? Seriously?'

'I'm not rich like one of your... bankers.' He spat the last word out.

'For the last time, Rob, I am not *with* any of the bankers. They don't even look at me. I am just the drinks bitch to them. And besides, I've not worked in months. Everything is closed, you know that!'

Rob remained silent but his anger and insecurity still seeped from him into the room. Every muscle in his body was taut, ready to inflict damage should he choose to. Beth tried very hard not to show her fear in case it further enraged him, and she was certainly afraid now. Before, his low self-esteem had been almost endearing, that he couldn't see how wonderful he was, how safe he had made her feel when she was so far away from home and alone, but little by little as his temper came out at the same time, Beth had learnt not to do or say anything that might make him feel low. She had thought she was being supportive, but now she realised she had been enabling this. And now, when she was showing him that he could have the future he so often narrated for her, he was angry?

'We'll have to get married.'

'What?'

'At some point your visa will expire, won't it? And I don't know what the implications for the... baby would be. About staying here. It'd just be easier all round if we got married.'

'Do you... want to get married?'

It had not been the proposal that Beth had expected. She had been scared but excited to tell him; she had expected him to sweep her up in his arms, shower her with kisses and affection and beg her to make him the happiest man alive. Or at least look happy. He looked sick. This was not how it was supposed to be.

He didn't answer. He paced furiously up and down the room until it made Beth feel dizzy to watch him. She'd never seen him this angry before. She briefly wondered if she ought to... get rid of the baby, but she took her hand to her stomach as her internal monologue told her 'No'. If he didn't want this then she could just go back home when the borders reopened. He could have his life, she could have hers and although returning home broke and knocked up was not exactly what she had planned, she knew her family would support her.

It was not what she wanted though. She wanted the dream. She wanted what he had promised her during all those late nights when they had lain in each other's arms. She felt cheated.

He turned to her. 'Well, I don't really have a choice now, do I?'

At his cold dismissal, Beth burst into tears, and it was like a switch had been flicked. Immediately, Rob wrapped her in his arms and held her as he stroked her head.

'Oh, Pooky. No. No, don't cry. I didn't want you to cry. I'm just... surprised. Shocked, that's all. Sssh, it's okay. I'll make it okay. Stop crying. Stop. Stop!'

Beth's breath stuttered as she tried to stop crying. She didn't want his rage to flare up again. Even in this new softness from him, the hard edge was still discernible.

'Rob...'

'It was just out of the blue. I love you, I love us. We'll work this out.'

Beth tried to ignore the practicality rather than the emotion in his voice. This was still a problem to be fixed, not a joy to be embraced.

'I need you. *We* need you.' She placed his hand on her stomach and appealed to his love of being the protector. She needed him to show her some affection. She felt wretched.

'I'll take care of this. I promise.'

Beth nodded, her eyes still full of tears unshed. She wanted to believe him. She chose not to hear his choice of words – 'this', not 'you'. So she took the growing pebble of doubt that sat heavy in her stomach and ignored it. Pushed it to one side and hoped it would go away.

It had not.

'Beth? Beth? Are you all right?' Dee was by her side and Beth reached out for her. She blinked hard over and over to try to get her mind to reset itself to where she actually was, not to where it was that she had just been. The room was swimming around her and she felt as though she was underwater. She needed to get to the surface. She couldn't breathe.

'Where did you go?' Dee asked, concerned. 'It was like you

disassociated for a moment. You were here, but you were very much not here. Are you okay?'

Beth shook her head. 'I just remembered... the day I told Rob I was pregnant and how badly he took it. He didn't think it was his, that was his first thought.'

'Wow. That's cold.'

'I don't know if it was just a shock, a defence mechanism kicking in or something or if he genuinely believed they weren't his from the start. God, I've let them down so badly.'

'No. No, don't say that. You're a wonderful mother.' Dee squeezed her hand.

'Am I? I got pregnant by accident by a man who doesn't want them or love them and is prepared to hurt them for his own purposes. I had depression when they were born. I gave them a terrible father. And now I'm hiding away from them, trying to chip enough power back from him to get back to them. I should go, now, take them and run away somewhere.' She thought of the sheer hatred that she'd seen in his eyes back at the house. 'I have to go. Now.'

'Where?'

'Home. Natasha found my passports, our passports.'

'Beth, babe, I don't want to be defeatist but with what money? And to where? You don't know where your folks have moved to yet, do you? I don't want you to stay with him, no, but I don't know if just getting on a plane is gonna work? We had a plan, didn't we? To get things all sorted, all above board.'

'Yeah, I've messed that up.'

'What did you do?' Dee looked from Beth to Natasha. 'Always honesty, babe, remember? You can tell me anything.'

'He came home. Raging drunk. Angry. I... I fed him my painkillers to knock him out. I was scared. I needed him away from me. And... well, he threatened to kill me. Me and the kids.

When he wakes up, he's going to be raging. And by then I need to be gone.'

Both Natasha and Dee's faces paled as the scale of the urgency of the situation dawned on them both.

'He will always find you though. If you run. He's obsessed with you. You know that. Surely you can see that. From all this... weirdness? He wants you locked up in a little bubble where he can keep you just for him,' Dee said.

'Is he? Surely he'd move on. Just find someone else to put on a pedestal and control.' She glanced at Natasha. 'Sorry.'

Natasha shook her head. 'No. Don't worry. You're right. I can see that now. But I think Dee is right too. He has no intention of letting you go. You or the kids. Not against his wishes. It has to be on his terms.'

'His terms? What are you saying? His terms means he kills us. He literally drove us into a ditch and then drove away, leaving us to drown! We have to go.'

Natasha looked at Dee in horror, but she held her palms up in a 'you know she's right' gesture.

'Okay, you're right, Beth. You need to go, and you need to go tonight. It's fine, we can make this work. Can't we, Tash?'

She nodded, overwhelmed. 'I'll... go wake the twins?'

'Not yet. No. He'll sleep for a few hours at least, I think. We have time to set things in motion before waking them. Let them sleep,' Beth said. As much as she wanted to scoop them into her arms, get in the car and just go, she knew it would be better all round if they got a few ducks in a row first.

Dee opened up her phone and checked a list she had been working on.

'I've made a list. I've done some research. Getting a bank account is going to be more difficult than I thought, I'm afraid.

We need addresses, proof of residence, ID. I don't know if we have those?'

'They might be in the box I found, with the passports? You could take the whole thing with you and go through it?'

'In the meantime, I've taken out as much cash as I could, babe. It's here.' She tapped her bag. 'We'll try to reset your PayPal account so you can access it. If you send the money to me, I'll withdraw it and give you cash instead. It's not ideal but it will do. I've spoken with the local women's refuge about what support you might be able to access.' Dee listed them as she looked over the notes she had made. 'The house is more complicated, I'm afraid, as the mortgage is entirely in his name. We'll need somewhere for you to go while we work out where to go from here.'

'I think we need to get as far away from him as possible. And... well, I think you too, Natasha. In case he works out that you helped us and decides to... take revenge or something.' Beth looked at her hands. She turned them over in each other again and again, trying to stop the shake in them. This was all such a mess. There seemed no way out.

'I could go to my mum's. He doesn't know where that is.'

'That's perfect. I'm so sorry. I messed up, I made it worse...' Beth said.

'No. I get it. It's okay.'

Dee looked back at her phone. 'Legally, you would need to contest his access to the children, so I wondered about setting up an appointment with Citizen's Advice about how to start that. He might not request any access or custody, but I suspect if he wants to lash out, he will...'

Beth rubbed her aching temples. She sighed, closing her eyes, feeling utterly defeated.

'I can't do this.'

'You can, babe, I promise. I know it must feel like you've got a bloody big mountain to climb, but you just have to put one foot in front of the other until you're at the top. And we're here to help.'

'It's like climbing a mountain being chased by a bear though.'

'I know, babe.'

'I should just shoot it. The bear,' Beth said dismissively.

Suddenly the atmosphere in the room changed. Beth had voiced the solution that had first come to her that evening, in the kitchen with Rob. Her or him – who would be the last one standing?

'I should... I could...' Her voice rose as her anger grew. 'He's taken everything from me. Everything. My children, my home, my money, my connection to my family, my belief in my own memories, my freedom, my body, my self-belief and my self-worth.'

Dee stood up to face Beth, her eyes questioning.

'I want him gone. I do. I want him dead. So he can't ever hurt anyone ever again,' Beth repeated in case either woman was in any doubt as to her meaning.

Dee looked shocked, her eyes flickering from Beth to Natasha and back again as she took in what Beth had just said. Her face set into an expression of hard resolve as she turned to Beth and asked, 'So what do we need to do?'

23

'Are you serious? You're not serious? You're... you mean it?' Natasha stuttered as she looked back between the other two women, who stood statue like, determination on their faces.

'No. That's insane. I can't... I can't be a part of that. I don't want to be. What... what about the twins? He's their *dad*. You can't just... Besides, how would you even? No. Don't tell me, I don't want to know. No. You're insane, this is insane.'

Natasha started gathering her things.

'What are you going to do?' Beth asked, panic in her voice.

Natasha turned to face her. 'Do you mean am I going to tell him? Or tell someone? The police?'

'Yes,' Beth said.

Natasha exhaled loudly. 'I don't know. I understand he's not a good person, I get that. Truly. But you can't just play God like that. You're being unhinged. This isn't TV, this isn't some drama where you get to decide who lives or dies, for God's sake! You'd be as bad as him! It's not fair on anyone and you... How would you live with yourself?'

'How would *she* live? How would *she live*?' Dee shouted. 'Do you even know what hell he's put her through? Do you? I know you understand that Rob is not going to be winning any good husband awards, and he apparently couldn't give two shits about his own kids, but I don't think you really understand just what he's *done* to her! Even after what I've told you already.'

'Dee, it's okay, you don't have to.' Beth said, shaking her head. 'She's right, we can't...'

'Maybe she is right, but I want her to *know* why you feel like this.'

Natasha shook her head. 'I'm sorry but I don't think there is any way that you can convince me of this. I've got to go. I can't be here. But. The twins. I can't leave them with you, not like this.' She looked conflicted.

'I can't *tell* you without...' Dee looked at Beth, her face full of rage but her eyes filled with sorrow. Her voice dropped. 'I can't tell you, Natasha, without telling Beth what she doesn't yet know. I remember. I know what he's done to her over the years. And I tell you what? I *hate* him for it. *I hate him.* I am not a violent person, not at all. I don't agree with fighting or capital punishment or war. I try to practise kindness and help raise children with a good sense of right and wrong and to always, always try to do their best for others and themselves. I believe in the innate goodness of people, but *him*? Him I would happily take a shotgun to if I thought I could. The world would be a better place without him. The children are the only good thing about him ever existing at all and even they would be better off if he wasn't here. He will only poison them with his twisted thinking. Or worse still, take it out on them. He *deserves* to die. And I will not take you standing here, judging Beth, or me, for wanting to find some way, any way, of allowing her and her children a life free from him. Because he won't ever let them go if he's still here. I know it. He would ruin his own life first in order to ruin theirs just because he thinks he *deserves* them. The only thing he deserves is to be six foot under. Or two foot under in a shallow grave and utterly forgotten.'

Dee sank down onto the side arm of the sofa, shaking and breathless.

'What did he do?' Beth asked, quietly, softly, as though her own voice scared her. 'Cos you *really* hate him. I know why I do, but you? What did he do to me? I thought I knew the worst of it even without all my memories.'

'I can't... You need to remember in your own time.' Dee shook her head. 'I don't want to blurt it out here, just like that. It's... a lot.'

'I want to know.'

Natasha stopped packing her things and put her bag down again. 'I want to know too. I know it's not about me, but I am involved now, aren't I? Whether I like it or not.' She sounded rattled, as though she was properly scared for the first time. Like the cold reality of this scenario was finally sinking in. That Rob's violence wasn't a one-off.

Dee pursed her lips and blew out the air. She nodded before turning to Beth. 'If you're really sure?'

Beth nodded in reply. 'I'm tired of not knowing, of there being this creeping sense of danger but not knowing what it is. Or if it's just my brain being in fight or flight for too long and always feeling afraid. I'm exhausted. I don't want to do it any more. I want to know and then I want to work out what to do with what I know.' She glanced at Natasha. 'Whatever that might be.'

'Okay, but I'm going to ask you to sit down and if it's too much you must absolutely tell me to stop. All right?'

'I will, I promise.' Beth moved to the sofa and Dee came and sat beside her.

'When I first met you, you were a scared, unsure, unsupported first time mum of twins, trying to work out what you were doing. But that wasn't so different to other mums I know. Every parent is just trying to figure it all out as they go while feeling like they ought to know already and pretending sometimes that they do. But slowly, really barely noticeable at first, you changed.'

'How?'

'It was hard to pin down. Your voice got less sure, quieter, you said less, chatted less, withdrew. You got paler, you smiled less. You... shrank. You got thin, never more than picking at any food we had, and you got quiet, like you didn't trust your own voice. Your own thoughts. And then there were the bruises.'

'Bruises?' Natasha asked.

Dee looked at her feet to hide the pain on her face, but Beth caught it. She looked up at her again.

'The ones I first noticed were on your neck. Like someone had grabbed you around it. I could see you'd tried to cover them up with make-up, but hot smudgy toddler hands had wiped it off. At first, I thought they were just hickeys. But then I noticed more, and one day the kids were clambering over you like kids do and it hiked your dress up, and you had them all over your thighs. Bruises... And bite marks. Bite marks all over you. You looked like you'd been attacked. I saw it and you saw me see it. You froze. You looked utterly terrified but then your eyes welled up and you excused yourself to the toilet.'

Natasha was quiet, observing. Her face was ashen. She had fallen for the same false charm that Beth had. Would this have been her future?

'He began to control other things. He'd already taken your phone. He didn't need to track you if he'd taken your own money, your bank account and your passport. And your house keys. Where were you going to go? He kept the petrol in your car low, so you'd never be able to go on a long journey. He'd thought of everything. Or at least he thought he had.'

'What did he miss?'

'Me. He underestimated that you have friends. People who care about you and were looking out for you. And that I was not going to let him do this to you. Or to the twins. He had forgotten that you mattered, you matter to people other than him. He hadn't isolated you completely. Because of that day, we made plans to contact each other in a way he couldn't track, didn't know about. We started getting you out from then. He got worse while we were making plans and he got worse faster than we could work out how to get you all free from him.'

'I'm sorry. I didn't know. But you still can't just...' Natasha whispered. She couldn't even bring herself to say the words.

'Why would you? He's clever, or at least to a point. He knows how to pull someone in with his lies. He's just not as clever as he thinks he is,' Dee said, venom in her voice.

'I owe so much to you,' Beth said.

'You can get me some thank you flowers, babe,' Dee joked, trying to lighten the mood.

'Flowers...'

Beth's breathing suddenly became ragged, shallow, and she was finding it hard to speak. Her face paled of all its colour. She was no longer in the room with the other two. She was in another room, at a different time...

'Oh, I'm sorry, have I come at a bad time? I just wanted to drop off these flowers to say thank you for such a wonderful photo shoot and beautiful photos. I love them! And you handled the children, being, well, children, so well. I will be recommending you everywhere!' the lady at the door had beamed at Beth before handing over a huge bunch of beautiful flowers. She had a sleeping baby strapped to her chest and a fidgeting toddler holding her other hand. Beth took the flowers and tried to smile.

'No, no, it's fine. It's just my... husband isn't well and is home today,' Beth said as her stomach dropped. How much had he heard? She could tell without looking that he was hovering, listening, just around the corner. She could sense his anger from here. It made her skin bristle as though it was burning as she forced herself to smile at this kind lady who had no idea what she had just done.

Her secret business, with the money it had been bringing her, the independence, freedom and the joy it gave her, would be discovered. And if it was discovered, he would take it. Like he took everything.

'Oh, I hope he feels better soon! I won't keep you any longer. I know how men are with their man flu! Thank you again!' the lady said. 'Come on then, poppet, let's go get you some lunch.'

Beth watched them as they walked down the path of the front garden and into the street. She did not want to go back inside, yet she was already trying to work out where she could safely keep the children away from Rob when she had to, so they didn't have to watch their father, red faced, sweaty, furious and unpredictable. Right now, they were just playing in the living room. They'd been looking at picture books when the doorbell had gone. She needed to get back to them and get them into their bedroom perhaps. But she also needed time, seconds even, to work out what she could say, what she could tell Rob, how much she could still withhold and have him believe it. He mistrusted and twisted everything she did tell him and so she needed to have a story, a backstory, an answer for every angle that he might demand to know about. She was dizzied by it all.

But one single piece of information stood out for her. She couldn't do this any more. She didn't want to. She wouldn't.

He was stood, arms crossed, nostrils flaring with indignation as Beth returned to the living room, arms full of flowers. The scent of them was making her feel sick and her eyes itch. She would forever associate their scent with fear. She was terrified.

'Who's bringing you flowers?'

'Just a lady from one of the playgroups.' *Don't give any more information than he is asking for. He doesn't know. He will only* know *if you tell him.*

'Why?'

'Because she's kind?'

'Don't patronise me. Why? What photoshoot? What photos? You aren't a photographer any more, if you ever really were one.'

Beth winced. That stung. He had never seen her dream, her love for the art, for the interaction, for the skill of truly capturing the essence of a moment or the soul of a person in a single second of time. He'd belittled it almost as soon as he could once she was trapped by him in their life together. Indignation, fury and her own hatred burned for how little she had allowed him to let her be. It felt like the words she wanted to say to him were scorching the back of her throat as she swallowed them down.

Not now. Keep your cool. Spitting rage at him will not serve you best here, she reminded herself and kept silent. *Do not give him what he wants.*

'Well? Aren't you going to say anything?'

Beth remained wordless, silently placing the flowers down on the coffee table and scooping the children up in her arms and walking them to their bedroom.

'Just play in here a little while, okay? Mumma will be back in a minute. Do not leave the room until I come and get you.'

She surveyed the room for any hazards. Anything they might accidentally put in their mouths, anything heavy they might pull onto them. Any danger in here was lesser than the danger out there. Their own father who, when feeling put upon, had no compunction at lashing out at whoever he felt best deserved his wrath.

Back in the living room, Beth found the floor covered in small bits of bashed and torn petals. The bouquet had been smashed repeatedly against the wall, staining the white paintwork with green smudges, and the remainder of it, limp and broken, was back where she had first placed it. Rob stood smiling maliciously, like he was proud of his work and waiting for glowing feedback on what he had done.

Beth looked at him with utter disdain. Why was he like this? He had the emotional development of a toddler. He'd never talked much about his family or childhood. All that he had ever been drawn on to say was that he and his own father had had a spectacular row when he was a teenager and he had packed his bags, moved to London and not seen or spoken to his family since. In her naivety, Beth had seen him as a tortured soul whose own family hadn't loved him properly in the way that she would love him. She would heal him. She would make him better. She had not considered the emotional damage that she could not reach, nor the fact that generational trauma often repeated itself. She had not considered that, without knowing Rob's family background, she wouldn't be able to predict what sort of father he might be. To know what he might repeat, what he might inflict on their own children. Well, it stopped here. She would not allow her children to grow up like him, or to think that his behaviour was normal. That this was what a marriage should be, or that this was love. This was not love.

'Always putting them first,' he spat at her. 'What about me? I was talking to you.'

Beth bit her tongue between her teeth to keep her words unsaid. She would not do this. She would not rise to his taunting. Something inside her shifted. Suddenly she realised that she was no longer afraid of him. He was a small, hurt little man who, instead of using his freedom to make his own life, to allow himself to be happy, was focused on creating a world where everyone hurt like he did. Well, not any more. She wouldn't let him do that to her nor to her children. She would not allow it.

'No.'

'I beg your pardon?' Rob said, a look of utter disgust on his face.

'No. I'm not going to say anything. I don't have to tell you anything. Someone kind bought me flowers for something I did for them. That's all. There's nothing more. I'm done.' Beth was shocked at the dead tone to her voice. She was stripped of all emotion; she was numb. Her only focus was on getting the children and herself safely away from him.

'You *won't* leave me. You can't. I won't let you.'

'I didn't say anything.' Again, Beth's voice was monotoned. She would not get drawn into this. She would not let him control this. She knew she was in a dangerous position. Leaving someone violent, someone controlling, was a delicate balance and she had to remind herself not to forget that, not to downplay what he might be capable of. She needed to de-escalate things so she could get away.

'*Say* something, dammit!' He turned around and blasted his fist into the door, cracking the wood. Paint splintered onto the carpet, like little flakes of snow. It made Beth's blood run cold.

'Like what, Rob?'

'Fight for us! Fight for me.'

'I don't want to fight. I'm tired of fighting. I'm done.'

It was like he had used every single cell of her; he had broken, abused, crushed and belittled so much of her that there was nothing left for him to grab hold of. She had elevated herself above it all, to the part of her that he couldn't reach.

He could see it. She knew it made him furious. Like a child who'd been told they could not have the one toy they wanted, the one thing they thought would make them feel good, only making their desire of it all the greater.

'We're not done! You aren't! You aren't until I *say* you are.' Flicks of spittle flew out of his mouth as he raged at her. He pushed all the clutter off the shelf he was standing near to and watched gleefully as it crashed to the ground. He started picking books, her favourite things, off another shelf and throwing them at her, using his full force. She ducked and watched him as he had what could only be described as a tantrum, flinging things everywhere, raging until his words were undiscernible. She kept her distance, all the time keeping one eye and her ears on the bedroom where the children were. How could she best escape with them? She needed him to expend all his rage now, here, to get to that point where his own self-disgust and remorse kicked him. He would be spent, weeping, apologetic. She knew how it went. A thought came to her. Should she *let* him hurt her? In the times that he had hurt her, it seemed to expend his rage faster. Should she let him do it, goad him into it even, so as to be able to get the children out of here sooner?

Just as she was considering this option and took a step closer towards him to gauge whether or not it would work, he stopped. He stopped throwing things and looked at her. Stared at her. His expression scared her more than it had ever done before. His eyes looked black, his pupils so dilated with fury that there was barely space for the colour around them to be seen. He was breathing hard, his breath rasping out of his nose, his mouth clamped shut in a hard line. He looked like a bull ready to charge at its victim.

He walked towards her.

Beth swallowed her nerves and willed her body to stop trembling. She clenched what felt like every muscle she had to keep herself utterly still. She held her breath as he came close to her, her whole being tensed in preparation for whatever he was going to do. She would let him do it, this one final time, and then she would take the children and run. She and Dee had been working on a plan, a way to get out, to get money, somewhere to go, a new life in blueprint form. It wasn't ready yet, but she wouldn't wait any longer. She couldn't. And so, knowing that this was the final time, she lifted her head to look at him, face to face.

He brought his face so close to hers that he was out of focus. She couldn't see his features but could feel his hot breath on her skin. She took a sharp breath inward. Her mind reminded her of how once, this closeness would have been erotic, a precursor to passion. Now, she felt only the frost of fear.

'You. Will. Never. Leave. I will *burn* this house down with you all in it before I let that happen. I will set fire to everything rather than let you walk away from me. You. Are. Mine. Do you understand?' He ran his finger down her cheek and cupped it over her chin. Beth lifted her face defiantly to his. She couldn't tell if his intended effect was supposed to be charming or chilling, but she felt ice creep through her veins as he held her face.

She nodded. 'I do.'

'Good.' He let her go. He walked away, readjusting his shirt and hair as he did so. 'Tidy up this mess,' he said, his voice almost back to normal as he gestured to the books, the clutter and the remains of the bouquet. 'The kids might do something stupid and hurt themselves on it.'

As Beth's mind returned to where she was now, the room was silent and both women were looking at her.

Beth realised now that she'd never had the chance to tell Dee about this threat. Because directly after, Rob went for a shower, Beth had picked up the children, got as much as she could carry, packed them into the car and left. She had been trying hard to work out where to go, what do to do. What was the best plan of action? She had driven to a side road for a while. She'd left Dee a rambling message and then and just sat, trying to decide what to do before driving off into the fens. She was trying to concentrate on the road with all of this swarming through her mind like angry wasps, stinging her thoughts into oblivion. The kids were confused as to what was going on, picking up on her stress. She hated the fen road, but it was the best one to take to escape. The fastest way out of her life with him. To freedom.

Only it had betrayed her. And it had delivered her straight back to him.

'Are you okay?' Natasha asked. 'You went really quiet. Like you weren't *here*.'

Should she tell them what he had said, what he'd threatened? He'd really meant it. Then and now. Surely they would understand what she had do to?

'Yes. Sorry. I... it's all a lot. What you've told me. What I remember. More and more is coming back to me.'

'I know, babe. I'm sorry. But we're here for you. Both of us.'

'We are, yes,' Natasha said, 'I... I still don't think we can just... *off* him. Morality aside, if I was even okay with that, which I am not, I mean, where would we even start?'

Beth looked at these two women, who had absolutely no reason to put themselves in danger in order to help her, and yet here they both were. She could not drag them into this any further. She could not have them know what she was going to do. She would be incriminating them, more than she had done so already, and she wouldn't do that to them. She knew she had been good at keeping her secrets locked away, and so one last time she put what she knew into a cage inside her and she turned the key.

'You're right,' Beth said decisively, hoping she could hide her real feelings from them. She had done it from Rob for years, after all. 'I was being ridiculous. I can't kill him. That would make me as bad as him, wouldn't it?'

She did need their help though, but she couldn't let them know it.

'But... maybe we could *scare* him a bit? Show him that I won't take his shit any more and that he needs to leave me and the kids alone. He's a coward really, he's a lonely little boy who wants to hurt people like he's hurting. I think if I showed him that he has lost his power over me, that I won't let him treat me like this any more, then I think he'll cave.'

Dee wrinkled her nose. 'Really? I mean, I loathe the bones of him for what he did to you, is still doing to you, and I know I said the world would be a better place without him, but yes, actually getting rid of him wasn't next on my to do list. But... you would be free of him.' She caught Natasha's expression. 'Hey! I'm just saying. It's true.'

'Beth is right with this, Dee, he is a coward. I think we could scare him off. She's not asking for anything from him other than the kids, right?'

'Why should she leave with nothing though? She deserves half of everything. The house, his money, everything.'

'I just want to be away from him. I met him with nothing. I can leave him with nothing. Other than our children. And if he gives nothing for them then he can't come for them, can he? If he's not supporting them financially then it'd damage any claim he might make for them. Surely?'

'I guess,' Dee said, unconvinced.

'I think the best plan is to gather your money, what you have, scare him off and go.'

'What, and leave him for you? Is that what you want?' Dee turned to Natasha accusingly.

'Oh, absolutely not!' Natasha said, shaking her head vehemently. 'I want to move on and forget this part of my life ever happened. How can you think that still, Dee? You know me. I know it sounds like I'm trying to get rid of the inconvenient family, but I've been taking care of those kids for weeks now. I love them. I want what's best for them and I can see now that Rob absolutely isn't that. They need to be safe from him. We all do.'

Beth closed her eyes to think. Could she do this? Make one plan with them while really considering something else? Would that put them in the clear if it went wrong, or would they still be implicated? What were the legal ramifications? After all both women had done for her, she didn't want to cause them any trouble. They were her literal saviours. She owed them her life.

'I think Natasha is right and I think that she is telling the truth. She's looked after Henry and Ammy all this time and she's going behind Rob's back now for what? If she wanted Rob, then surely she'd have just told him about this, about us? Wouldn't you?' Beth turned to Natasha.

'I would have. Look, I know you hate him, I get it. I do too. I can't believe I ever fell for him and his false charm. Which is why I think we should scare the shit out of him. I think we should metaphorically hold him over a cliff edge by his balls and tell him we'll cut them off and let him drop if he doesn't back the hell off and let us all go.'

'Jesus!' Dee said, shocked. Her eyes widened in surprise but then settled into an expression of respect. 'Wow. I… absolutely.'

Beth smiled. They were both on board with messing with him, with teaching him a lesson he'd never forget. She would just not tell them that she might decide to take things overboard once they had got Rob right where Beth wanted him – with his life in her hands.

'It has to be now. He's already out of it. Once he wakes up, he will be too strong, too angry, and it'll put us in danger. I want him incapable of hurting me while I teach him a lesson. That's all.' *That's all I'm going to tell you, at least.*

'Okay,' Dee said, chewing her lip. 'So what do we do?'

'I want to take him to where I crashed. To where he nearly killed us all. I should have escaped him that day. I would have done, except for the accident. I'm done with him. I want it to be over.'

'Are you sure you shouldn't just go now? Leave him to his hangover and regret?' Natasha asked.

We're going round in circles. We haven't got time for this. It'll be daylight again before too long.

'And let him come for me? Or you? Or the twins?' Beth asked, infuriated that Natasha still didn't quite get it. Then again, it wasn't her who Rob had threatened three times. Or three times that Beth could remember.

'What happened with the metaphorical cliff?' Dee asked.

'Fine. I'm jittery. This is not the sort of thing I'm used to.' Natasha said, looking tense.

'I need you to stay home with the twins anyway, Natasha. Just double lock the door and don't let anyone in and if he does turn up then call the police. Okay?'

'We're just scaring him, right?' Natasha asked cautiously.

'It'll be fine,' Beth assured her.

I don't care if it isn't fine, but I need you to play your part.

'Makes sense, babe. Then I'll come with you to what? Help you get in him in the car? He's gonna be heavy.' Dee looked worried. 'I don't think even two of us could carry him.'

'We'll work that out when we get to it,' Beth snarled.

She'd had enough of talking. It was time to act.

Rob's time was up.

24

'Don't stress,' Beth said, feeling a strange sense of calm. She wasn't nervous. She wasn't worried. She was almost... excited. As though she could taste how beautiful her freedom was going to be. She could picture just how happy things were going to be from here on in. Her and her babies without Rob anywhere in the picture. That was the only bonus to having hit rock bottom – that from there, absolutely everything else was up.

Dee's legs were jiggling as she sat in the passenger seat as Beth drove them back towards Natasha's house, back to where they would find Rob, in whatever state he might be in.

'I just... I've waited so long to be able to help you. To be able to free you from him. I don't want us to get this wrong.' Dee chewed her lip. 'So we're going to get him into the car, take him out to the fen road, threaten him and then bring him back to wake up to the mother of all hangovers and an empty house? Yes?'

'Yes.'

'Are we over complicating things? Moving him about? Why

the fen road, why not just threaten him there and leave him where he is?'

'I know it sounds insane, dragging him all the way out there. But it's to do with power and getting mine back. In that house, the power was his; he feels in control, I feel... weak. There, where I survived, I am going to make him fear for his life in a way that I don't think I can do anywhere else. I don't think he will believe me. Here, he knows the lay of things. There, he's out of his comfort zone. I want to scare him, like he scared me, so that he won't ever be able to do that to me again. I want to take *me* back and walk away with my head held high rather than scurrying away into the night.'

'I guess that makes sense, in a sort of poetical way.'

'Exactly,' Beth agreed. It had to be this way. 'I'm going to make him see how all he has done, including his part in my accident, means he *has* to leave us alone. Forever. And when he wakes up tomorrow, we'll be long gone.'

They pulled up outside the house. Neither spoke for a moment. Both preparing themselves.

'How are you so calm? Cos I'm bricking it. I thought we'd just be flitting you and the kids away into the night rather than playing fast and loose with Rob's temper.'

'I know but I *have* to make sure he knows never to come for us. This is the only way I'll be free of him,' Beth stated firmly, though whether for her own reassurance as much as Dee's she couldn't tell. She looked at her hands. They were trembling now, she didn't feel calm any more. She was like a frightened rabbit around Rob. What had he done to her? She had to pull it together so Rob wouldn't know something was up.

'The only way?' Dee asked, but then she shook her head in a way that indicated she knew what Beth might mean but also that she knew it was best not to say it out loud.

'Exactly. Let's go and see what we're dealing with? Or you don't have to come with me.' Beth realised she better not assume anything.

'Oh, hell no, I'm by your side, babe.'

'Thank you,' Beth whispered.

The two of them walked up to the house and found the front door ajar. Beth looked worriedly at Dee, who nudged her, encouraging her to keep going.

'I've got your back.'

Beth pushed the door open and gingerly stepped inside. Even with the low level of light, she could see Rob, stood up but leaning heavily on the living room wall. The outline of his bulk was immediately threatening, and Beth started questioning the sanity of her plan. Could she really pull this off? Did she still want to?

Without thinking any further, Beth stepped into the room, followed closely by Dee.

'Rob?' Beth called out, trying to work out if he was *waiting* for her or something else. 'Are you okay?'

He reached out towards her.

'I don... I don't know,' he slurred. He held his own hands up in front of his face, looking at them as though they surprised him.

'Rob? What's up? You don't seem... right.'

Emboldened by his slurring speech and his laboured breathing, suggesting the drugs had taken their effect, Beth turned on the light. He flinched and he was clearly unsteady on his feet.

'Woah,' Dee said quietly behind Beth. 'He looks *rough.*'

'I slept. I woke up... I'm... fine...' he said, his head rolling back on his neck as he blew air out of his cheeks. He brought his face back down and looked at Beth, his expression scrunched up in confusion. 'I feel... feel wrong.' He blinked hard as though trying to re-set his eyes.

'Oh, you don't look good. Not at all.' She tried hard to keep the sarcasm from dripping into her voice, not to sound triumphant. She felt it. This was it. This was payback and she wanted to enjoy it.

Rob pushed himself off the wall, wobbling on his feet and using the sofa to steady himself. He looked chaotic. His eyes were wide, his pupils were huge. He looked like that person at the end of a gig when the lights come on and everything is too much for them, doused in whatever substances they had taken. Like the real world was an assault to them.

'I don't... I...'

'Are you okay? Are you... are you having a stroke?' Beth asked, feigning horror at his situation, though pleased at this suggestion that had just come to her unplanned. She liked the idea that she could now be the one to make him question *his* sanity, *his* health, *his* own mind. *See how he likes it.* It would also give a great reason for his sudden incapacitation; one she could not be directly blamed for. She tried not to enjoy the look of terror that settled onto his face. Sure, a little of this plan was revenge, but mostly it was about the future, about making sure that he knew *never* to mess with her again, *never* to come for her and the kids. This was about leaving him firmly in the past.

'Shiiiiit.' He touched his temple as though his fingertips could tell him what his brain was doing. His face was flushed, the alcohol and the drugs making him messy.

Beth moved towards him. 'I think we ought to get you to a hospital, don't you?'

Rob nodded, compliant, his face white as a sheet. His head lolled, the effort of holding it up too much. When he forced it back up again, Beth could see drool forming at the edge of his mouth. Had she not known what was wrong with him, this could have been terrifying. He looked really sick. Her resolve started to waver.

She went to Rob and steeled herself before putting her arm around his waist, helping him to stagger to the door. Even though he was diminished physically in his current state, the close proximity of him made her feel faint. He had caused her so much pain, of all kinds, that being pressed up against him, feeling his muscles tense as he walked with her, made her shaky.

You can do this. He can't hurt you like this. You are in control now. Find your anger and use that. Think of everything he's taken from you.

'Steady now, one step at a time,' Beth said to Rob, 'not too fast. If you rush, you'll fall and you'll take both of us with you.'

'I...' Rob looked as though he was falling asleep again. She couldn't have that. She needed him awake and listening so she could make him understand, make him realise why she had to do this. As Beth stepped them through the front door, it was almost as if the very air itself tasted of freedom. The world already felt different. She knew this was the last evening she would have to worry about Rob. Her shoulders felt lighter already despite the current dead weight resting on them.

'Is he okay?' Dee whispered, a concerned look on her face as she stepped up to Beth, keeping behind Rob's line of sight. 'How much did you give him? I mean, I don't care how he *is* but is he even conscious?'

'He's fine,' Beth snapped back, though she was worried herself. How much *had* she given him? A handful? More? She hadn't paid that much attention. And she hadn't known what or how much he had drunk too. Or if he'd already taken something himself. 'Help me. Open the car door?' She indicated her pocket with a jerk of her head, and Dee reached into it, pulling out the keys and pressing the button. The lock clicked. Dee swung the door open and stepped back.

'Who...' Rob slurred, trying to move his head in Dee's direction but clearly finding it too heavy.

'Just a neighbour, helping out,' Beth said, positioning herself between Rob and Dee. 'We need to hurry. Get in,' she said, her voice hardening. She was impatient to get him to the place where she had total control over him. She wanted to see him scared. She wanted to see him afraid, and afraid of her.

Rob fell headfirst into the car and Dee and Beth manhandled his legs in after him, swinging his body around until he was seated. Beth reached across him to fasten his seatbelt and brushed across his face with her cheek. He was sweaty, clammy, and his breathing was slow. Was he having a reaction? The meds had never done this to her. Did he really need to see a doctor?

'Let's get you going,' Beth said, slamming the door shut behind him.

'I don't like the look of him, Beth. He looks wrong.'

'I know. I didn't expect him to react quite like this. He's... worse than I thought. Perhaps the whisky with the meds? I... I don't know. I'll work something out.'

'I'm coming with you,' Dee asserted.

Beth reached out to Dee, taking her hand and shaking her head. 'I can't let you do that.'

Dee looked at her, a pleading expression on her face. She really wanted to help. For a moment, Beth wanted to let her, this woman who she really had only known a few days and yet, Beth realised, she trusted with her life. But a voice inside herself told Beth that she needed to do this alone. She needed to stand on her own two feet, and she needed to make Rob see her for who she was. A woman who would not be messed with. Not any more.

'If I'm not back in an hour, then call me. But not until then, okay?'

Dee sighed. 'Okay. If you're really sure. Turn on your location share so I can see where you are?' Seeing Beth's confused expression, Dee took Beth's phone, selected a few options and then handed it back. 'There. So at least if he tries anything I will know where you are. Be safe. I love you.'

'Love you too,' Beth said as she got into the driver's seat and fastened her seatbelt. She felt terror kick in as soon as she did. She would be returning to the scene of the crash. Would she make another bad decision when driving? She closed her eyes firmly to try to rationalise. The last time she drove there was different. She was different. She took deep breaths until her mind stopped racing. She opened her eyes and looked across at Rob. She felt a tidal wave of anger surge inside her and she turned the key in the ignition. The engine roared into life and Beth drove off into the night. When dawn came, it would be the start of her new life. Just one thing stood between her and her freedom. And she was going to take him down.

25

Beth's hands shone bright white against the darkness inside the car, gripping onto the steering wheel as she drove out into the night. The sky was a dark blue, the horizon an inky black where air and land merged. The wide open skies were both beautiful and terrifying in their scale as they reached out across the landscape. The traffic was non-existent, just as Beth had hoped. She only had one chance at this, and it had to be done right, and she didn't need an audience for it. The only question still remaining in her mind was just how far would she push this? How far would she need to go in order to make herself crystal clear to Rob? Would he listen to her for once in his life or would he make her need to hammer home her point?

She glanced across the car to the passenger seat where Rob was slumped, seatbelt on, drowsily trying to speak but not managing to make any sensible sounds. Today it was him who was rendered helpless. *Good. Let him feel what that's like, to be the one with no power.*

Looking back at the road, she kept her eyes about her for the exact place she had in mind. She knew what she was looking for. After a winding section, there was another slight curve, almost a blink-and-you'd-miss-it kink in a then otherwise straight-as-a-ruler road stretching between the dark, dense fen fields. It meant that the roadside had a slightly larger grassed area that you would be able to pull your car up onto, without being too close to tipping into the water that ran in channels either side of the road, where the water drained away from the below sea-level fields into murky, silt-filled ditches.

There.

She saw it and, checking again to find no traffic was behind her, she pulled over, turning off the headlights but leaving the side lights on for safety. She turned off the engine and sat in the surrounding silence for a moment, collecting the calm it offered to her. Rob was shifting about in the seat but hadn't said anything in a while.

Her heart rate was still hammering in her chest as she got out of the car. She dipped down to the ground and scooped some of the peaty earth from beneath the grass into her hands. Then she quickly went to the back of the car and smeared some, just enough, over the rear registration plate. She then walked around the car and did the same at the front, the side lights spotlighting how her hands shook as she did so. She didn't want to make it obvious but just enough to make anyone passing find it difficult to read the registration plate. She wanted to be untraceable.

Just in case.

She wasn't really going to go through with this anyway, was she? Not all the way. She had told Natasha and Dee that she was just going to mess with Rob, to scare him in a way that he had scared her over and over and over. She was going to make him feel how she had felt, and she was going to make sure he never did that to her or to her children again, so that he would leave them alone. Then she would pick up the children and go, somewhere, anywhere, far away from him. That was all. Wasn't it?

The adrenaline pumping through her body made her feel both light-headed and also more powerful than she had ever been. She now understood why fighters, enemies, people in moments of power or influence could almost *growl*. She felt like the predator after years of feeling like the prey. Now it was her turn, and, dear God, she was going to enjoy it.

A lone car sailed past, its headlights glinting on the dark waters at the side of the road, and Beth crouched behind the side of the car, as though inspecting a wheel. She had her story ready if anyone did stop or approach them. He was drunk and she was trying to get him home safely. She'd gone over a pothole and had decided to stop and check that she hadn't bent the wheel or burst a tyre. Nicely straightforward, plausible. But this car drove off into the night without so much as a pause to see if she needed any assistance and the road fell silent again. She and Rob were out there all alone. Time to put her plan into action.

Slowly but with purpose, Beth carefully walked to the side of the car, wiping her muddy hands on her jeans as she did so. With each footstep, she gently twisted her foot side to side and back to front, hopefully making any footprints unrecognisable. She needed nothing to connect her to this in the case something went wrong.

Beth opened the passenger door wide and then returned to the driver's side, making sure to place her feet in the same marks that she had already made, literally muddying them further. Back at the driver's seat, Beth leaned in, reached over, unbuckled Rob's seatbelt and pushed him, hard, to the side. At first, his limp body simply sagged to the door arch but then slowly, gravity took hold and it pulled Rob's bulk to the cold, mulchy ground with a satisfying thud. Beth felt it as his shoulders then his head hit the ground. A small moan escaped his lips, like the groaning of an old wooden door easing shut.

She walked over to where he now lay, a crumpled heap of a man, stripped of his strength, stripped of his dignity, stripped of his control over her. She looked at him and smiled.

'Not so clever now, are you? Not so sure of yourself,' she spat at him. 'It's so easy to be in control when you're taller, when you're stronger. But now? You're the weak little man that you truly are. You've always been like this. I just didn't see it at first.' She shook her head and looked up. It was the middle of the night, the darkest before dawn. She needed to get back to the children. Her children. It felt strange to be so primally protective of children that she had to keep telling herself were hers. It was unnerving.

She stood over Rob's crumpled form. He wasn't moving. She had to step over him in order to see his face, half illuminated in the glow from the side lights of the car. She had a moment of anxiety that she was running down the car battery unnecessarily and would end up stranded out here, but without them, it was practically impossible to see anything. Night was night out here, which was why she'd chosen it. It scared her. She wanted to use it to scare Rob too.

'What was that?' Beth asked as Rob started making noises. He was slurring badly, and nothing was making much sense. His jaw was taut. Beth could see the muscles in his face stretched tight as he clenched his teeth together, maybe with rage or maybe with the encroaching cold. Either way, Beth had to crouch down beside him to hear. She felt her stomach lurch as she got closer to him. How could she ever have forgotten that this was how he made her feel? How could she have had him sat next to her in her hospital bed and not feel this revulsion?

He was writhing, trying to push himself up but not having the strength or co-ordination to do so. He was breathless and it made him hard to hear.

'I can't understand you.'

'What... you doing? What...'

Beth raised her eyebrows at him.

'What am I doing? Well, I guess you've worked out we're not going to see a doctor. Don't worry your little head about it... *Pooky.*' She smiled as she sneered the term of endearment. She hated being called that. It made her feel like an animated squirrel. She was not cute, she was not adorable, she was not to be underestimated. And Rob was about to learn that.

'Or what do I want?' she said as she formulated her response. She opened her mouth to continue but then stopped. She was about to say that she wanted never to have laid eyes on him but then, if that had been the case, she'd not have her children. Would that be better? To lose them, in order to lose him? No. No, she didn't think so. The idea of not getting them back was abhorrent to her. Getting back to them was now her entire focus, the only thing that mattered to her.

'I want you to leave me alone. I want you to leave *us* alone. Me and Ammy and Henry. Who you have had your *mistress* care for all these weeks! Don't try to deny it again, I *know* you've been lying to me about it. I know the truth. You have manipulated us, you have terrified us, you have' – her voice halted as she tried to get across the depth of horror that he had inflicted upon them – 'you have *tortured* us and then when I tried to leave you... you couldn't let us go, could you? To let us both just move on from the *mistake* that was us. You couldn't stand to lose, to admit defeat and move on, so first you tried to *kill* us by driving us into the ditch, *knowing* how dangerous that was, and when that didn't work, and I was handed back to you, memory wiped clean of your misery, you decided to create a false world, a fantasy in which you were trying to make me live, existing only as you saw fit, in order to fulfil some twisted version of yourself as a good guy, a good husband, the perfect man. When in reality, you are a sad, twisted individual who can't cope when things don't go your way. You're a toddler in the body of a man. You are... you are *nothing*.' She turned away from him, putting distance between them as she realised that all she wanted to do was to kick him and keep kicking him until she was spent.

Beth pulled her coat around her. She was hot with rage, but her toes were numb. She stamped her feet where she stood, trying to get the blood back into her toes so she could feel them.

'So what do I want?' she said almost to herself. Then, louder, to Rob, 'I want my life back. I want to walk around without fear. Without you. You're a sad, pathetic excuse for a man and I want never to lay eyes on you again. Do you understand me? So either you agree to let us go forever or... well, take a good look at where you are and you know what I'm saying, don't you? Agree to let us go or you will never leave this place.'

She walked away from him then to the other side of the car and leant against it. She hadn't thought this through. She had wanted to scare him but other than that, other than dragging him out here, what could she do? And after threatening him, then what? He was too heavy for her to lift. She couldn't even get him sitting up by herself, let alone lift his whole weight up high enough to get him back into the car. If she left him here, he'd get dangerously cold. Especially as drunk as he was. The air temperature was dropping still, the ground was damp; it was due to drop below freezing overnight. The road was empty. He'd freeze out here if she left him. What was she going to do with him? Should she scare him a little more? Drive off and get help for him? She could call Dee but even the two of them might struggle to lift him and she didn't want to risk either of them getting hurt or caught trying.

Still trying to work out her plan of action, Beth walked back to where Rob had been lying to see if some other idea would miraculously come to her.

He wasn't there.

Her stomach flipped. Where was he? She turned her head from side to side, anxiously trying to locate him in the gloom. Something brushed her foot. Her heart stopped. Whatever it was touched her and moved on. A rabbit? A water vole perhaps? She didn't know English wildlife well enough but was grateful she wasn't at home. Things in the dark were dangerous there. The only dangerous thing here was Rob. Or maybe her, depending on who you asked.

Outside of the beams of the side lights it was difficult to see much. She looked around for something, anything, to protect her if he came for her. If Rob had somehow managed to regain control over his limbs to even some degree things could go very badly wrong very quickly. She had only guessed at how the painkillers would incapacitate him and for how long. She could have been wrong. He could have been messing with her, pretending. Lying – that came so naturally to him, didn't it?

Scanning the darkened road, she spotted a large pothole with road debris scattered around it, which was briefly illuminated by the moon. She ran to it and picked up two heavy pieces of broken tarmac. In the absence of anything better, she could hit him with them if it came to it. She walked back to the car gingerly, edging round it until she finally saw him. He'd fallen down the bank a little – perhaps the grass was slippery with dew – and his movement had dragged him down. He was dangerously close to the edge of the ditch and Beth had to choose her footing carefully to reach him. When she did so, she stood just more than an arm's length away so he couldn't get to her, couldn't reach her. She loomed over him, still relishing this difference in power now that her terror had subsided. His fate was still in *her* hands. For a fleeting moment she realised that maybe this feeling was what drove him to do what he did, this intense feeling of power. Then she remembered herself, remembered all he had done to her and to their children in order to have that control, and suddenly the taste of it in her mouth went sour. She swallowed, sickened by it all.

'Is this what you wanted? You wanted to drag me down to your level? How does it feel, eh? To be the one without any power. You scared?' she yelled at him, the rising fen winds whipping the words away from her almost as they left her mouth. 'You should be scared, you should be utterly fucking terrified of me. I could do anything here. *Anything*, and you couldn't stop me, could you? No one knows you're here. No one knows I'm here either. We're just shadows in the night.'

A harsh sound came from Rob's lips. At first, Beth thought he was choking. He was face up now. Perhaps he had vomited, or the drool had gathered in the back of his throat. A wave of panic hit Beth, which pulled up sharply when she realised what was causing the noise.

He was laughing.

He was laughing at her. At this. At her feeble attempt not to be scared of him any more. Even now, lying face up in the cold fenland mud, he thought he was better than her.

'Don't laugh at me,' she said. She had meant to sound strong, but it sounded whiny. She heard it with his ears. She did not sound as though she meant it.

'We could have been what you promised, you know. We could have had something beautiful. We could have been happy,' she said, her voice softening temporarily as though she were mourning what could have been. 'But you were too broken, too weak to give yourself up like that, weren't you? Too scared. Did the control make you feel strong? How about now? Eh? How strong are you now!' she yelled. The wind whipped her hair into her mouth and she put down the pieces of tarmac to have enough hands to tie it up out of her face.

There was a pause, just the briefest of moments before Rob's arm flung out towards the pieces, trying to grab one. Beth caught the movement and jumped back, grabbing them and bringing her foot down onto his hand hard, stopping him.

'Nuh uh,' she said, shaking her head. 'I don't think so. You don't get to win this time. I thought I'd made that clear but apparently not clear enough so let's try a bit harder, shall we?' She started to grind her foot into his wrist, her weight behind it, but the idea that she might be leaving bruises, traces of her on him, made her stop. She had to be untraceable. He wanted an invisible wife? Well, he would get one. She would leave no trace, and she would disappear, with the children, forever. She felt the resistance go out of him, his muscles slackening as he gave up.

Would he ever really give her up though? Her heart sank as she knew he would not.

'I just want you to leave me alone, leave the children alone. I want to never, *ever* see you again after today, do you understand me?'

He said nothing. He had stopped moving. Was he reserving his strength to try something else?

'You *have* to.' She could hear the desperation in her own voice. 'You can't be part of our lives any more. I can't do it. You had that, you ruined it and when you had the chance to do the right thing? You didn't. You never can. You never do. And I can't risk that for them, for me. I will not let them think that *this* is love. So this is how it is going to be. Okay? We're going to go back. You're going to sleep this off. Then in the morning, you're going to pack your things and you're going to go away. I will meet a solicitor, sort out a divorce and get the house on the market. You can have fifty per cent of everything. I can be reasonable, see? But then, we will never see each other again. That's it. You don't get the children. They come with me. This is not a negotiation; this is a fact. Do you understand?'

She stood over him, her breathing fast and her heartbeat faster.

'Well?' Her voice was trembling, whether through fear or cold she couldn't tell. He had to agree to this; it was the only way. She wouldn't spend her life looking over her shoulder for him. He had stolen enough from her; he wasn't going to have her peace of mind as well.

She looked down at him, the moonlight patchy as the moon moved in and out from behind clouds. It was hard to see his face clearly and yet she still saw it. His expression.

It was pure *hatred*.

Anger. Violence. He wanted her dead. She could see it in his eyes. In the tautness to his jaw, in the prominent vein on his forehead. His fists were clenched. Pure unadulterated rage flowed through him. And as she saw it; she knew.

He would never let her go.

That understanding came to her, loud and clear. It was not a case of then and now. She had been right before, it was a case of him or her.

Just as that sank in, he lurched again, flinging his body sideways towards her, grabbing her ankle with his hand furthest from her and squeezing. He may have lost co-ordination, but it was clear that he was still much stronger than her as he started to pull her towards him, down the muddy bank towards the ditch.

Her throat felt like it was closing over, and she was suddenly finding it hard to breathe, the memory of going under the water flooding into her brain. He pulled harder and she lost her footing on the wet grass and fell, heavily, landing with a painful thud as her backbone hit a rock in the grass.

She was smarting from the pain, and it somehow cut through her panic to let her think. She raised a hand to check that she still had hold of the large, ragged chunk of tarmac. She could... she could just... His head, one quick strike. Could she? Her hands were shaking with even the thought of it. No. No, she couldn't do that. That was too much. His blood literally on her hands. Instead, she raised her arm and brought it down hard on his hand over her ankle, forcing him to let her go.

'Fuck!' he yelped as the rock cracked his fingers.

He released her and she took the split second to scramble back up the bank. She looked over the top of Rob, to the dark, muddy water beyond him. The drainage ditch. Full of mud and weeds, full of silt. A jolt of fear ran through her. The same fear that she now knew she had felt when she realised the car was going to crash into that same dark water. Pushed into the ditch by Rob. Who did that to their wife, to their children?

Someone who didn't care if they died, that was who.

A cold wind blew across the fields. Beth shivered and a resolution settled in her mind. She would not live her life in fear of him any more. She would *not*. This ended here and now.

Beth gingerly stepped towards Rob and swiftly kicked him hard in the groin. The one place that she knew would incapacitate him fast and effectively. He called out and bunched up into a foetal position, giving her access to his back pocket where she could see his mobile phone. She reached out and grabbed it, placing one of the pieces of tarmac into his jacket pocket as he writhed on the ground. Then she grabbed his hand roughly and placed his fingertip on the phone screen before throwing his hand back at him. She opened the chat with Natasha and messaged:

I can't. I'm sorry. Forgive me.

That should keep Natasha in the clear should it come to it. A confession of sorts from Rob. Then Beth wiped the screen roughly with her coat sleeve and threw it into the ditch where she heard it land with a splash.

Taking a deep breath, she then bent down to his side.

'This is for everything,' she whispered at him as she put the other piece of tarmac into his jacket. He was still balled up in pain and breathing heavily.

Beth stood up, planted her feet firmly on the ground and then kicked Rob hard towards the ditch. He moved slowly at first, but as he met the steeper gradient of the ditch where it curved downwards towards the water, he picked up speed and rolled away from her. She stood back to watch. She was full height when he toppled off the grass entirely and into the water with a resounding splash. He briefly bobbed, with his arms floundering on the surface, trying to make his limbs listen to his dulled brain until the fenland water soaked into his clothes and the weight of it and the rocks in his pockets pulled him down into the weeds. Soon, within seconds, he was under the surface. Out of sight. Like he had never been there at all.

Gone.

Beth waited, almost expecting a dramatic resurfacing, a gasping for air, a flailing of limbs like in the movies, but there was nothing. Silence.

He was just gone.

She leant back on the car and waited, checking her watch to

be sure. Two minutes. The water was still black, inky. The surface chillingly flat. Five minutes. She looked up and down the ditch for any sign that he had somehow swum away to climb out further down, but there was nothing.

Ten minutes. Just her and the night breeze and the sky striped violet and indigo.

She was still alone.

Beth expected to feel horror at what she had just done, but she did not. She felt light. Relieved.

Free.

After everything he had done, after everything that she had survived. She was still standing. She had won. It was a game she had not wanted to play, but she was the survivor, the victor. Rob had underestimated her, and he had lost.

Taking one last look at the water, treacle-black and still, Beth walked back round to the driver's seat and got in. Turning on the headlights, she could now see the track marks in the grass from another, heavier vehicle still imprinted on the verge. The dredging lorry, she guessed. The ditches were de-silted every so often. She hoped that either the rain forecast tomorrow would wash both sets of tyre marks away or that in the clear light of the morning, her own car tyre marks would be camouflaged by these ones, with no one bothering to look close enough to realise there had been two vehicles. No one knew there was any reason to look any closer. No one but Dee knew that she had been here. She had *not* been here. She was never here at all.

Beth turned the engine on, checked the road was clear for traffic, and, turning in the road so as to avoid the pothole, she drove away without looking back. Now the only way was forwards. Onwards. To a future she could control.

26

Back at Natasha's house, Beth pulled the car up to the kerb, turned off the engine and rested her head briefly on the steering wheel. As she did so, some muscle memory brought her back to the last time the two had been in contact when her forehead had slammed into it, and the whole scene of the accident played out in her mind. The screeching of tyres as she slammed on the brakes, the noise as the metal of the car crumpled behind her as the car following impacted it, the scream that escaped her lips, mixed with a terrifying silence from the back. The utter silence from the children had been the worst thing. Had they been crushed? Then, before this thought had even had time to be processed, the sensation of her car skidding across the road, uncontrollably, as the steering wheel moved by itself, momentum forcing it sideways as the car shot towards the ditch. The hot feel of blood and the metallic smell of it on her face as the wound on her head burst her skin open. The crash as the car hit the water and then the silence as it sank.

It was silent now. It was night, and barely a handful of lights were showing in the street as Beth sat in the car. She took her hands and head off the steering wheel, and the glint of her wedding ring caught her eye as it flashed in the beam of the streetlight.

He was gone. He was really gone. She was free.

She wrenched the band from her finger and her stomach muscles pulled inwards as sobs wracked her body, making her judder with the intensity of them. All the tension of the past few weeks and the feeling of being trapped that had plagued her was forcing its way out in one giant torrent.

Suddenly the passenger's side door was wrenched open.

'What are you doing to her you utter bast— Oh,' Dee said. 'Oh, babe, it's just you.' She leaned into the car and looked around. 'Where's Rob?'

She stood back and looked at Beth, who was gulping deep breaths of air into her lungs and trying to regain composure. She had a lot of explaining to do.

'Beth? Beth, what happened? Where is he? Are you okay? You're covered in mud – what happened?'

'Let's go inside,' Beth managed to say.

Dee dipped her head to the side, aware that she was about to learn something big.

'Okay…' she said slowly, cautiously. 'Are you hurt?'

Beth shook her head.

'Let's go inside,' Beth repeated, pulling herself out of the car, feeling both weakened and yet also stronger than she ever remembered feeling. She felt taller, wider – as though she were suddenly taking up more space. Taking up space she had always fit into and yet had not claimed. She stood up tall at her full height and as she did so, she realised that this had been her before. Before Rob. This feeling of belonging within herself was a feeling she recognised. She liked it.

'It's really strange,' Beth said as she walked into the house, 'how everything feels different, even though it's the same place I left barely hours ago.'

Dee's face was dark. 'What happened, Beth?' Her voice was low, filled with concern.

'I told him. No more. That he had to leave us alone.'

'And?'

Beth looked at her feet. 'He didn't listen.'

'Right. As we suspected, I guess. So what did you do?'

Beth lifted her head again, to look Dee right in the eyes. 'I made him listen.'

Dee's mouth formed an 'O' as she exhaled slowly. 'What did you do, Beth? Where is he? Did you leave him somewhere?'

'You could say that.'

'Babe. Enough with the cryptic chat. This is *me*. With Natasha, you said you wanted him dead. She heard you loud and clear. And now? Now you took him out somewhere to scare him off, as all three of us eventually agreed, and then what? You come back alone?'

Beth clamped her lips shut. In her mind she went through how to phrase this, but one version made her sound psychopathic and the other sounded apologetic. She was neither. She was not mad, and she was not sorry. She searched her mind for any shred of regret and found none. She was glad she had done it, and she would do it again.

The two of them stood in silence. The only sound was the ticking of the clock on the wall that seemed to get louder with each *tick*. Dee paced, looking worried. Beth stood still, looking calm. Both of them waiting for the other to speak first. Neither did.

The high-pitched beep from Dee's phone broke the tension. She reached into her pocket. She opened the message and read it.

'Natasha.'

Beth nodded.

'Who has the twins with her. Remember? Now, before I call her, I want you to tell me what the hell happened with Rob, where the hell he is so that we can work out what on earth we're going to tell her so she doesn't march your kids straight to the nearest police station. Do you understand?'

Beth's face paled.

'Do you? You know I am on your side, Beth. Whatever it is you have done, I am here, okay? But you *have* to be truthful with me. I can't work with lies. Ever. That's not me, babe. You know that.'

'I do know.'

'So, what am I telling Natasha?' Dee opened her eyes wide and crossed her arms.

Beth filled her in on all that had happened on that muddy bank in the middle of nowhere, her voice trembling as she spoke.

'He definitely...?' Dee asked.

Beth nodded slowly. 'I waited. I waited ten minutes. I checked up and down in case he was hiding somewhere. It was dark, I admit that, but... I couldn't see him. He was fairly out of it. I don't think he could have swum far. The water, the weeds, the mud. I... I think he's still down there. He is.'

'Fuuuck.'

'I'm sorry. I know that was not the plan.'

'Wasn't it? Or was it just not the plan you shared with me?' Dee said, a bite in her tone.

'No! No, I really hadn't planned on it. You and Natasha were right. Just scaring him and then leaving was better. That *was* my intention but... it felt like he'd never let me go and... the idea of him chasing me, chasing us, always. I... He'd find me, and he'd kill me. Or worse, hurt the twins in order to hurt me. I know he would.'

Dee's eyes were all over the place. She couldn't look at Beth. She sat down, looking at the floor as she thought.

'You're right,' she finally said.

'I am?'

'He'd never have let you go. But...'

'But?' Beth's voice wavered.

'We don't know for sure he didn't get out, do we?'

A jolt of terror ran through Beth as this truth sunk in. 'I guess not. No.'

'Babe. Do you want to hear what I think? About what we should do? Or did you want time to think yourself?'

'We?'

Dee smiled at her. 'Yes. We. I'm in on this now, always have been. As is Natasha. Whether we like it or not. If anything comes of it, it's going to be our word against whoever. Isn't it? So yes. We.'

'I'm so sorry.'

'Don't be.'

'I am. For pulling you into this.' Her voice cracked. 'Yes, please. What do you think we should do? I'm tired, so tired. I can't think any more. I feel like I need to sleep for a decade.'

'I think we should stick to the original plan. That's what Natasha is expecting. That's what she agreed to. That is what will get you back with the twins and the fuck from away here. We can't know he's... he's dead, until we see a body. And, well...'

'One to two years.'

'What?'

'The ditches are de-silted every one to two years. About that. I think. There were track marks by the road. I think... I think it had just been done.'

Dee narrowed her eyes. 'How do you know that? Did—'

'No! No, I promise, I'm telling the truth. I swear.' She held her hands up in front of her in surrender. 'I did not intend to do... what I did. This was not planned, not researched. No, you know how much that road scared me, how much those ditches...' She shuddered. 'I looked it up once, ages ago. To make me feel more in control, less scared.'

Dee nodded. She believed her.

'Okay. Right. So if he is... still down there, then they probably won't find him for a good while at least. And then, I guess...' Her skin took on a tinge of green. 'It might be... difficult to...'

'Identify him.'

'Exactly.'

'His work let him go. I know that. The only people who might miss him are me and Natasha. She will be expecting him to want to know where the children have gone. Where I have gone. That's why... I...'

'You sent the text.'

'Please don't judge me. I needed a way out. I had to get out.'

'Do you think she'll buy it?'

'She has to. We have to make sure that she does.'

Dee swallowed. 'OK. So we work with that. Plan A.'

Beth closed her eyes. She was beyond thankful that Dee understood. She had done a terrible thing. But she had done it for the good of everyone else. She would have to live with that. But it did mean that she could live.

'But how would he have got there? I mean, if we want it to look like it was him topping himself? It's not like he could walk there, is it? Where would his car be?'

'I...'

'If we took the car back and abandoned it then they'd look for him and we don't want that either.'

'Shit. I... I hadn't thought.'

'And frankly you need the car to get where you're going. So...'

'His bike?'

'Eh?'

'He used to go on bike rides. Could we... could we take his bike out there and drop that in with him?'

'Jesus... you're scaring me now, babe. What your brain is coming up with.'

'Sorry. I'm just thinking out loud.'

'Remind me never to piss you off!' Dee laughed.

'Don't joke, please.'

Beth's face was stony. Dee looked admonished.

'Sorry. But yes, that could work. We'd have to be beyond careful doing it. That is the sort of shit that gets people caught.'

'We need to do it now. It's dark, the road will be quiet. It'll be light again soon and if we wait until tomorrow then it'll get in the way of my leaving. It has to be now. Doesn't it?'

'I agree.'

'Let's just wait a moment though, think this through, work out if we're missing something. You need to get changed. I can wash your clothes. Is there anything you need from this house? Before we go?'

'I just need my laptop, to contact my mum.'

'Pack whatever you need, let's ditch the bike and get you back with your kids and the hell away from here. Tonight.'

27

'It's really late. I was expecting you earlier. Where have you been?' Natasha asked anxiously as she opened the door. She peered past them both to see if Rob was with them. Rattled nerves radiated from her. Beth could almost hear her shaking.

'Sorry. We had... things to clear up,' Beth said quietly as she stepped into the house.

'How did it go?' Natasha asked, taking Dee by the arm. 'How did he take it? He... sent a cryptic message to me hours ago now. He sounded... almost remorseful. Do you think he'll leave you alone now? Do you think he got it?'

'Yes, I think so,' Dee said, watching Beth wander about almost in a daze. 'What did he say?' she asked, trying to look like she had no idea.

'He said he was sorry?'

'Right. So, maybe he was trying to get back in your good books, knowing he'd burnt his bridges with Beth?' Dee suggested.

'Typical Rob.' Beth scoffed, trying to back up Dee's suggestion.

'He's burnt all his bridges. Text message or not. He's going to be so angry when he wakes up and realises everyone is gone. I've already packed. I'm going to stay with my mum. I can't be here when he realises that I've been helping you. He'll have worked it out by now, I'm sure. He's a bastard but he's not stupid.'

'That's a good idea. About going to your mum's,' Dee said. 'Best to be on the safe side, eh? Fresh start for everyone. Sort everything out once everyone is safe. Right? Beth?'

Beth turned to look at the two other women. She was drawn and pale.

'Right.'

'What did you say to him? What did he say?' Natasha persisted.

'He didn't really say much. He listened. I... made him listen. I made him understand,' Beth said, not lying so much as withholding the truth. Natasha didn't have to know. It was better for her that she didn't. What she didn't know she couldn't tell, and what she didn't know couldn't haunt her. She had suffered enough in this mess that was not hers; she didn't need to suffer any further. Beth had freed herself and she wanted to free Natasha too.

'Good. Look, are you okay?' Natasha asked. 'You look absolutely exhausted.'

'I am. I... I was planning on getting the kids into the car and going. Tonight. But...'

Natasha glanced towards the stairs.

'They're asleep. I don't think waking them is a great idea. They've not seen you in weeks. It'll be a shock. A happy one, don't get me wrong, but small children when they're tired aren't the best travel companions.'

'Agreed. I don't think you should be driving right now anyway. You need some sleep. Rest. Today has been... a lot.'

'They tend to wake early. Around six. Rob will likely wake up with a sore head later in the day. Right?' Natasha looked at the other two nervously.

Beth smiled weakly.

'Right,' Dee said, a strained expression on her face.

'Sure. You're both right. I do need some sleep. I... I need to work out what to say to the twins too. I don't want to scare them. I was going to say we were going on a holiday, somewhere fun.'

'Good idea. I'll go make up a bed for you.'

'Thank you. I appreciate it. Really.'

Beth's heart flooded with joy. After all the horrifying mess of the past few weeks, she was home, the twins were here, they were all safe and would be safe tomorrow and all the days from here onwards. She would be reunited with them in a matter of hours and all would be well.

'So,' Dee said once Natasha was out of earshot. 'What's the plan now?'

'I think I want to go home.'

'You are home.'

'No, *home* home. To Melbourne. Despite so much of my memory coming back to me here, such a large part of my time here has been ruined by him. Tainted. I just want to start over somewhere where everything doesn't make me think of him.'

Dee's face dropped. 'It's just so far away.'

'I know. But the only person I'll miss here is you. But there, I miss everybody.'

Dee smiled a sad smile. 'I get it, I do. Have you heard anything from your family yet?'

'Not yet.'

'When did you last check? Check now?' Dee suggested.

'Good idea,' Beth said, grabbing the bag she had packed the laptop in.

She tried to ignore the flicker of hope in her stomach as she opened the laptop, and it auto connected to the Wi-Fi. She hadn't closed any of her tabs – that could have been stupid. She felt her core retract before remembering that Rob couldn't find this, couldn't hurt her any more. Any of them, ever again. A smile settled on her lips. A smile that grew wider still as she refreshed the page and saw the new message. From her mum! She gasped.

'You okay?' Dee asked, but Beth couldn't answer.

Lovey, it is wonderful, wonderful to get this email, but I'm worried. Complicated? What do you mean? Are you all right? Call me, whenever you get this, night or day, doesn't matter. Okay? Our new number is...

'She's given me her number. I can call her. I can call her now!'

'What time is it over there?'

'I don't know, I don't care,' Beth said, grabbing her phone and dialling the number. She held the phone in her trembling hands, willing her mum to pick up. She did.

'Mum?'

'Bethany? Beth, is that you?' her mum said, her voice rising as it flooded with excitement.

'Mum. Oh God, I've missed you.'

'Me too, lovey. I'm so sorry,' her mum said.

'For what?'

'For our stupid fight.'

Beth's voice cracked. 'I...'

'I've been so worried. I am worried. How are you? What's

been going on?'

Beth was on the phone until her credit ran out and then her mum called her back immediately. They had so much to say and by the time Beth reluctantly hung up, Dee had fallen asleep on the sofa and Natasha had gone to bed. Beth covered Dee with a blanket and went to sleep in the room that Natasha had made up for her. When the morning came, her new life was going to begin.

The first thing Beth was aware of was a chink of light pushing its way through a gap in the curtains. She had barely had time to register where she was, or to remember all that had happened, when suddenly the door burst open and Ammy and Henry came running into the room and jumped on to her bed.

'Mummy!' they yelled as they clung to her. 'Mummy is back!'

Beth had both wanted and feared this moment, frightened that she wouldn't know what to do, terrified that she would somehow feel nothing and that the twins would be damaged by it. But as she wrapped her arms around them and brought them close to her, one either side as they snuggled under the blankets with her, she realised that her fears had been unfounded. This felt like it was supposed to be. She knew them, they knew her. They chattered at her as though she had never left, yet still clung to her in a way that suggested she had been away too long.

'Mummy is back,' Beth repeated to them. 'And I'm not going anywhere again. But we are. All. Together. We're going on a big adventure!'

'To where?' Natasha said as she popped her head around the door from the corridor where she had been waiting.

Beth looked up at her.

'Home. My mum is wiring me some money to buy plane

tickets and we're going back to her new place. She told me to just come home and we can work out everything else once we get there. Our fight – it was nothing. Rob made it out to be more than it was and Mum thought I didn't want to speak with her, but now it's all going to be fine. You're going to meet your granny and gramps!' Beth said to the twins. 'And to get there, we're going on an aeroplane!'

'Are you allowed to do that? Take them out of the country?'

'A holiday,' Beth lied. 'I'll sort everything else out from there.'

She could learn how to be a mother all over again, with help from her family this time. They could all swim in the sea and play on the beaches and be thousands of miles away before Rob was ever found. *If* he was ever found. It was all going to be okay.

He had not broken her. He had tried his best to make her nothing but his. He had underestimated her, her friends, her fight for a life that she loved.

A life without him.

A life where she was free.

ACKNOWLEDGEMENTS

As always, I am grateful for a whole list of people whose help and involvement has made this book possible. Firstly, thank you to the women who shared their stories of coercive control and abusive relationships in order to help others. The research for this book led me to read about some horrific experiences, but also inspiring stories of strength and resilience.

To my editor, Emily Yau, for being such a joy to work with and for collaborating with me to tease the book out of itself. To my fantastic agent, Marianne Gunn O'Connor, for all her support and understanding. To the always fantastic Team Boldwood, Jenna, Ben, Claire, Issy, Nia, Wendy and the wider team whose dedication to their authors is always uplifting. To the other Boldwood authors who are a support network to be proud of.

To Jennifer Davies, my copy editor who makes sure that my days in the book aren't either 127 hours or 45 minutes long! To Rose Fox, my proofreader for catching the things I can't see after having read the book so often!

To Aaron Munday for his brilliant cover design.

Thank you to Nicolette Chin for the audio recording of this book and the team at Ulverscroft for bringing the book to life for audio book listeners.

Grateful thanks to Dr Edward Neeham, Consultant Neurologist at Addenbrookes Hospital, Cambridge, for his assistance with my research into retrograde amnesia to ensure that the medical details were correct.

Thank you to Francis Pryor for his insightful conversation about fen ditches and their maintenance, that sparked an element of this book.

To the wonderful book community, who are as always, supportive and encouraging. To fellow writers, to bloggers and reviewers including Julia Laite, Emma-Claire Wilson, Sara Cox & The Cheshire Novel Prize, Ellie Hawkes, Jo Leevers, Asha Hick, Strap in Patricia debuts, the 2023 Debuts and the Faber gang.

To the Cambridge book community, Cambridge Literary Festival, Lucy Cavendish Fiction Prize team, Cambridgeshire Libraries, Heffers, Waterstones and Bodies in the Bookshop and all their booksellers who champion their local authors, thank you for your support.

To the lovely Julia & Tracey at Emerald Foods on Cambridge Market who sell the best coffee to keep me going!

To my wonderful friends and family who make it possible for me to ignore the world and write, thank you. To Malcolm, Beatrice and Madeleine who are what it's all for. To Daisy, my cat, who keeps me company when it's just me and the laptop.

And to readers everywhere, thank you for sharing your time with me and my characters.

If you are currently experiencing domestic abuse, here are a list of organisations who may be able to help:

www.nationaldahelpline.org.uk 0808 2000 247

www.thehotline.org 1-800-799-SAFE (7233)

www.gov.nl.ca/vpi/domestic-violence-help-line 1-888-709-7090

www.1800respect.org.au 1800-737-732

ABOUT THE AUTHOR

Alison Stockham has worked in film and television production for BBC and Channel 4, before working as the events coordinator for Cambridge Literary Festival. Now a full time writer, she lives in the city with her husband, their children and their cat, who keeps her company while she works on the next book. Her debut novel *The Cuckoo Sister* was a top 10 bestseller and was also longlisted for the Lucy Cavendish Fiction Prize.

Sign up to Alison Stockham's mailing list for news, competitions and updates on future books.

Follow Alison on social media here:

facebook.com/AlisonStockham-Author
x.com/AlisonStockham
instagram.com/astockhamauthor

ALSO BY ALISON STOCKHAM

The Cuckoo Sister

The Silent Friend

The New Girl

The Man She Married

THE

Murder

LIST

THE MURDER LIST IS A NEWSLETTER DEDICATED TO SPINE-CHILLING FICTION AND GRIPPING PAGE-TURNERS!

SIGN UP TO MAKE SURE YOU'RE ON OUR HIT LIST FOR EXCLUSIVE DEALS, AUTHOR CONTENT, AND COMPETITIONS.

SIGN UP TO OUR NEWSLETTER

BIT.LY/THEMURDERLISTNEWS

Boldwood

Boldwood Books is an award-winning fiction publishing company seeking out the best stories from around the world.

Find out more at www.boldwoodbooks.com

Join our reader community for brilliant books, competitions and offers!

Follow us

@BoldwoodBooks

@TheBoldBookClub

Sign up to our weekly deals newsletter

https://bit.ly/BoldwoodBNewsletter

www.ingramcontent.com/pod-product-compliance
Ingram Content Group UK Ltd.
Pitfield, Milton Keynes, MK11 3LW, UK
UKHW021231200125
R3786800001B/R37868PG453414UKX00001B/9 781835 615775